Shadows on a
Morning in Maine

Praise for *Shadows on a Maine Christmas* by Lea Wait

"Wait's seventh outing for antiques dealer Maggie Summer...is as frothy as eggnog....The book's highlights are its loving descriptions of the Maine winter and the area's strong sense of community."
—*Publishers Weekly*

"Wait touches on social issues and women's history in a compelling mystery. She blends Christmas observations, small town beauty, a little antiques background, with personal relationships. It's not easy to combine charm and tragedy, but Lea Wait succeeds beautifully in *Shadows on a Maine Christmas*."
—*Lesa's Book Critiques*

"...a solid entry in this series. The mystery plot is well structured, involving issues such as elder care, adoption, child abuse, and abortion. But it is the characters and setting that are so engaging, drawing the reader into the story and keeping the pages turning. On a side note, each chapter opens with interesting facts about antique prints."
—*Hidden Staircase Mystery Books*

"Intriguing characters and a snow-covered Victorian town provide a lovely setting to a compelling plot. Recommended reading over the holidays."
—*Buried Under Books*

"Wait captures the atmosphere of a small town beautifully. She also has great insight into human relationships. The story moves at a leisurely pace that will appeal to cozy readers, who will love taking time to enjoy the wintry setting and the interactions of the cast."
—*Booklist*

BOOKS BY LEA WAIT

In the Maggie Summer
"Shadows" Antique Print Mystery Series
  Shadows at the Fair
  Shadows on the Coast of Maine
  Shadows on the Ivy
  Shadows at the Spring Show
  Shadows of a Down East Summer
  Shadows on a Cape Cod Wedding
  Shadows on a Maine Christmas
  Shadows on a Morning in Maine

Novels for children & young adults
  Stopping to Home
  Seaward Born
  Wintering Well
  Finest Kind
  Uncertain Glory

"Mainely Needlepoint" Mystery Series
  Twisted Threads
  Threads of Evidence
  Thread and Gone
  Dangling by a Thread

Shadows on a Morning in Maine

AN ANTIQUE PRINT MYSTERY

by

LEA WAIT

PERSEVERANCE PRESS / JOHN DANIEL & COMPANY
PALO ALTO & MCKINLEYVILLE, CALIFORNIA, 2016

A Perseverance Press Book
Published by John Daniel & Company
A division of Daniel & Daniel, Publishers, Inc.
Post Office Box 2790
McKinleyville, California 95519
www.danielpublishing.com/perseverance

Distributed by SCB Distributors (800) 729-6423

Book design by Eric Larson, Studio E Books, Santa Barbara, www.studio-e-books.com

Cover image: gregobagel/iStock

10 9 8 7 6 5 4 3 2 1

LIBRARY OF CONGRESS CATALOGING-IN-PUBLICATION DATA
Names: Wait, Lea, author.
Title: Shadows on a morning in Maine : an antique print mystery / by Lea Wait.
Description: McKinleyville, California : John Daniel & Company, 2016.
Identifiers: LCCN 2015048060 | ISBN 9781564745774 (softcover : acid-free paper)
Subjects: LCSH: Summer, Maggie (Fictitious character)—Fiction. | Prints—Collectors and collecting—Fiction. | City and town life—Maine—Fiction. | Antique dealers—Fiction. | GSAFD: Mystery fiction.
Classification: LCC PS3623.A42 S5349 2016 | DDC 813/.6—dc23
LC record available at https://lccn.loc.gov/2015048060

Shadows on a
Morning in Maine

1. Untitled

Black-and-white engraving of small sailboat heading into storm, from Lynd Ward's *Gods' Man: A Novel in Woodcuts*. Published in 1929, the week of the stock market crash, *Gods' Man* is considered one of the first graphic novels. Ward went on to win the Caldecott Medal in 1953.

4.5 x 6.5 inches. Price: $35.

I DON'T NEED ANOTHER mother. I get by fine on my own." Brooklin Deschaine clutched a worn stuffed animal tightly to her chest.

The words rang in Maggie Summer's ears and heart.

Brooklin was small for nine years old. Skinny, wearing a faded red T-shirt and jeans that were too large for her. Shaggy brown hair unevenly framed her face and partially covered her dark eyes. Her thin legs were planted solidly apart. She'd rejected a seat on the faded couch next to Maggie, or on any of the other half dozen mismatched chairs in the small room arranged to relax nervous prospective parents and the children they were meeting for the first time.

"Why don't I leave you two alone to get acquainted," said Sandy Sechrest, the young blond social worker who'd brought them together. "I'll be back in a few minutes." She smiled at them both and closed the conference room door behind her.

Don't leave, Maggie thought. *I don't know how to do this. I'm not ready.*

Framed photographs of pounding surf and paths through dark green pine woods hung above a low bookcase full of worn picture books and toys. The agency had tried to make the institutional room homelike, but no way was this a comfortable meeting.

Brooklin didn't look at Maggie. She stared at the door, like a cornered animal ready to run.

9

This was the daughter she'd dreamed of? Maggie swallowed. Hard. The daughter she'd planned to buy pretty clothes for and read to and take to museums and zoos and the beach? The daughter she'd wanted so badly it had almost broken her relationship with the man she loved?

Will Brewer was the man she'd been waiting for.

Except that she'd also been waiting to be a mother, and Will refused to consider fatherhood.

She hadn't let that stop her from dreaming and planning. She'd read all the books about adopting older children. She'd told social workers in New Jersey, and again here in Maine when the agency in Augusta updated her home study, that she was ready. She'd even convinced Will this decision could be right for both of them.

She glanced down at the green tourmaline ring Will had given her at New Year's. He'd said it was a promise to love her, for now and forever. To love her, even if she adopted a child. She wore it on her left hand.

But now she wasn't talking about adopting a theoretical child.

She'd seen a picture of Brooklin the week before. It must have been taken a year or more ago. In person the girl looked older. Tougher.

Was she ready for this? Ready to be rejected by a homeless child?

She'd dressed up for this meeting, choosing a yellow sweater and tan slacks. Bright, optimistic, but steady. Reliable.

Right now she didn't feel optimistic.

The room was silent. Maggie held out the teddy bear she'd brought as a first gift for her daughter. "This is for you, Brooklin."

"I'm nine. I don't need no teddy bear. Teddy bears are for babies." Brooklin tightened her hold on the gray stuffed animal she'd brought with her. "I'm no baby."

The Call had come last week. Sandy Sechrest had said there was a child waiting. Brooklin was a girl, just as Maggie had hoped. Nine years old. A rough nine years, by all accounts. But she'd been in counseling, and the agency believed it was time to try a permanent placement. And, Sandy had added, the foster family where Brooklin was living had decided she needed to move on.

Sandy'd shown Maggie that one out-of-focus picture, and medical reports that said Brooklin was underweight and needed dental work, but was basically healthy and of slightly above-average intelligence.

When Maggie'd told Will about Brooklin he'd uncorked the bottle of champagne he'd been saving for just that moment. He and his ninety-one-year-old Aunt Nettie had toasted Maggie and the girl the State of Maine thought might become her daughter. That night she couldn't stop smiling and couldn't sleep, she was so excited.

For the past five months she'd been racing between her college teaching job in New Jersey and Waymouth, Maine. She'd had her completed home study transferred to Maine, and consulted with Will about the renovations he was doing to the stately home they were turning into Victorian House—an antiques mall with an apartment for Maggie and, she hoped, her daughter-to-be.

Two weeks ago the semester had finally ended. She was now officially on sabbatical and she'd arrived in Maine, fortuitously, on Mother's Day. She'd spent the past two weeks nervously painting walls and arranging furniture in her new apartment. Her home in New Jersey was rented to the professor taking her place for the school year. She'd brought notes for the book she planned to write.

Her life was organized. Ready.

Victorian House was scheduled to open July Fourth; only six weeks from now.

Winslow Homer, Maggie's large gray cat, had already chosen his favorite seat by a window overlooking the river, and although Maggie was still waiting for her stove to be delivered, she was beginning to learn which Waymouth supermarket aisles stocked what she needed for her kitchen.

Sandy Sechrest had suggested that, if all was going well, in five or six weeks Brooklin could come to live with her. School would be over by then, and Maggie and Brooklin would have the summer together. The agency was aiming at placing Brooklin by the Fourth of July.

Between Brooklin's placement and the opening of Victorian House, Independence Day now loomed as the official beginning of Maggie's new life. In Maine, and as a mother.

From now until then Maggie and her new daughter would gradually spend more time together, getting to know each other before Brooklin moved into the sunny room Maggie had already painted and furnished with books and stuffed animals and a WELCOME HOME! sign on the bulletin board over the bed.

Were six weeks enough to make them a family?

Maggie and Brooklin stared at each other.

Finally, Maggie spoke, certain whatever she said would be wrong. "Brooklin, I hope I can be your mother. That's up to both of us."

"My name's Brook. And I had a mom. And lots of foster moms. I don't need another mom."

"I'm not your birth mother. But I'd like us to see if we could be a family, together. A forever family."

Brook shook her head. "Families are stupid."

"Sometimes they are," Maggie said. She had to be honest. "But they can also be good. A place to be safe. A place people care about you. Love you. No matter what. They can be home."

Brook shook her head as though Maggie had just said she lived on Mars. "Not," she muttered. She shuffled her feet and then looked up. "Miss Sechrest, she said you live in a big house. You got pictures?"

Maggie reached into the red canvas bag she used as a pocketbook. "I do live in a big house. But you and I would only live on the top floor." She held the photograph out cautiously, the way she remembered holding out treats for a puppy she'd been given when she was Brook's age. The scared puppy had taken the treats, biting her hand in the process. She still had the scar.

Her childhood hadn't been perfect, but it was far from the one Brook had survived.

Sandy had instructed her not to mention Brook's history, not at their first meeting. Not until Brook brought it up, which could be days, weeks, or months from now. Or never. Not to mention the father who'd abused Brook's mother and then stabbed her to death in front of five-year-old Brook and her baby brother, Toby. Not to mention Toby, who'd been adopted as soon as the court terminated their father's rights, three years ago. His new parents, a couple in western Maine, hadn't wanted a child as old as six. Hadn't wanted Brook.

Not to mention the five foster homes where Brook had lived during the past four years. One family had moved out of state. One placement ended because an older foster sister accused the foster father of rape. Two families said Brook was difficult; she was disobedient, didn't do her chores, and ran away. One set of foster parents divorced. The home where Brook was now living had five other foster children, and said they couldn't handle six. Brook was their oldest; the first on their "move them on" list.

Two prospective adoptive couples had been told about Brook. Neither was willing to take a chance on her, so the agency decided to try a single parent. If the placement with Maggie didn't work out, Brook would be moved to a group home for emotionally damaged teenagers. She was young for that kind of placement, Sandy admitted, but that was the only alternative left at the moment. Maggie was probably Brook's last chance at having a forever mother and family of her own. A mother who'd cheer for her at softball games and help her with her homework, and in a few years, help her pick out a prom dress.

Looking at Brook right now, the possibility of prom dresses seemed dim.

The girl edged closer to Maggie and snatched the photograph with her right hand, ripping the corner. She didn't let go of her stuffed animal. Was it a teddy bear? No. Teddy bears were for babies.

Maggie put the bear she'd brought as a peace offering in the corner of the couch.

Brook backed up, studying the picture. "Who lives downstairs?"

"Downstairs is a business. Antiques."

"Old things?" It was an accusation.

"Special old things, yes. Silver, and jewelry and pictures and furniture." Maggie didn't mention that the pictures were hers; that she was an antique print dealer and a professor. Sandy had said to keep this first meeting simple.

What had Brook been told about her, other than that she lived in a big house?

Brook shook her head. "Old things are dumb. I like new things." She stared at the photograph of the three-story Victorian House.

"There's a bedroom for you, and one for me. And a living room and kitchen that are really one big room. And see that little room at the top of the house? That's a cupola. You can look out those windows and see the whole town, and the river."

"A whole room just for me?"

"Just for you. We can paint it any color you'd like." Maggie immediately realized she shouldn't have painted the room until she'd met Brook. The room was now a warm peach color she'd thought would be more grown-up than pink, and cozy on cold winter days. But she could paint it again. Paint was cheap. "What's your favorite color?"

"Red."

Maggie winced. But she'd promised.

"Then your room can be red."

Brook stuffed the photograph into the pocket of her baggy jeans. They looked like hand-me-downs, probably from another, larger, foster child. "I'm keeping the picture." She looked straight at Maggie, as though waiting to be told she'd crossed an invisible line. Taken something that wasn't hers.

"Good," said Maggie. "I hope someday soon I can take you to see the house."

"And my room. My red room," Brook said.

"You and I could paint it red together."

"You looking for someone to do work for you?"

"I'd expect you to do some chores. Painting the room would be fun."

Brook snickered. "Sounds like work." She hitched up her jeans. "Other kids live in that house?"

"No other kids," Maggie said. And then added, "But I do have a cat. His name is Winslow. And children live near there, in other houses on the street. Maybe they'll be your friends."

"I don't need no friends." Brook plopped down on an armchair across the room from where Maggie was sitting. "Does your cat bite?"

"Not unless someone hurts him. Or he gets scared."

Brook shrugged. "Cats are boring. I like dogs."

The stuffed animal in her lap was a seal. A well-loved seal.

"And there's a school, only four blocks away." Maggie brushed her long brown hair behind her ears and kept talking, hoping something she said would appeal to Brook. This meeting felt eerily like a blind date. Would she and Brook find anything in common? Would they like each other? Was this the beginning of a lifelong relationship? Or was it a one-time meeting? "The school's close enough so you can walk to it in September."

Sandy had told her they'd first aim at two visits a week; then a visit to Waymouth; and an overnight by the third week. Sometimes adoption visiting periods lasted several months, but the agency wanted to place Brook quickly.

When she first heard that schedule Maggie'd thought waiting until the end of June would seem like forever.

But maybe it was too soon. Maybe they were pushing too fast.

"I hate school," said Brook.

Maggie took a deep breath. "Everything about school? Is there one thing at school you do like?" It wasn't the time to tell Brook she was a teacher.

Brook considered. "Recess. And lunch. Some schools give good lunch. Does your school have good lunch?"

"I don't know. But if you don't like it, we could make a lunch you could take with you."

"I never took lunch," said Brook, as though considering. "I like peanut butter and jelly and ice cream."

Maggie nodded. "So do I. You could take peanut butter and jelly sandwiches for lunch."

"You're dumb. Schools don't let kids bring peanut butter to school. Other kids might be allergic."

Maggie inhaled. "I didn't know that. I'm glad you told me. We'll find something else for you to take for lunch, then. What else do you like?"

"Just jelly is okay. Strawberry jelly."

Plain jelly wasn't healthy. But this wasn't the best time for a lecture on nutrition. Would food be something else to argue about? She'd looked forward to introducing her new daughter to baking bread and making vegetable soup and chowders from scratch. "What do you like to do, Brook? When you're not in school."

"Computer games. Some people have computer games."

"Some people do. I don't have any now. But if you came to live with me, we could think about getting one."

Brook shrugged. "It's not important. I'm used to not having any. I just know people have them. I've seen them on TV."

The silence was like a gulf between them. What did they have in common?

"I've always wanted to have a daughter," Maggie ventured.

"So, why didn't you?"

She wanted to be honest. But Brook didn't need to hear about the marriage that had ended with a car accident. About the decision making. About Will, who said he loved her, who hadn't wanted to be a father, but who was now trying to be supportive. "I'm hoping you'll want to be my daughter."

"Good luck with that," Brook said. "Miss Sechrest said you ain't even married. Why'd you want a kid? Kids're trouble."

"I think I could help someone grow up. Love them, and be there for them, no matter what."

Brook was about to answer when the door opened, interrupting whatever she was going to say.

Sandy Sechrest looked like someone who'd dried a lot of tears, and kept a pocket full of tissues just in case. She looked at both of them. "How did today go?"

Neither Maggie nor Brook answered.

"First meetings are hard. Brooklin, now you come with me. Your foster mom is here to take you home, but before that you can tell me about today's meeting."

Brook looked at Maggie, reached in her pocket, and obviously crumpled the picture of Victorian House.

"Maggie, you stay here. I'll be back in a few minutes."

Maggie nodded. What would Brook tell Miss Sechrest? They'd made a couple of connections, she thought. The room, and food. If she came for a visit they could make cookies. *When* she came for a visit, Maggie corrected herself, a little guiltily.

She'd wanted to adopt for so long. Completed all the home study requirements in two states. Spoken with other people, single and married, who'd adopted older children.

And yet, face to face with a real child, at a moment she should feel thrilled and full of love, she'd felt totally inadequate. What could she offer a child like Brook? A girl who didn't even want a family. Maybe Brook wasn't the daughter for her. Maybe, somewhere in Maine, there was another little girl who wanted a mother. Who wanted her.

She paced the small room, focusing on the photographs of happy adopted children on one wall. But all she could see was Brook's face, half-hidden by her hair.

Weren't you supposed to fall in love with your child the first time you met?

All she felt was fear. And an increasing headache. Had she made a giant mistake? Maybe adoption really wasn't for her. Will had never wanted her to adopt anyway. Aunt Nettie would be disappointed. But Aunt Nettie hadn't met Brook.

The door opened and Sandy came back in.

2. June

Lithograph showing young girl holding a bunch of yellow daisies. Original painting by Maud Humphrey (1868–1940) from *Babes of the Year*, published by Frederick Stokes in 1888. Maud Humphrey, a suffragette and commercial artist known for her sweet portraits of children, was also the mother of actor Humphrey Bogart.

6.5 x 8 inches. Price: $70

*Y*OU MADE A GOOD first impression," said Sandy, tucking a strand of hair behind her ear and sitting down, notebook in hand.

"I did?" Maggie blurted. For the first time she noticed Sandy's blond hair was beginning to gray. If she told Sandy she'd been wrong, that she wasn't ready for a child like Brook, would that mean the end of her adoption dreams? Would the agency even consider referring another child to her?

"Brooklin told me she was going to have a red room," said Sandy. "That's a positive sign. She's already thinking of a future with you."

"She told me she didn't want a family."

"Of course she did. That's to be expected. She's never had a good experience with a family. She's lived with six families, counting her birth family. Most were pretty bad experiences. And when they were positive, they ended. In her mind she's been rejected by every family she's ever known. She's learned not to trust. Because of her father, and at least one foster father, she has particular trust issues with men. That's why we thought you, being single, could be the right parent for her."

Will was a big part of her life, even if they weren't married. He hadn't wanted children. Brook was nervous about men. How was that going to work out?

"I understand why she doesn't trust people. But what can I do about it?"

"Just relax, be yourself, but let her know you're in control. You don't want to be her best friend. You want to be her mother. That's why whenever possible with older children we have this 'getting to know you' period," said Sandy. "You can meet her again, early next week. Is Tuesday good for you? We encourage children and prospective parents to meet at least three times before we ask them if they want to proceed." She paused. "Brooklin's nine. She won't be placed with you if she doesn't want to be. You both have to agree to at least give the placement a try."

Maggie nodded. "Next week. Tuesday. Same time, same place."

"Exactly. And if you want to talk to me in the meantime, feel free to call. Brooklin has a history of running away, so we'll keep the first couple of visits contained. If you'd like, you can bring a snack to share next time. She'll be coming here right after school."

"She said her name was Brook," Maggie said.

"That's right. Sorry, I forgot. I have so many children to keep track of. She decided to change her name after her last placement."

"Brooklin's an unusual name."

"That's where she was born: Brooklin, Maine."

"And that's where her family lived?"

"For her first couple of years. They lived with her grandmother, her mother's mother. After her grandmother died they moved up near Gray."

"So I'll bring a snack next week. Pizza?"

"Pizza's always good."

"Or—she said she liked peanut butter and jelly sandwiches."

Sandy Sechrest stood up. "Your decision. She may soon be your daughter. Snack choices will be the easiest part of it."

Maggie didn't say anything.

"You'll be fine, Maggie. Expectations are different from realities. I believe you and Brook will work out your differences. It'll just take longer than one or two short visits." She hesitated. "Brook knows this may be her last chance to have a family of her own. She's getting older, and not many families are willing to accept the emotional baggage she comes with. But, underneath, she's just a scared little girl."

Maggie nodded. She'd wanted to be a mother for so long. But how could she be strong for a scared little girl if she was scared herself?

3. 'They are only dreams,' said the crow.

Black-and-white illustration of scared young girl holding a lantern. Frightening shadows of animals and people are reflected on the wall in back of her. Two large crows are in front of her, trying to reassure her. Arthur Rackham (1867–1939) illustration for "The Snow Queen" in *Andersen's Fairy Tales*, 1932. Rackham was a major illustrator during the "Golden Age," a period in England when illustrated books were highly valued and produced with brilliant lithographs.

5 x 6.5 inches. Price: $45.

*A*LITTLE OVER AN hour later Maggie was back in her Waymouth apartment pouring herself a glass of sherry and giving Winslow his dinner.

Luckily it was late enough in the afternoon so all the workmen at the house had left for the day.

She didn't want to see anyone. She wanted to think.

But Aunt Nettie had been anxious to hear all about how the meeting with Brooklin—Brook, Maggie corrected herself—had gone, so last night Will had invited her to join them for dinner after she got back from Augusta. They'd be expecting her to be excited and positive. Could she tell them how confused and scared she was? Would Will be relieved? Aunt Nettie disappointed?

Probably.

Since Aunt Nettie's minor stroke almost a year ago, Will had moved in with his aunt. He and Maggie might be "promised," as he put it, and business partners, but for now she lived over the antiques mall they'd named Victorian House, and he lived a few streets away.

Usually she wished he were closer. Today, she was glad he was across town.

She'd wanted to be a mother since she was in elementary school.

When *she* was a mother, she'd planned, she'd give lots of hugs and encouragement and never tell her daughter she wasn't smart enough, or pretty enough, or brave enough. She wouldn't leave her little girl alone all night because she was partying. She wouldn't make her wear hand-me-downs. She'd make sure her daughter had shoes and sweaters like the ones other girls in her school wore.

But the child Maggie'd dreamed of decorating a Christmas tree with and sharing old movies and helping with homework was nothing like Brook.

And what about Brook? What did Brook think of her?

Sandy had said Brook was positive about their meeting, but she sure hadn't looked positive. Maybe Sandy just said that to make them both feel better.

Maggie sipped her sherry, gave Winslow a pat, and quietly panicked.

Maybe she wasn't wise enough, or patient enough, or loving enough to be a parent.

What if her dreams of motherhood were fantasies?

What if deciding to adopt had been a big mistake?

She got up and walked from one window to another, not noticing the boats on the Madoc River or the red-and-purple sky deserted by the fading sun.

Sandy Sechrest had said that if she didn't adopt Brook then the girl would have no one. How could she walk away from a child? But Brook was angry and tough and didn't want her. What would her life be like with a daughter like that? She'd thought about what it would be like to love a child. She'd never imagined that a child wouldn't love her.

When she'd decided to move to Maine she'd made Aunt Nettie and Will her family. Would Aunt Nettie be shocked at how she felt? Would Will say, "I told you so"?

But the decision to adopt was hers. Not theirs.

How open should she—could she—be about how she'd reacted? But she had to be honest with her social worker, with Brook, and, especially, with Will and Aunt Nettie. If Brook came to live in Waymouth, they'd be a part of her new world.

She gulped the rest of her sherry. She should be ecstatic with happiness. Instead, she felt confused and inadequate.

She picked up the rejected teddy bear and held him for several long minutes. Then she placed him carefully on the bed in Brook's room.

Right now she had to face Will and Aunt Nettie.

She walked slowly down the three flights to the street and headed toward their house. The streets of Waymouth were quiet on this early evening. Occasionally a car or pickup passed, or she heard the low hum of a lobster boat's motor on the river. Chickadees, cardinals, and sparrows filled the air with busy chirping. May was the season for nest building and egg laying. The time to start families.

"Maggie! You're finally here. I've been thinking about you all afternoon. Come. Tell us all about her," Aunt Nettie called out from the living room as soon as Maggie opened the front door.

Maggie sniffed the air. Tomato sauce. Will had spent so many hours working at Victorian House this spring he hadn't had much time for cooking. He made great spaghetti, but she'd eaten it four times in the past two weeks. As soon as her stove was delivered, and the elevator installed that would let Aunt Nettie visit, she'd invite them both for dinner.

Would she be able to entertain after Brook came to live with her?

Not at first, for sure. In a couple of months? But it wouldn't be the same as having an "all adult" evening. Would she ever have privacy again?

Aunt Nettie was wearing a gray-blue sweater that matched her eyes and was sitting in the wheelchair she'd been using recently. Will got up from the couch and Maggie let herself be hugged.

She sat next to him on the couch and looked at the crackers and cheese and pâté Will had put on the coffee table.

"I have a bottle of champagne waiting in the refrigerator," he said. "Shall I pop the cork?"

"Why don't you just get me a glass of red wine," said Maggie. "Let's save the champagne until we know for sure she's going to move in."

Will and Aunt Nettie exchanged glances and Will went to pour her a glass of merlot.

"Well? How did it go?" said Aunt Nettie, leaning forward. "I'm guessing from your expression the meeting wasn't what you expected."

"No. It wasn't," Maggie answered as Will handed them each a glass. "Brook—she wants to be called Brook, not Brooklin—is a tough kid. I'd thought she'd be more—positive—about meeting me. I guess I expected too much."

"She's already been through a lot of rejection, hasn't she?" Aunt Nettie said.

"Yes. But I think she's a survivor," said Maggie.

"That sounds good," Will put in. "What did it feel like? I mean, did you feel as though she was going to be your daughter?"

"You mean, did we bond? I don't know. I don't think so. It was only a short visit, and it was over so fast. We're going to meet again next week." She took a sip of wine. "I made the mistake of telling her she could have any color room she wanted."

"Black? Purple?" Will grinned.

"Red." Maggie couldn't help smiling. Will's years teaching high school sometimes gave him insights she didn't expect. "I'll take paint samples the next time I see her."

"Red! I always liked red," said Aunt Nettie approvingly. "Much better than the usual 'pink for a girl' some people paint a child's room. And if you paint the furniture white, with red handles or knobs on her bureau, it would look very cheerful. And cozy in the winter."

"Or you could go for a patriotic theme and make it a red, white and blue room," suggested Will. "Sounds like you'll have to repaint that room you just finished. So when will we get to meet this young lady who likes red?"

Maggie shook her head. "I have at least one more meeting with her before I can bring her to see Waymouth and the house. No sleepovers for a couple of weeks. I'll have to see how it goes."

"Sounds exciting, anyway," said Will. "Excuse me a few minutes while I put water on to boil for the pasta."

When he was safely out of the living room Aunt Nettie leaned over toward Maggie. "Are you all right? The meeting didn't go the way you hoped."

"No. It didn't."

Aunt Nettie was silent for a moment. "I've never been a parent. But from what I've seen over the years, being a mother or," she glanced toward the kitchen, "father, is never what you think it's going to be. Like any relationship, it has its highs and its lows. But everyone needs family, Maggie. You need to be a parent and this little girl needs to be a daughter. The pieces will fit together. If it's meant to be, you'll both make it work."

Aunt Nettie's only pregnancy, over sixty years ago, had ended in a stillbirth. She still grieved for her lost daughter. "You're probably right. I'm just nervous."

"You can always back off," said Will, coming back into the room. "You don't have to do this. Maybe Brook isn't the right one for you. There must be a lot of other children needing homes."

"Many. Here and abroad. But today I sat and talked to one girl who needs to be able to trust someone. She needs a place to come home to." Maggie looked from Aunt Nettie to Will and back again. "I can't give up this quickly." As she said the words, she knew that was what she believed.

"You mean, give up on her? Give up on this Brook being your child?" asked Will.

"No," said Maggie. "Give up on myself. Give up on thinking I can do this." She'd never forgive herself for not trying. For her own sake, as well as for Brook's.

"That's decided, then," said Will. "Dinner's almost ready. And we need to talk about tomorrow. I forgot to tell you. Yesterday I hired Brian's friend Annie to help set up the accounts for the business, and build us a website. She'll be coming in tomorrow morning. I thought you could show her what we need done."

"Annie?" Maggie asked.

"Eric Sirois's girlfriend. You remember Eric—Brian's friend. He helped you move in."

"I remember Eric. Nice kid." Muscular, not too tall, and a big smile. A lobsterman, he'd said.

"I agree. Annie stopped in with Eric today, while you were in Augusta. They were looking for Brian. Mentioned she was looking for a job. Turned out she knows computers—she's had a couple of years at a technical school. Said she could set up our website."

"That would be great," said Maggie. "We need someone to do that. You and I aren't computer whizzes."

"Exactly. And she seems to have her act together. Anyway, Giles and Brian and I are going to work in the front room tomorrow, and I have to walk around with the electrician, so I'd like you to spend some time with Annie. I want to make sure she understands what we're looking for. We need to get the website up as soon as possible, so we can start listing some of the antiques the dealers will be bringing in. And the accounting system has to be set up."

"Not to worry. I'll talk with her. I think I met her once before, with Eric at The Great Blue. I liked her. I didn't realize she had computer skills."

She'd planned to do some more unpacking and look for paint samples. But Will had plans, too, and his first priority was getting Victorian House ready to open by July Fourth.

Although right now that didn't seem as important as it had yesterday.

"I'll be available whenever Annie arrives tomorrow," Maggie promised.

After all, she wasn't going to see Brook until next Tuesday. Her "to do" list could wait.

4. Honeybees; male, female and worker

Delicate hand-colored bees on black-and-white steel engraving. As was the custom at the time, the bees are hand-colored with watercolors, but the background is unpainted. From *The Naturalist's Library*, 1843, Edinburgh, edited by Sir William Jardine (1800–1874) and engraved by William Home Lizars (1788–1859).

4 x 6 inches. Price: $60.

*S*LEEP DIDN'T COME EASILY that night. Maggie went over and over the afternoon in her head. Had she said the wrong things? Come on too strong?

Or maybe she'd been too weak. She should have taken control of the situation.

But how could she have done that? Sure, she was a teacher. She could control a classroom. But dealing with college students wasn't the same as coping with a nine-year-old. And she didn't want to control Brook. She wanted to establish parameters. How did that work with parents and children?

So much she had to learn. Books, the sources she always went to when she wanted to know something, wouldn't have all the answers this time. They might head her in certain directions. But they didn't know Brook. Or her.

She woke up three hours later with cramps, and tears in her eyes. She'd been dreaming she was giving birth, but the doctor refused to let her see her baby, and she was convinced the child had died.

She got up and scrounged for aspirin in the carton of bathroom supplies she hadn't unpacked because her bathroom wasn't equipped with a cabinet yet. She'd remind Will about that tomorrow. He'd waited until she'd picked the one she wanted, but for the past week it had been sitting in a carton on her living room floor.

27

Before Brook spent the night at least the bathroom should be fully functional.

Speaking of "functional," the stove would be delivered Monday. She hated to think what the men delivering it would say when they found out she was three flights up, with no elevator. They were hoping to soon have a small elevator installed where the old dumbwaiter was, but putting in new wiring and plumbing, and replastering and painting walls were higher priorities.

The aspirin helped. When sleep came this time, it was deep.

"GOOD morning, beautiful." Will stood over her bed and reached down to kiss her lightly. "It's almost eight. Giles and Brian are downstairs, the electrician's on his way, and Annie should be here by nine. Rise and shine!"

Maggie reached for Will's hand, but he'd already moved into the kitchen area of the living room. "I'll turn on the coffee," he called back. "Bring me a cup when it's brewed, would you? Giles and Brian are building bookcases for the two front rooms while I walk around with the electrician. I wish we didn't have to pay an electrician to do the final work on the lights, but that's the only way we'll get approval from the state electrical inspector."

She sat up. "Will, could you ask Brian or Giles to install the cabinet we bought for my bathroom? I want to get my stuff unpacked and put away."

"Don't worry—I'll take care of that later. The bookcases are critical for the dealers renting space in those rooms. That antiquarian book dealer you suggested, Joe Cousins, left a message that he has a show to do in New Hampshire in ten days, so he'll be here next weekend to set up even though he knows we won't open for another month. Don't forget my coffee. Black." The door closed in back of him.

Maggie sighed. Will's cousin Giles and his son Brian worked for Brent Construction during the week, but had been moonlighting all spring, helping Will by working for him weekends and some evenings. In New Jersey Saturday had been a sleep-in and relax day. Here in Waymouth Saturday was definitely a work day.

She pulled herself out of bed and headed for the bathroom.

An hour later she'd delivered Will's coffee (she didn't drink the stuff, but he'd made sure a percolator was in her apartment when she'd moved in) and sipped half of the Diet Pepsi that was her go-to morning beverage. Victorian House's front hall was now equipped with a massive mahogany office desk Will'd bought at an auction to serve as both a receptionist's station and a place to pay for merchandise. Already it held a telephone, computer, and cash register.

Joe Cousins would be the first antique dealer to set up his room. She hoped Will had explained their tagging and pricing system to him, and that Joe had listened. If the codes on the tags weren't correct, it would be hard to enter sales in the computer, and harder to figure how large a check Joe would be getting once a month, and how much would go to the mall. Depending on how much space they'd rented, dealers would pay between $50 and $400 a month to show here, and seventy-five percent of the receipts for their merchandise that sold would go to them.

The other twenty-five percent would go to Will and Maggie, to pay utilities and taxes and salaries for anyone else, like Annie Bryant, who'd be working here. Maggie and Will hoped there'd be enough profit to live on. If not the first year, then the second.

All the inventory tracking had to be in place before the dealers moved their antiques in. Not even Will, who planned to display his iron, brass and copper fireplace and kitchen equipment in Victorian House's kitchen and barn, or Maggie, who'd claimed the hallway and one of the first floor rooms for her prints, had set up yet.

Victorian House was still under construction. Dust was everywhere.

At first Will had assumed he or Maggie would be at the front desk most of the time the House was open. But between Aunt Nettie's needs and Maggie's adoption plans, they'd realized that, at least for the summer, they needed someone else to be there on a regular basis. After school opened and summer visitors left Maine they'd reconsider staffing and hours. They planned to keep Victorian House open all year 'round, but that could change. Many

Maine businesses found January and February such slow months for business that they closed, and their owners were able to take vacations.

Of course, with Brook in school, Maggie wouldn't be able to travel then.

Annie Bryant walked in a few minutes after nine, wearing a loose sweatshirt over tight black yoga pants.

When she saw Maggie she put her hands over her ears. The noise from the hammers and saws in the front room was so loud Maggie had to shout.

"Good morning, Annie. I know—it's impossible in here. But we'll try to go over this once before we lose our hearing. Will said you'd be working here full-time beginning the Tuesday after Memorial Day?"

Annie nodded. "I've given my two weeks' notice at the clothing store; I'm all set. Whatever hours you need me, I'll be here. I'm excited about working so close to home. And to Eric. He gets up before dawn to pull his traps, and he's ready to fall asleep by the time I get back from South Portland." She looked at the stack of papers Maggie had just taken out of one of the desk drawers. "Unless he's out drinking with the other guys. Then he manages to stay awake. I need to learn the systems here. But do you think today I'll need to be here more than this morning?"

"I don't think so. I'll just run through the basics today. We can go into more detail when you're here in June."

"Good. Because," Annie lowered her voice, glancing over her shoulder at the men working on the bookcases, "I have an appointment with a wedding planner later today."

Maggie stopped. "That's exciting! I didn't know you and Eric were engaged! When's the big event?"

Annie reached up, pulled her long red hair streaked with white into a ponytail, and held it in place with an elastic band she'd picked up from the desk. "We're not exactly engaged. I just wanted to find out how expensive it would be to have a small, elegant wedding and how far ahead we'd need to plan."

"I see. Does Eric know you're doing this research?" No wonder

Annie'd lowered her voice. Brian, in the next room, was one of Eric's best friends.

"No. I mean, he hasn't exactly proposed yet. But I'm sure he's going to soon. I just want to be prepared when he does. You know?"

Maggie smiled incredulously. No, she didn't know. Planning a wedding before you were engaged sounded more than a little strange. On the other hand, young people did things differently today. Annie must be very confident about her relationship with Eric.

"I've been thinking Columbus Day weekend," Annie was saying. "Rates are lower then, and Eric should be able to take a week off for our honeymoon. I'm hoping he could find someone else to check his traps then. Abe knows where they all are."

"Abe?" asked Maggie.

"Abe Palmer. Eric's sternman." Annie paused. "Will there be any problem if I take a week off in October after Columbus Day?"

Columbus Day weekend. Maggie'd always taken her antique prints to the Rensselaer County Show that weekend. Because of moving into her apartment, setting up Victorian House, and preparing for her adoption, she'd cancelled out of the Memorial Day show. She'd hoped to do the Columbus Day event.

How many shows would she have to cancel out of this year? If she cancelled out of too many, she wouldn't be able to get back in unless she went on waiting lists for dealer spaces. The best shows had several-year-long lists of people hoping to get in.

"You could take time off then. But why don't you wait to ask officially until you're really engaged and setting a date." October was months away, after all.

"Okay." She pointed at the tourmaline ring on Maggie's left hand. "What about you? When are you and Will getting married?"

"We haven't set a date yet." Maggie turned to the papers on the desk. "Now, why don't I begin by explaining how the mall will be set up?"

"Will said there'd be sales from different dealers. I've never handled anything like that."

"It won't be that complicated," Maggie assured her. "We'll take it one step at a time."

She pulled out a list of dealers and their codes, and she and Annie bent over them as the hammering from the room in back of them said the bookcases were in progress.

This was Maine. But no one this Saturday was treating it like Vacationland.

5. There was an old woman who lived in a shoe...

Illustration of large worn boot on a hill surrounded by lines of children eating or waiting in line to be whipped by an angry woman. From *The Volland Mother Goose*, 1915. Eulalie Osgood Grover, editor; Frederick Richardson, illustrator. P.F. Volland & Co., Chicago. Lithograph.

7 x 9 inches. Price: $70.

*A*FEW MINUTES AFTER Annie'd left for her appointment with the wedding planner, Brian came over to talk to Maggie. She was entering a list of codes into the computer.

"I saw you talking to Annie," said Brian, leaning over the desk. "Eric told me you'd hired her. How's she doing?"

"She'll be fine," said Maggie. "But it will take a while. From the noise coming out of that room you've been working in this morning, you and your dad must be making a lot of progress on those bookcases."

"They're almost done," he agreed. "Come and see."

Maggie followed him into the front room where Joe would be displaying his antiquarian books. Six-foot-high bookcases were now between every window and door. "What about the space above them?" Maggie asked.

"Will said not to build them higher. People couldn't reach shelves above that, and he doesn't want any ladders, in case someone would fall."

"That makes sense," Maggie agreed. Would Will mind her hanging some prints above the bookcases? Or had Joe Cousins reserved every inch of this room? She made a mental note to check after Joe set up.

"We're going to build some lower bookcases next; back to back for the center of the room," Brian explained. "Of course, they all need to be sanded and varnished and painted or stained. I'll ask Will what he wants us to do."

"Will thinks you're doing a great job, and he and Maggie can do the finishing," said Will, coming up in back of Maggie and giving her a hug.

"How's the electrical work coming along?" she asked. So she and Will would be finishing this room. Her plans to finish unpacking and set up her desk flew out the window.

"We had to add more power to the house because of the spotlights the dealers want," Will said. "And all new grounded electrical outlets. It's taking longer than I'd hoped. How did Annie do this morning?"

"She'll be fine. It'll be easier to work when the place is a little calmer and quieter. I have an errand to run at the hardware store. Is it a problem if I go now?"

"We need more finishing nails," Brian put in. "I can take you, Maggie."

"All right. But, both of you, come back soon," said Will. "Only ten days until the first dealer moves his stuff in. And this is his room."

"If you're going to stain the bookcases, they need to be done in the next couple of days." Giles, Brian's father, stopped measuring #2 pine boards and joined them. "Books'll be ruined if the stain isn't wicked dry. This time of year there's a lot of rain. Humidity'll keep stain from drying fast."

"Good point, Giles. Why don't you and Brian pick up some stain while you're at the hardware store, Maggie," Will agreed. "A medium pine shade. Pine says 'Maine.'"

"You'll need gallons of the stuff for this many bookshelves," Giles pointed out.

"We'll start with one gallon," said Will. "Make sure we've got the right color. Then we can get more."

"Giles, while we're at the hardware store, would you mind installing the medicine cabinet in my bathroom? The hole's already cut. It just needs to be put in and secured, but I've never done anything like that," asked Maggie.

"Maggie, why are you bothering Giles about that? I told you I'd take care of it later," said Will impatiently.

"Why don't you come up with me, Will? The two of us should be able to get it done, no problem," said Giles. "Keep your lady happy." He winked at Maggie.

"Thanks," said Maggie, as she and Brian headed out the door.

She climbed up into the passenger seat of Brian's faded pickup, brushing fast-food bags off the seat. Thank goodness she'd worn jeans. Come to think of it, except for the meetings with the social worker, she hadn't worn a skirt since she'd moved to Maine.

"I'm looking forward to working with Annie," said Maggie. "Have you known her long?

"Just all my life." Brian started the truck and headed down Route 1. "She and Eric and I went to Waymouth High together. Well, sort of together. They were a couple of years ahead of me. So were Hay and Jill. Hay dropped out in tenth grade, but the rest of us graduated. We all live close, in town. We've known each other since we were kids."

"Hay and Jill?"

"Sorry. Thought you knew them. Will does. Hay tends bar, nights, over at The Great Blue. Jill's his girl. She waits tables there."

"I see."

"We all hang together. I haven't seen them as much this spring. Will's had Dad and me working at Victorian House." He shrugged. "Will's family. We're second or third cousins or something. I never figured it out exactly. But family helps family."

"You like construction?"

"It's what Dad does, and he's taught me. Been doing it summers since I was a kid, and full time since high school. Never tried anything else. Pays, and there's always work. Can't beat that."

"Are you saving for something special?"

"I'd like to get my own place. Mom and Dad are pretty relaxed, but," he glanced at Maggie, "living at home is for kids. And someday I hope I can start my own company."

"So do your friends all have apartments?"

He shook his head. "Nah. Annie and Hay live with their folks. Eric's dad is long-gone, and his sister left, too, but he lives with his mom. Jill's the only one who lives alone. She rents a room up on Federal Street. Her mom died years ago, and she and her stepmom don't get along."

"How old are you now, Brian?"

"Twenty-one last month."

"No girlfriend?" she teased.

Brian didn't answer at first. Then, "Not since Crystal."

She'd opened a painful door. "I'm sorry, Brian. I didn't think. It's been, what? Two years since Crystal was murdered."

"Two years this August." Brian turned the truck in at the hardware store. "You need any help finding things here?"

Maggie shook her head. "I'm picking up paint samples, and then looking at the stains. Why don't we meet at the check-out?"

She headed for the paint section and started looking through red wall colors, trying to pick three or four she'd find acceptable for a room in her apartment. Brook should feel the color was her choice, but Maggie would have to live with it, too. So, nothing shiny, she thought, as she looked through the colors. Smoldering Red, Shy Cherry, and Rhubarb were the best, she decided. Their cool names were a plus.

Ahead of her in the aisle a small boy wearing shorts and a Red Claws T-shirt was methodically reaching up and pulling dozens of paper tabs of color samples out of their slots and dropping them on the floor.

"And how much paint would I need if I paint all four walls with two coats?" his mother was asking the older man putting her cans of paint on the mixer.

"Your son over there, he's making a mess of the place," said the man, gesturing toward the boy. His tone was remarkably restrained.

His customer reached over, grabbed the child, and swatted him several times on the rear. "Arnold, why don't you ever behave? I should never have brought you here. How could you do this?" The boy's eyes glimmered with tears. "I'm taking you to the car right now." She turned to the man who'd been helping her. "Hold my paint, would you? I'll have my husband pick it up later."

She strode out of the store, carting her son with her, loudly chastising him all the way.

The hardware store clerk bent to pick up and sort the dozens of color samples on the floor. Seeing Maggie looking at him, he asked, "Can I help you with anything?"

"No. I've found what I need."

"Good. At least you don't have a kid who leaves a mess for other people to clean up," he said, muttering to himself as he started carefully replacing the paint samples in the right slots.

No, Maggie thought. *I don't have a kid like that. Not yet, anyway.* How would she have coped? She hated seeing the boy yelled at. But he'd definitely been misbehaving. She could hear her own mother's voice. "Maggie, keep your hands to yourself in the store. Don't touch anything."

What would she do if Brook misbehaved in public? She was a lot older than that little boy. She wouldn't drop paint samples. But who knew what else she might do?

Maggie took a deep breath and dropped the free paint samples into her red canvas bag.

Stain. She had to find pine stain.

6. "Tell me the way, then," she said, "and I'll search you out."

Small girl clings to tall bedpost as elegant woman reassures her. From *East of the Sun and West of the Moon: Old Tales From the North* illustrated by Kay Nielsen (1886–1957), Doubleday, Doran & Company, Inc., New York, 1930. Nielsen was born in Denmark and studied in Paris before he moved to England, and then to the United States, where he worked for The Walt Disney Company.

7 x 5.25 inches Price: $80.

SATURDAY AFTERNOON Brian and Giles moved on to replastering the ceiling of the room where Maggie planned to display her prints. She'd stopped on her way to Maine to replenish those for sale at her friend Gussie's shop on Cape Cod, but most of her inventory was still in her van, waiting to be unpacked when the room was finished.

"There wasn't a pine stain," she'd explained to Will. "I got the 'Early American' because it was closest to what you were thinking of."

He glanced at it and shrugged. "It'll do. Did you think to pick up some wood patch or shellac?"

"Wood patch and sandpaper," she answered, pointing to the bag on the floor. "I wasn't sure you'd want to use shellac."

"Sealing the wood will keep the grain from showing through more than it should. But we need to patch and sand first," he said, handing Maggie a mask. "These are a nuisance, but as soon as we start sanding there'll be a lot of dust."

Maggie gamely tied her mask on.

"You take one can of the wood patch and I'll take the other. By the time we finish, the first patches should be dry enough to sand."

The patching didn't take long. But the sanding seemed never-ending. Talking was difficult while they were wearing the masks, so they worked in silence, sanding until they were both covered with dust and tiny fragments of pine and their hands hurt.

"I need to stop for a while. At least drink some water," she said, finally.

"It's almost five o'clock," Will noted. "Giles and Brian will be leaving. It's time for us to stop."

"Great." Maggie got up from where she'd been sitting on the floor, working on the bottom half of a bookcase, and added the sandpaper she'd been using to the box of supplies balanced on a board between two sawhorses. "What I want is a hot shower." She shook her head and tiny particles fell from her long brown hair. Will's gray beard was spotted with dust.

"Do you want to come over for a leftover spaghetti dinner?" Will asked. "We didn't finish it all last night."

Spaghetti again? "I'm tired, Will. It's been a long day. Would you mind if I just stayed here? I have bread and sandwich makings. That's all I need. I'd like to get some more cartons unpacked tonight. I'll be more comfortable when the apartment is finished."

"When will Brook be able to visit?"

"She won't be able to stay the night for at least another ten days, but I'm hoping she can visit here next Friday afternoon."

"Okay. You get some rest. But why don't we plan dinner tomorrow, just the two of us, at The Great Blue? I'll fix something for Aunt Nettie at home first."

"I'd like that," Maggie said. "We're spending a lot of time together, but it's almost all work time. I'd like an excuse to shower and get cleaned up and relax."

"And now you even have that medicine cabinet you've been nagging me about," Will teased. "A place to put all your womanly necessities."

"I wasn't nagging. But I'm glad it's installed. One more carton I can unpack." She reached up to kiss him and then turned toward the staircase.

"One more thing," he said. "I forgot to tell you. I've gotten a couple of estimates on the elevator we wanted. I found one that'll fit

in the corner of the pantry on the first floor, where the dumbwaiter is
now, and have exits on the second and third floor landings."

"And?"

"We can afford it."

"Good! I was worried about that."

"I was, too. I still hope we can open the second floor to dealers
later this summer, and I wanted all the rooms to be handicapped
accessible. The wheelchair ramp is finished, and the elevator will
let customers get to the second floor. Plus, you won't have to cart
groceries up three flights, counting the one up to the porch. The exit
on the third floor will be close to your door."

Will had built a small entryway at the top of the staircase on
the third floor, and circled the old hallway with walls. No mall customers could wander into the apartment thinking there were more
antiques upstairs.

"I can't wait," said Maggie. "I'm just sorry there wasn't an elevator when you and Brian and Eric moved my furniture and cartons
upstairs."

"The elevator will give you and Brook more privacy," Will pointed
out. "You won't have to walk through rooms of antiques and customers to get home."

The elevator would also limit the possibility of Brook's damag-
ing any of the antiques in the rooms below, Maggie knew. Will'd
once mentioned that children and fragile antiques didn't mix. Some
antiques malls didn't allow dogs or children inside. But so far the
only dealer signed up who had a fragile inventory was the smalls
dealer, who had china teapots and cups and was renting a locked
display case to hold her crystal.

"Can they install the elevator before July Fourth?" Maggie
asked.

"I hope so. I'll talk to the dealer Monday," said Will. "Construction is going to be a mess, and noisy, so I'd like it over before we
open."

"And you won't be able to set up your exhibit in the kitchen until
they're finished," Maggie pointed out.

"So let's hope we can get it done soon," he agreed.

"And the security system?"

"This week. We already have locks on the windows, and a special lock on the room where Jim Tyson's silver and jewelry will be. The cameras and motion detectors will be installed Tuesday or Wednesday."

"Make sure you tell the security company about the elevator." Maggie hesitated. "I'm a little nervous about that security system. I don't want to set off an alarm every time Brook or I come and go when Victorian House isn't open."

"But you will," Will cautioned. "You'll have to enter the code at one of the doors, and then, once you're in your apartment, reset the alarm. If either of you leave the apartment during the night you'll set off alarms."

"We can manage that. I hope Brook doesn't sleepwalk." Maggie smiled. The security would definitely be a pain. But with the antiques here it was necessary.

"Good. Because several dealers have asked about what security we'll have."

"Be sure to tell them someone will be here all night, after hours," Maggie pointed out. "That's got to mean something. Although I don't know how much I'd hear from the first floor if I'm sleeping in the apartment."

"We won't mention how far away you'll be from the antiques. My insurance guy liked the idea that someone would be living here. He figured it would discourage burglars. I don't think he was counting on your catching them."

"Enough talk. I'm heading up. I suspect it will be an early night."

"Love you, lady. See you tomorrow morning."

Will's hug was lingering, but his kiss was not. Like an old married couple, Maggie thought. Not exactly romantic. But they were working toward the same goals. Or some of the same goals, she amended as she wearily climbed the three flights of stairs to her apartment.

Until she'd officially moved into the apartment two weeks before, she'd stayed with Will and Aunt Nettie when she visited Waymouth.

Sleeping across town from Will already was awkward, although having her own space was positive.

But after Brook moved in—if she moved in—the space would no longer be hers alone. That would present further complications to the way she and Will were living.

Life, and their relationship, would never be this simple again.

Had it ever been simple?

Maybe two years ago, when they'd met at that Memorial Day weekend antiques show in New York State.

But even then, they'd both been nervous. Not just with each other…although most new relationships begin with some trepidation. But they'd met because a mutual friend, an antiques dealer, had been murdered. Will had taken his booth space at the show.

And then there'd been another murder.

Maggie shook her head, remembering. So much had happened since then. But here they were. "Promised," and in business together in a small town in Maine.

Where would they be, in their relationship, in another two years?

7. Monk Seals

Eleven monk seals basking in the sun on a beach, palm trees in the mid-distance. Hand-colored lithograph from *A History of the Earth and Animated Nature* by Oliver Goldsmith. 1878 edition. London, Edinburgh and Dublin: A. Fullarton & Co.

6.5 x 7.5 inches. Price: $60.

*M*AGGIE TOOK A long bath in lavender bubbles. Then she sipped a glass of sherry and ate a tuna sandwich while she and Winslow watched the local news from Portland. Will had made sure she had cable and Wi-Fi hookups before she moved in.

Half an hour later she was relaxed and ready to unpack her bathroom cabinet supplies. She put all her over-the-counter pills in her bureau drawer, away from nine-year-old hands and curiosity.

Brook hadn't even visited the apartment, but she was already influencing how it was organized.

Three days until Tuesday. She had the pre-approved red paint samples to show Brook.

But what should she bring for their after-school snack? Pizza would get cold. And what would Brook like on it? So many things she didn't know.

Peanut butter and jelly sandwiches would be safe. But if she made them with whole wheat bread, would Brook reject them? On the other hand, if she brought white bread sandwiches, did that mean she wouldn't bring her child up with healthy choices? And should she bring a sandwich for Sandy, the social worker? And what about jelly? Brook had said she liked strawberry. With seeds or without? Did Brook even know the difference between jam and jelly?

What about dessert? Her stove wouldn't be delivered until Monday, so she couldn't commit to baking cookies before Tuesday.

Ice cream (what flavors?) in a cooler? That would mean bowls and spoons.

She knew she was obsessing about minor issues, but her mind wasn't letting her body relax.

She vowed to unpack at least one more carton. Will had equipped the "L" shape off her bedroom with a built-in desk, a file cabinet, and a wall of empty bookshelves.

For several years she'd been taking notes for a book comparing the early work of Winslow Homer with that of Norman Rockwell. Both had focused on the social issues and everyday life of their times, and had an eye for detail and humor. "Publish or perish" was still the rule at colleges, so she hoped to finish her manuscript before either she went back to New Jersey or looked for a job in Maine.

She filled the filing cabinet with her notes. She wouldn't be able to do much work on the book until fall, when Brook was in school and Victorian House wasn't as busy as she and Will hoped it would be this summer.

If, of course, Brook accepted her and agreed to move in.

It all sounded so easy when Brook wasn't with her.

Tuesday she'd know more.

She stood in the door of the bedroom that would be…could be…Brook's in six weeks. The room that would soon be red. It had a single bed with a bright patterned bedspread, a bureau and mirror she'd bought at a house sale the week before, and a floor-to-ceiling bookcase, where the children's books Aunt Nettie had given her last Christmas were side-by-side with other books she'd bought in anticipation. More children's books were in cartons she hadn't unpacked yet. Would Brook like books? Like to be read to? She'd assumed so. She'd loved books when she'd been a child. But now she wasn't so sure. Maybe Brook would prefer drawing. Or games.

She'd mentioned computer games. Should a nine-year-old have her own computer? She could insist it only be used in the living room. Or should she give Brook access to her computer?

So many questions.

So many unknowns.

Maggie moved the teddy bear from the bed to one of the empty shelves.

By ten o'clock, despite the thoughts racing through her head, she was asleep.

SHE woke Sunday morning with the sunrise.

Her bedroom window looked out on the Madoc River. A light layer of fog covered the opposite shore and part of the water, but she could hear the engines of two lobster boats. Another was still docked at the town pier. Lobstermen got to work hauling traps early.

Maine was beautiful. Sure, Somerset County in New Jersey was lovely, from a New Jersey perspective. But it couldn't compete with the view from this window.

How many more mornings would she be able to take a peaceful early-morning walk alone? Quickly she pulled on jeans and a sweatshirt, picked up a diet soda for sustenance, and headed down the stairs and toward the town pier.

There it wasn't as quiet. Brian's friend Eric Sirois was arguing with an older man.

"You're no good to me if you show up drunk," he was saying. "I need a sternman I can depend on. Not one who'll stumble around the boat and get his foot caught in the ropes."

"Eric, I'm not that drunk. I just had a few drinks." The man tried to smile convincingly, but failed.

"You're stinking. How am I supposed to do two men's jobs? I'm already late getting out, since I was waiting for you." Eric looked furious.

"Sorry, man. Won't happen again." The man stumbled and then headed up the ramp to the wharf. He swayed as he passed Maggie on his way to Water Street. She watched him a few minutes, hoping he wouldn't fall off the wharf—or get into a car. He did neither.

Eric was standing on the deck of his *Lucy II*, calling someone on his cell phone.

When he put the phone back in his pocket, Maggie waved. "Morning, Eric! Beautiful boat."

"Hi, Maggie. C'mon down. I won't be going out for a while." He smiled, but he was tense. "Yup. The *Lucy II*'s special."

"Why Lucy? I thought your girl was Annie."

Eric grinned. "My Gram was Lucy. Grandpa named all his boats after her. It's bad luck to change a boat's name. Almost as bad luck as painting it blue."

"I see," said Maggie, walking down the long wharf to where Eric's boat was tied up. "Don't you go out about now?"

"Usually by five I'm out running traps," Eric agreed. "Today I'm burned. I should be out there now."

"Why aren't you?"

"I'm missing a sternman. Most days Abe Palmer sterns for me. He sterned when the *Lucy II* belonged to my Grandpa. Now the boat's mine, he wants to keep working. I get that. I need someone, and he's experienced, and stronger than he looks. When he's sober he's a good man to have on board. But then this morning he showed up late and drunk." Eric shook his head. "I just called a friend and asked him to help me out."

"Brian?" Maggie asked.

"Nah. Brian's working at Victorian House today. And he's more comfortable on land than water. Other guys know boats better. I just woke up Hay Johnson. He works nights, so early mornings aren't his choice of times to work, but he said he'd come down and help out." Eric shook his head. "I hate not being able to depend on someone."

"Hay Johnson. He's the bartender at The Great Blue, right?" One of the friends Brian had mentioned he'd grown up with.

"Right. But he fished with his dad for years, so he knows the ropes."

"How's lobstering been this summer?" Maggie asked, hoping to change the subject.

"Not great," Eric admitted. "Canadians aren't importing lobsters anymore, so prices are down. I wanted to get another Sunday or two in before summer rules take effect."

"Summer rules?" Maggie asked.

"State of Maine says first of June 'til first of September you can't haul traps after four o'clock Saturday afternoon or any time Sunday."

"Why?"

"Not sure. Maybe showing tourists we respect religion, or some-thing. The rest of the year we can haul seven days a week, sunrise to sunset."

"How many traps do you have?"

"Close to four hundred." Eric's smile said he was proud of that number.

It sounded like a lot of work. "And you haul every one every day you're out?"

"I hit every trap about every two days. Can't leave them longer, or the bugs—the lobsters—that get caught will start eating each other. But that's still a couple of hundred traps a day."

"How many lobsters do you pull in most days?"

Eric hesitated a moment. "I suppose I could say that's classi-fied. Grandpa knew where the bugs were, and he showed me. A lot of those in the traps have to be thrown back, of course—they're too small or too large, or they're females with eggs. Or notched females. I'd say one or two keepers per haul would be a good day. Eighty-five percent of what we haul we have to throw back."

Maggie was surprised. "That many?"

"Maine has strict rules for keepers, so we can sustain the lobster population."

"And what's a notched female?" Maggie's degrees were in Amer-ican Studies, not biology. Eric had lost her a few sentences back.

She batted at a couple of black flies as she tried to concentrate on what he was saying.

"If a lobsterman finds a female carrying eggs, he or she puts a triangular-shaped notch in her tail. That tells other lobstermen she's a breeding female, and can't be taken out of the water, even if she has no eggs then. It's a conservation thing." Eric slapped at another black fly.

"Makes sense." Maggie looked at Eric's *Lucy II*. One or two hundred lobsters a day was a lot. But at wholesale prices? And how much did it cost to keep a lobster boat working? Fuel, bait, repairs to traps, ropes. Not counting the cost of the boat and engine itself. A hard way to make a living.

"I'm hoping to put out some more traps this summer. But they cost about a hundred dollars each, and that doesn't count all the buoys and ropes. Or the time." Eric grinned. "My girl, Annie, she'd like me to have five or six hundred traps. Maybe I will someday." He slapped the black flies again.

"I don't remember there being this many black flies when I was in Maine before," said Maggie, killing one that had landed on her hand.

"They're most common Mother's Day 'til Father's Day," said Eric. "At dawn and dusk." He grinned. "Only the females bite, though. Like mosquitos."

"Then there must be a lot of females out here," said Maggie, swatting another one.

Eric looked up toward the street and waved. "There's Hay. He made it faster than I'd thought. He's a good man."

A tall, sinewy young man ran down the ramp toward them. "He likes the twenty percent of the haul's profits, too," he said. "Want me to cast off, Eric? I can get on my gear while we're heading out."

"Good luck to both of you," Maggie called as the two young men pulled up the bumpers and untied the ropes holding the *Lucy II* to the float. "Have a successful day!"

She walked back up the ramp, and down Water Street, toward the center of town. Sunday morning was quiet.

She and Will would have dinner at The Great Blue tonight. Her brief conversation with Eric Sirois made her think of lobsters. Not lobsters in traps; lobsters on plates. Maybe a buttered lobster roll would be on the menu tonight. Or a bright red steamed lobster, pulled out today. Some restaurants had summer menus now; some didn't. Year 'round Maine restaurants seldom featured fried clams and lobster rolls in months when tourists were few and far between. Haddock was the fish of choice for most locals, with steamed mussels in wine and herbs as an appetizer. Chefs added selections of other seafood around Memorial Day.

I'm now a resident, at least for the moment, Maggie thought. But I haven't been here long enough to prefer baked beans or haddock sandwiches to crab cakes and lobster.

Would that ever happen?

Not as long as oysters and lobster and clams tasted as good as they did. In terms of food she didn't mind being a tourist: what some locals called a summer complaint.

She was looking forward to making haddock chowder for Brook from Aunt Nettie's recipe.

Life in Maine was going to be good.

It was. It would be. No matter what the challenges.

8. A Picture of Good Health

Lithograph of a man's head, on an aqua background. The head opens and contains five pages that fold out, like a small book, showing cross sections of the head's muscles, bones, nerves, blood vessels, and sections of the brain labelled "Aspiring," "Moral," "Reflectives," "Self-Perfecting," Animal," and "Domestic," considered the divisions of the mind in 1894, when this was published in *Warren's Household Physician* by doctors Ira Warren and A.E. Small.

5 x 8.5 inches. Price: $75.

I HOPE YOU WON'T MIND; I asked Nick Strait to join us," Will said as he and Maggie walked in the door of The Great Blue.

Maggie glanced at him, trying not to show her disappointment.

"He called late this afternoon and sounded down. You and he know each other. I hoped seeing you would cheer him up."

Nick was a Maine State Trooper, a homicide detective. He and Maggie hadn't always agreed on the relationship between law enforcement and an amateur sleuth with key information. But he was also one of Will's oldest friends. "I'll be glad to see Nick," Maggie said. "Although I'd hoped tonight would be just for us."

"We'll have the rest of our lives together," said Will, putting his hand on Maggie's back and guiding her to the only empty table left with a view of the harbor. "Nick's alone."

"I know." Maggie picked up the menu. "He's lucky to have you as a friend."

"Us. He's lucky to have *us*. Beer or wine tonight?"

Maggie glanced at the menu. "I've been thinking about lobster rolls all day, and they're on the menu. A glass of the house white would be fine."

Will ordered their drinks. "We'll wait until Nick joins us to order food. So—lobster rolls? And here I was hoping you'd been thinking of *me* all day."

"I've been *working* with you all day," said Maggie. "Shellacking bookcases is not my favorite chore." She could still smell the stink of it, despite the gloves and mask she'd worn and the long shower she'd taken.

"But it gets us one step closer to being ready for our first dealer," Will reminded her.

"Early this morning I walked down by the harbor. I saw Eric Sirois on his lobster boat. That's why I've been thinking of lobster."

Will nodded. "Eric's a good kid. Probably the steadiest of Brian's pals. Inherited his grandfather's lobster boat, so he has a good start on making a living. And I like Annie. Nice couple."

"I hope she'll be as much help as she promises she can be," agreed Maggie. "She'll be starting May twenty-sixth—eight days from now. I can't believe three weeks ago I was still grading reports and cleaning out my office at the college."

"And now you're doing hard labor at Victorian House!" Will grinned.

"And Tuesday I'll see Brook again," Maggie reminded him.

"Hey, there's Nick!" Will stood and waved over the crowd.

Nick waved back and joined them at the table. "Good to see you again, Maggie. Understand this time you're here to stay."

"Seems that way," said Maggie. Nick was Will's age, mid-forties, but he was clean-shaven and trim…two things Will was not. In fact, Nick had lost weight since she'd last seen him, during the Christmas holidays. But he still looked good. "How've you been doing?"

He shrugged. "Been a rough spring. But I don't want to talk about that. How's the antiques mall—excuse me—Victorian House coming along? I saw your sign up last week. Good name."

"We're aiming at officially opening Fourth of July weekend," Will said. "Although we hope to open the doors a few days before that if we're ready, just to make sure everything's set."

"Test the place out?"

"Exactly," Will confirmed. "So, how's crime in Maine these days?"

"Always something. I'm working on a nasty domestic violence case in Whitefield now. Hope to get that finished up before anything else comes my way."

"With summer visitors, does that mean more crime?" asked Maggie.

"Depends. Folks don't go on vacation to kill each other. But with warmer weather people are outside, partying, drinking…and that can all go wrong. Homicide doesn't take a holiday."

"That sounds like a book title," said Maggie.

"Someday I might just write one of those." Nick smiled. "Have you guys ordered?"

"Just drinks," said Will. He signaled to Jill Pendleton, who was waitressing.

As she wrote down Nick's order (a Pemaquid Ale) Maggie took a good look at her. Jill was the other friend Brian'd mentioned; a shapely blonde whose Great Blue T-shirt was tight, and cut a little low for bending over tables. Maybe low necklines inspired higher tips. Next to Jill, Annie, despite her streaked hair, would hardly be noticed.

"Good to see you all," Jill said, who'd already put down Maggie's and Will's drinks. "I'll get your beer," she almost purred to Nick. "When you're ready to order food you just let me know."

"Kids grow up fast," said Nick as Jill walked away. "I remember when she was a toddler."

"She isn't toddling any more," Will replied. "She's Hay Johnson's girl now."

Nick shrugged. "Could be. Hard to keep track of all the relationships around this town. I may live in Waymouth, but I don't spend much time here. Most of my cases are further inland. Mom keeps track of what's going on in town and tries to keep me informed, but I don't always pay attention." He turned to Maggie. "Hey! Mom told me your adoption plans are working out. She's been talking to Aunt Nettie. Congratulations!"

Nick lived with his mother, Doreen, who was one of Aunt Nettie's closest friends. Of course he'd heard about Brook.

"Thanks, Nick, but no congratulations yet. I have to meet with her a few more times before she and I and my social worker all agree it's a match."

"You'll be a good mom. I don't understand why the state doesn't just admit that, and give her to you," said Will.

"Families aren't that simple." Nick looked at Maggie. "I've seen a lot of kids taken away from families because of neglect or abuse. I'm assuming your young lady has some rough times in her background."

"She does," Maggie affirmed.

"Then she needs to feel she has some control over her life. She needs to be part of the decision about what happens to her," Nick continued. "If she buys in, the whole situation'll be easier for both her and Maggie," he said to Will.

"Exactly," said Maggie. "You get it, Nick."

"Being a trooper means I see a lot I'd rather not remember," he said. "I also know what it's like to be a single parent to a daughter. No matter what, you'll have your hands full, Maggie."

"Thank you. I appreciate the support. I know there'll be a lot of challenges." Nick certainly had had problems with his daughter, Zelda. And some of his coping strategies weren't ones Maggie approved of. She'd already vowed—and promised to her social worker and the State of Maine—that she would never hit a child.

"Challenges, no doubt. But you're up to it," Nick said. He looked around for Jill. "I could use that beer about now."

Jill was serving a man sitting by himself in a corner. As Jill moved away from his table, Maggie could see it was Abe Palmer, Eric's grizzled sternman. Jill was giggling and laughing. Flirting with customers must be one of her shticks. Maggie smiled to herself for thinking of a word like that on the coast of Maine. Her New Jersey heritage was showing.

Will said, "Nick, do you know anyone local who plasters and could help me out in the next week or two? We had to tear holes in a couple of walls to get wiring in for the new lights, and Giles and Brian are only free evenings and weekends. I could use some help. We've got dealers moving in soon, and their rooms have to be ready."

"Can't say I can think of anyone offhand," said Nick. "I have a few vacation days coming and could help you out myself next week if

you still need someone. Thought I'd lengthen Memorial Day weekend into a week off if my case load is still down."

"But it's your vacation!" said Maggie. "Don't you think you
should just take some quiet time for yourself, Nick?"

"I'll do that, too," he assured her. "And Mom has a list of house
and yard chores she wants me to take care of. But I could still find
some time to help you guys out. What are friends for? As long as
you both promise not to murder anyone. It'll be relaxing to work on
something I can see the results of right away."

"Great! I'll give you a call to confirm when you can help out.
And in the meantime, if you think of anyone else who could help…"

"I'll think about it. A couple of guys around here are on probation. Maybe one of them's looking to make a few extra dollars. I'll see
if I can come up with anyone."

Maggie swallowed. Guys on probation? They deserved a new
start. But what if Brook was around? What if any of the men were
dangerous? She could handle it. But with a child…

By the time she'd decided to ask Nick not to send them any
sexual predators he and Will were deep into a serious discussion of
the current Red Sox lineup.

After Jill delivered Nick's beer (with a wink) they ordered their
food, and chatted through a leisurely dinner.

Maggie sipped her wine, looked out at the river, and savored
her lobster roll and the company of both men. Nick had certainly
understood what the situation with Brook was. He'd had firsthand
experience that wasn't all positive. Good to know she wasn't the only
one who had a glimmer of what might happen.

The restaurant had emptied as they were lingering over raspberry bread pudding when loud voices from the bar distracted them.

"No reason you can't serve me," came a rough voice, clear across
the room. Maggie turned. "You serve every other damn person who
asks." Abe Palmer had moved from his table to the bar.

Nick sighed. "Sounds like Abe's had a bit too much again. Guy
can be a problem. I'll see if Hay Johnson needs any help." He got up
and headed toward the bar.

"Abe Palmer. He's Eric's sternman, right?" asked Maggie. "I saw him down at Eric's boat today. Eric sent him home; said he was too drunk to work."

"Lobstering's not easy. And it can be dangerous. Abe's had his problems in life. Most people have some rocks in their paths. Abe just hasn't been dealing with his recently. Makes sense Eric wouldn't want him drunk on the water," Will pointed out.

"I've been drinking at this bar since before you could wipe your own rear," Abe yelled. "If I have money I should be able to get a beer! Or any other damn thing I want."

By that time, everyone still at The Great Blue was listening.

"Abe, it's time for you to head home." Nick's voice was strong and steady. Authoritative.

"I don't need no cop telling me what I can do," said Abe. "I'm a law-abiding citizen."

"Then why don't you let me take you home," said Nick.

Abe muttered something Maggie couldn't hear. But Nick waved to Maggie and Will as he took Abe by the arm and steered him out of the restaurant.

"That ends the evening on a sour note," said Will.

"Abe's in here just about every day," said Jill, handing him their check. "And night. Sweet enough when he comes in, but he's a nasty drunk. Too bad your friend isn't here all the time to help us get rid of him."

"The man's harmless," assured Will. "He's more a danger to himself than to anyone else."

"He doesn't make it easy for those of us who work here," said Jill. "I wish he'd find another place to do his drinking. A place he doesn't bother the customers or staff."

"Understood. But, like he said, he's been drinking here for years. Old habits don't die easy."

"Maybe not. But they stink," was Jill's succinct closing remark.

9. Untitled

Peter Rabbit in his blue jacket, racing to escape the garden basket Mr. McGregor is about to drop on his head. From *The Tale of Peter Rabbit*, written and illustrated by Beatrix Potter (1866–1943). Potter grew up with only her brother, her pets, and her sketchbook to keep her company. She loved Scotland and England's Lake District, where she lived after marrying at the age of 47. Although her books are still in print, the earliest editions have the finest lithographs. This illustration is from the 1902 Frederick Warne & Company edition, the first edition Potter didn't self-publish. (All publishers at first rejected *Peter Rabbit*, which became one of the most successful children's books of all time.)

3.5 x 5 inches. Price: $35.

*M*ONDAY MORNING MAGGIE pulled on the old jeans she wore for painting and shellacking, and a worn yellow shirt her husband Michael had worn to meetings with clients. She'd kept a few of his shirts after he died, not for sentimental reasons, but because they were comfortable to work in. He'd have ten thousand fits if he knew his once-immaculate shirts were now stained with dirt and paint.

She opened a can of diet soda and walked to the window overlooking the harbor.

Soft early-morning light painted Waymouth's neat white houses. It was close to low tide. A wide ribbon of mud stretched along the Madoc River, under long wharves and around points and eddies. Wormers wearing heavy boots and carrying pronged rakes were digging on the tidal flats, filling their buckets with the large red bloodworms fishermen prized for bait.

This morning a dozen people were down on the town wharf

or below it, all looking at something lying on the mud. Several cars and trucks were parked nearby, including one of Waymouth's police cars.

For a few moments Maggie watched. Then she headed downstairs. What was on the mudflat? Images of the body she'd found on a Cape Cod beach last October kept filling her head.

Whatever was happening on the shore of the Madoc River wasn't her business. The police were already there. It had nothing to do with her.

Still, Waymouth was now her town, and she wanted to know what was happening.

The closer she got, the louder the voices grew.

"Enough, now," her old friend from the Waymouth Sheriff's Office, Deputy Owen Trask, was saying. "There's nothing to be done here. I've called the Marine Animal Hotline. They'll be here before the tide turns to pick up the body. We'll know more after they've examined it. For now, it's dead, and there's nothing anyone can do."

"Just as well," said Abe Palmer. "Them seals are messing with our lines. How's a fisherman or lobsterman supposed to make a living anymore? Seals should be out in deeper waters. It ain't the way it used to be."

"Enough, Abe. We get what you're saying. But we all know seals are now on the protected list. They may be a nuisance to some of you working the waters, but they have a legal right to be here." Owen looked around the crowd. "It's a crime to hurt a seal. And this one's going to be reported to the Marine Patrol."

"Clam cops? All they do is hassle folks trying to make a living," Maggie heard someone in the crowd mutter.

"They don't hassle you if you're obeying the laws," Eric called in response.

"You're young. You don't know the half of it," Abe grumbled. "Your granddad would've understood. In the old days, we took care of ourselves. Didn't need no clam cops then."

Abe was weathered, in his late fifties; possibly even sixties. His "old days" hadn't been that long ago.

"I'm not arguing with you, Abe. But Maine's had fishing

regulations for two hundred years. All the Marine Patrol's doing is making sure everyone working the waters plays by the same rules. And protects wildlife." Owen Trask looked down at the dead seal. "Like seals. What happened to this seal is against the law."

Maggie pushed her way through the cluster of men standing on the dock. The seal's large body was below them, on the mud.

"What happened?" she asked Eric.

"Came down to take the boat out as usual this morning, and saw the seal there." Eric shook his head. "Some folks think they're a nuisance. But they were here before we were, and they deserve their share of the fish. They don't bother me. I like seeing them. Sometimes they follow my boat and keep me company on an early morning. Unfortunately, not everyone in town feels that way."

"I'll admit I've cussed 'em out a couple of times when they've gotten caught in my lines," said an oiler-clad man nearby. "But killing them? No way."

"Someone killed that seal?" Maggie asked. Brook had a stuffed seal. Thank goodness she wasn't here to see this.

"Shot that poor fellow clean through the head," Eric said. "If you go down there, close, where some of those men are, you can see. I called the police. Deputy Trask got here right fast."

"What will happen now?"

Eric shrugged. "I suppose Marine Mammals of Maine'll do an autopsy. See what kind of gun it was, and if the animal was sick or anything." He shook his head. "Doesn't look sick to me. If anyone's sick, it's the idiot who killed him."

"Who would have done that?" Maggie asked sadly.

"Could have been anyone in Waymouth," Eric said. "Look around. Ain't much love lost between some fishermen and lobstermen and seals." He headed down the ramp toward his boat. "Hey, Abe! You coming or not?"

"I'm coming, boy. Nothing here for us, that's for sure. I ain't crying for a seal." Abe Palmer followed Eric, who was already pulling on his yellow oilers. "Seals ain't worth such a fuss."

How many seals were in the river? She'd never thought much about seals.

Later that day, as Maggie carefully applied stain to bookcases, she kept thinking about that dead seal. She wished she hadn't seen it. Why had someone shot a seal?

Maggie's hands were red and her old jeans were now spotted with stain, but the room where Joe Cousins would soon be displaying his books was looking better every day. She looked forward to seeing Joe again; she hadn't seen him since last fall's Rensselaer County Antiques Show.

Working all day kept at least part of her mind off Tuesday afternoon, and her next meeting with Brook.

BY noon Tuesday she'd packed pints of vanilla and strawberry ice cream in a small cooler, and added a package of sugar cones to a picnic basket with boxed juices, oatmeal bread, strawberry jam, and peanut butter. She had enough plastic dishes so Sandy Sechrest could eat with them, too, if she chose.

She clutched the steering wheel of her van as she headed to Augusta. What would Brook be like today? Would the lunch she'd brought be acceptable?

Did all prospective parents feel that way?

She wanted to ask someone. Prospective parents were supposed to share their thoughts with their social workers. But would confiding her doubts and fears to someone ultimately responsible for placing (or not placing) a child with her stop the placement? She might not look ready to be a parent.

Couples had built-in support systems. They had each other to share with, and plan with. To rejoice with, or share disappointments.

She'd tried explaining to Will what she was worried about. He'd laughed and told her it didn't matter what she brought for an after-school snack. She was worrying too much over a simple task.

He hadn't understood that this meeting was a critical test. Was she ready to welcome a difficult child as her daughter? Would Brook be willing to be adopted?

She loved Will, but today she felt torn between him and Brook. She needed him to care, really care, about what she was going through.

But Will had never hidden that he didn't want to be a father. Although he'd told her he now was willing to compromise, to get to know Brook, Maggie knew he wouldn't be disappointed if her placement fell through.

She was taking on this adoption on her own. She was going to be a single parent. She couldn't count on having anyone else to share her concerns with or help out or even listen. She'd gotten this far, Maggie told herself. She'd had a home study and an update. She'd done all the paperwork.

Naively, she'd thought that would be the complicated part.

She wanted to be a mother. Brook needed a family, whether or not she admitted it. *I can do this*, Maggie told herself. *I can.*

Sandy Sechrest smiled when Maggie pulled a red-checked tablecloth out of her picnic basket. "Nice touch. You didn't need to go to that much trouble. I hope you won't mind if Brook spills jam and juice all over that cloth."

"It's washable," said Maggie. "But I wanted our snack to be a little special. Will you be joining us? I brought enough for three."

Sandy glanced into Maggie's basket and cooler. "I'd say you brought enough for six! But, no. I have paperwork to do. This will be time for you and Brooklin."

"How long will we have?"

"An hour should be enough for now," Sandy said. "If all goes well today, Friday you could have a half day together. Brooklin's school has a half day then."

"Could I take her with me to Waymouth, so she can see where she might live?"

"I'll leave that decision up to you and Brooklin. But it's too soon for her to meet a lot of people. She needs to get to know you first. To trust you. Not get confused by other people. She needs to know she'll be the center of your life."

Maggie swallowed. "Of course. I understand. But there will be people working on the house...downstairs, though. You've seen my apartment. We're hoping to have an elevator to the third floor by July, but for now we have to walk through the rest of the building to get to our home."

Our home. She'd said it. Would Brook feel the same way?

"No problem with the construction crew. She'll understand the work is going forward, and will be finished soon. Those people won't be a part of her new life." Sandy hesitated. "Your house will be finished by July, right?"

"Definitely. You saw my apartment when you visited two weeks ago for the home study visit. I have a few more boxes to unpack, but it's pretty much finished now. Victorian House—that's what we named it—will be open in a little over a month. Dealers will start moving in soon. But it won't open officially until July Fourth."

"You have a lot going on in your life right now," said Sandy. "If this placement is too soon, if you feel pressured, then let me know now, before you and Brook start bonding."

"Brook is my priority," Maggie replied firmly.

Sandy nodded. "As it should be, at least until she's acclimated to you and Waymouth. By fall she should be ready to start school, and you'll be able to have a few hours a day to yourself."

She checked her watch. "Let me check my office and see if Brook's foster mom has dropped her off yet. I'll be right back."

Maggie put the tablecloth back in the basket. She and Brook could unpack the basket together. Should she have brought a small gift for Brook?

The teddy bear hadn't been a hit. Would a gift seem like a bribe?

If this worked, she'd have plenty of time. Years. To buy Brook clothes and toys and athletic equipment. Not everything she wanted; she was an antiques dealer and college professor, not a millionaire. And although she'd saved for an adoption, she was now on sabbatical: half salary.

Still, she looked forward to shopping with Brook for new clothes for the summer and for back-to-school. The Maine outlets in Kittery and Freeport should be a big help.

She told herself to calm down. This was going to work. It was going to be fine.

Brook should have been at the agency by three o'clock. By three-thirty Maggie had almost worn out the carpet in the visiting room.

When the door finally opened, she jumped. "Sorry to keep you waiting," said Sandy. "Brooklin's not going to get here today. I've been calling her foster mom, and finally she called back. Brooklin must have gotten up at dawn. She unlocked the back door, took one of the skateboards in the garage, and rode off. The whole family was out looking for her."

"Did they find her?" Maggie stood still, hardly breathing.

"They did. But she'd had an accident. She was a mile or more from where they live, on a back road. She must have fallen. A man driving by saw her and took her to the emergency room. At first she wouldn't tell anyone who she was, or what her telephone number was, so her family didn't know what had happened."

She'd run away? "How is she?"

"Her foster mother says she broke her ankle. I don't know exactly how she is because her mom was so furious with her. The younger children were supposed to have swimming lessons this morning, and they'd been promised a McDonald's trip while Brook was visiting with you. Now, no swimming, no McDonald's. Right now the other kids are angry, and the mom is, to put it kindly, frazzled." Sandy shook her head. "She said this is why she wants Brook gone. She can't handle a child who takes off without telling anyone where she's going, and then won't tell authorities who she is."

Maggie couldn't focus on what Brook had done. She'd think about that later. What was important was Brook's condition this afternoon. "How is her ankle? Is it badly broken?"

"I'm not sure. She's at the regional medical center near where she lives. I'm assuming it isn't too bad. It's only an ankle, after all."

Only an ankle?

"She was lucky someone kind took her to the hospital. She could have been on the side of the road for hours."

Or the wrong sort of man could have picked her up, Maggie added to herself. "So her foster mom is with her?"

"Not now. She went there, with all her other kids, but it looked as though Brooklin would be there for at least the afternoon, so she took the kids to a park nearby. She'll go back later today to pick

Brooklin up and bring her home. The doctors didn't think the ankle was bad enough to keep her at the hospital overnight."

"So Brook's alone at the hospital?"

"For the time being, yes. But we all know where she is, and the doctors and nurses are with her."

She was only nine, and alone. "I want to see her. How far away is the hospital?"

Sandy hesitated. "Going to see her there isn't the normal procedure. We don't let the prospective adoptive parents know exactly where children are. It keeps things simpler, if the placement doesn't work out."

"She's nine years old. She shouldn't be alone and in pain in a hospital," Maggie said, picking up the picnic basket and the cooler. "Tell me what hospital she's in."

Sandy threw up her hands. "I suppose it won't make a big difference. She's in Waterville, at the Medical Center there. About thirty minutes from here."

Maggie was already at the door.

"Let me know how it goes," said Sandy. "And don't stay long. You shouldn't meet her foster mom."

Maggie didn't hear her last words. She was already gone.

10. *Anatomy:* **Skeleton; Osteology**

Detailed steel engraving, black-and-white, of skeleton, with details of the hands and feet. From *The Cyclopædia: Or, Universal Dictionary of Arts, Sciences, and Literature* by Abraham Rees, 1819. Engraving by Jules Vallance.

8.25 x 10.5 inches. Price: $100.

*T*HANK GOODNESS FOR the GPS on her phone. In the past Maggie'd used it to find house sales and auctions and paper shows. Today it directed her north on the Maine Turnpike, toward a Maine hospital.

"I'm here to see Brooklin Deschaine. She was brought in this morning," Maggie said to the receptionist in the Emergency Department.

The graying woman looked at the computer screen on her desk. "She's here. Are you a relative?"

"I'm going to be her mother," Maggie said. Her voice sounded louder than she'd intended it to.

The woman looked at a paper on her desk and frowned. "Her mother was here earlier."

"That was her foster mother. I'm going to be her adoptive mother."

"May I see some identification?"

Maggie pulled out her New Jersey driver's license. The puzzled receptionist looked at it closely. "This isn't a Maine license."

"No. I just moved here. I live in Waymouth now. I haven't had time to get a new license." Which she should do, she now realized. It might be more important than she'd thought.

"Just a minute." She made a copy of the license, and handed it back to Maggie. "This is very irregular. I'll have to check with my supervisor." She got up to leave.

"That little girl is only nine years old, and she's alone in there. In pain. Please. I need to see her." For a moment Maggie considered just walking through the door she assumed was the emergency room entrance. But she suspected that wouldn't sit well with the security guard. Being thrown out of the hospital wouldn't help her, or Brook. This was crazy! She'd never considered that although she was already thinking of Brook as her daughter, she had no paperwork to prove it. Hospitals had tough regulations. "Please!"

"I'll see what I can do." The woman disappeared. No one else was waiting for her assistance. This wasn't a New Jersey emergency room where at any time a dozen patients were waiting to be seen.

A few minutes later a woman wearing jeans, a white jacket, and a stethoscope came out from behind the swinging door. The door that was keeping Maggie from Brook.

"Ms. Summer?"

"Yes."

"I understand you want to see one of our patients. You understand we can't let just anyone wander through the hospital."

"I'm not just anyone. I'm going to adopt Brooklin Deschaine. If she weren't here, we'd be having an afternoon snack together right now." That was stretching the truth. This had taken so long they'd have finished eating by now.

"I see your driver's license. But do you have any proof of your relationship with this child?"

"She's in foster care," said Maggie.

"We know that."

"You can call her social worker." Maggie rummaged in her canvas bag for Sandy's card. "Here. Call her. She'll tell you who I am."

The doctor took the card. "Wait here. I'll see what I can do."

"How is she?" asked Maggie, catching her before she left.

The doctor smiled. "She's going to be fine. She's on painkillers right now, so she's comfortable. The break isn't a bad one. We're icing it, waiting for the swelling to go down before we put her cast on. She's a tough young lady. Hardly a tear, even when we knew she was in pain."

"Thank you." Maggie went and sat down in one of the orange

plastic waiting room chairs. The doctor hadn't said anything about surgery. That was good. Brook was going to be all right. And she was tough.

Sometimes, too tough.

A few minutes later the doctor returned. "I talked to Ms. Sechrest. It's all rather irregular, but I've been concerned about that little girl being all alone this afternoon. You can see her now."

"Thank you!" Maggie followed her through the swinging door into a large room ringed with small curtained areas around a central station where hospital personnel were talking and filling out paperwork. "Would she be able to eat an ice cream cone?"

The doctor glanced at the small cooler Maggie had brought with her. "I think we could allow that."

Brook was in the third space on the right. Her right foot was propped on a high pillow, her head turned toward a small window near the bed. A wall-mounted television set was silently showing a soap opera.

"Brook?" Maggie said as she walked in.

Brook turned toward her. Her eyes opened wide. "You came here?"

"We missed our meeting. I thought you might like an ice cream cone."

"I'm starving. All they gave me here was yellow Jell-O." She made a face. "Yuck."

"Yuck, indeed." Maggie opened the cooler. "I have vanilla and strawberry. Which would you like?"

"Both. Two dips," said Brook, watching as Maggie opened the cooler and took out the ice cream, and then pulled a box of cones and a spoon out of her bag.

Apparently her broken ankle hadn't affected her appetite.

"One double-dip cone, coming up," Maggie said, filling the cone. "Are you allowed to sit up a little so you can eat this more easily?"

Brook fumbled for the controls on the bed, and then moved it so her head was a little higher. "I have to keep my foot up on the dumb pillow."

"See how this works, then." Maggie handed her the cone. Brook started licking it immediately. "Now my turn. I'll have both flavors, too."

They were still eating their cones when the doctor stuck her head in. "Hey! Those ice cream cones look good! How's the ankle feeling?"

"Better," said Brook, licking the dripping cone. "Not so bad. I was sleepy for a little while."

"The medicine we gave you sometimes does that. After you finish your cone we're going to put a cast on your ankle, Brook, to hold the bones in the right places so they'll heal well. What color cast would you like?"

Brook didn't hesitate. "Red."

"Red? Let me check. I know we have pink and blue and white casts. But I'll look for a special red one. You go ahead and finish your ice cream." She disappeared.

"I'm going to have a red room, right, New Mom?" said Brook.

"A beautiful red room," Maggie promised, trying to keep from grinning.

11. *Eggs—Common Gull*

Hand-colored lithograph of two large mottled brown eggs on tan background. From *Nests and Eggs of British Birds*, 1875, by the Reverend Francis Orpen Morris (1810–1893). The books containing the prints were printed and bound in the English village of Driffield, and shipped to London in tea chests.

5.25 x 8.5 inches. Price: $40.

"*D*ID SHE CHOOSE one of the colors you showed her for her room?" Aunt Nettie asked.

"Rhubarb," said Maggie. "But she made me promise not to make her eat any. In one of the homes where she's lived they served it without any sugar."

"That would be awful," said Aunt Nettie. She pulled her light blue shawl tighter around her shoulders. "I don't blame her one bit. Although I do like stewed rhubarb when it's sugared well."

"I'm going to buy the paint tomorrow. She's very set on her red room. I'd planned to have her help paint it, but with her cast that will be difficult so I've decided to go ahead and paint two walls before she visits. Maybe two walls will be all she'll want. After they're done she can pick out curtains and a rug, and other things for her room. I'd bought her a bedspread, but that can be changed. When I bought it I hadn't thought the walls would be red."

"I can hardly wait to see that room! And she sounds like a brave little girl," Aunt Nettie continued. "She'll be able to visit Waymouth Friday?"

"She will," said Maggie. "The social worker decided today was such a success that even though she's on crutches, she'll be able to visit. I can drive her around the town, and then we'll see if she can climb the steps to the apartment. I wish the elevator was installed now. Climbing three flights of stairs on crutches won't be easy."

"She's young. She'll be able to handle it," Will put in. "Tough on both of you she had to break her ankle now. It's good we'll have the security system installed before she moves in. If she decides to take off in the middle of the night she'll set off the alarm."

"She didn't leave in the middle of the night," Maggie corrected him. "She left early this morning." But, yes. It would be more complicated for her to leave from a third-floor apartment than from a first-floor bedroom.

"I'm looking forward to meeting her," said Aunt Nettie. "Can you bring her here?"

"I'd love you to meet her! But I can't bring her Friday. The social worker said she first needs to spend time just with me; see Waymouth and where she'll be living. The next time she visits we can come here."

"I understand perfectly," said Aunt Nettie. "It's just so exciting! Having a young lady in the family."

"It *is* exciting," said Maggie, with a smile. "I can hardly wait to see what she thinks of where she's going to live." *If she really wants to live here; if her words today weren't just because she'd been in pain, and was on painkillers.*

Aunt Nettie anticipated her thoughts. "When you saw her she was very vulnerable. And it sounds as though you did just the right thing. I can just picture her eating an ice cream cone in that hospital bed! But she may be different the next time you see her."

More like she was the first time I saw her? I've thought of that. I'm taking it one day at a time. I'll paint her room, and finish unpacking my things. I'll feel better, more established, once I get all those boxes out of the apartment. Plus, sorting through my stuff will keep me busy, even if my mind is somewhere else. I keep thinking of things Brook and I could do together. Now that I have a stove, I'll get ingredients so we can make cookies while she's here. She could cut out and decorate cookies sitting down.

"And she won't be running away too easily as long as she's on crutches," Will pointed out. "That's a plus. But I'd planned that this week you'd paint the back room on the first floor, where your prints will be. The electrical work is finished there, and last night Brian came in and spackled the walls. They just have to be sanded and painted now."

Maggie didn't say anything.

"You want to be able to get your prints unloaded from your van and in place soon. Closer to the opening we'll be getting the other dealers settled. And Annie came in while you were in Augusta. She's got some ideas for our website you need to look at."

"I have two days. And evenings. I'll talk with Annie tomorrow, for sure. But I'd like to focus on finishing my apartment this week. I don't think Brook will be here next weekend. I can paint the back room then," replied Maggie. "Or one of Eric's friends might have time to paint it. Nick said he might be able to find us a couple of guys to help, too."

"That would cost money," said Will. "We've already borrowed enough. I was hoping that with the two of us working we'd only have to pay Giles and Brian a few more days."

"One day at a time," said Aunt Nettie. "Like Maggie said. That's a very wise motto."

Maggie reached out and touched Will's hand. "I promise I'll help you, and we'll get it all done on time. But it's important to have the apartment ready for Brook."

Will got up and went to the kitchen to refill his glass. "I'll bet that kid has never had anyone make a fuss about her before. She won't expect everything to be perfect."

"You're right. That's exactly why I want it to be special," Maggie said softly. "As near to perfect as I can get it."

12. Seals at Rest

Three blue-gray seals and one brown seal sunning themselves on ledges above ocean waters. Hand-colored steel engraving from *A History of the Earth and Animated Nature* edited by Irish poet, naturalist, and historian Oliver Goldsmith (1728–1774.) First published 1774–1777, the eight-volume work was republished twenty times. This print is from the 1853 edition.

6 x 9 inches. Price: $65.

I CAN DO IT MYSELF," Brook said as she limped to Maggie's van, bracing herself with her crutches. Her worn gray stuffed seal was tucked securely under her arm.

Her cast was heavier than Maggie had anticipated, and the van's seat was high. She stood by, hoping Brook would ask for help, as the girl maneuvered herself and her crutches awkwardly up and onto the front seat. But she managed everything on her own.

"Make sure you fasten your seat belt," said Maggie, closing the passenger-side door.

So far Brook had been quiet, but hadn't hesitated about going with her.

"What's all the stuff in here?" Brook asked, peering between the two front seats at the back of the full van.

"I'm an antique print dealer. All those portfolios and boxes hold my inventory. The pictures I sell," said Maggie. "As soon as my room in Victorian House is finished those things will be out of the van." She glanced over at Brook.

"What's that sign mean? 'Shadows'?" The girl pointed at a white wooden sign. Maggie'd had three made before she left New Jersey: one for her prints at Gussie's shop on Cape Cod, one for Victorian House, and one to use at antiques shows.

"Shadows is the name of my business."

"Shadows are creepy," Brook pronounced.

"I've never thought about them that way. I named my business Shadows because old prints are views…windows…shadows of the past. Ways we can see through the eyes of people who lived in the past."

"Creepy," said Brook. "Who wants to think about dead people's eyes? They're gone. Over. Boring."

Maggie swallowed. "I like to think about the past, sometimes. It helps me understand what's happening now."

"Weird." Brook turned away and stared out the window. "How far away is this place we're going?"

"It'll take a little over an hour to get there," said Maggie.

"I'm hungry. Can we go to McDonald's?"

"We'll have lunch when we get to Waymouth. Not at McDonald's though. There isn't one in town." *Thank goodness*, Maggie thought.

"That's lame. McDonald's is the best," Brook proclaimed.

They were both silent as Maggie drove by newly plowed farm-lands and fields where cows or horses or goats grazed, and, every seven or eight miles, past a small white church and post office that marked the center of a rural town.

As they passed a school, Maggie said, "I'm glad you had a half day at school so we could spend time together today."

Brook shrugged. "School's boring." She glanced at Maggie. "My foster mom told the school my ankle hurt too much for me to go this week anyway."

Maggie glanced at her. "Are you in pain now? Are you sure you want to go to Waymouth?" They were already halfway there. Why hadn't Brook said anything?

"I'm okay. The pain's mostly gone."

"You're sure it doesn't hurt too much to come with me?"

"I'm fine." She suddenly grinned. "My ankle's almost better."

To ensure her prospective daughter didn't starve, they stopped outside of Waymouth at Will's favorite fried seafood place. Brook checked out the menu. "They have peanut butter and jelly."

"They do. But this place is famous for its fried seafood. How about scallops, or clams? Or fried fish?"

Brook looked doubtful. "I like PB and J."

"You can have whatever you want. But it's fun to choose new things. I'm going to order the scallops. And fries."

"I like fries." Brook looked at the menu again. "And fried chicken." She glanced at the counter, which featured a display case of different-flavored Whoopie pies. "And Whoopie pies. The peanut butter one."

"Okay!" She shouldn't press the issue. Brook's life had already changed too many times. Maggie ordered for both of them, and they sat in a booth by the window.

"I thought we'd drive through the town first. I'll show you the school and the river, and then we'll go to see our house," said Maggie, eating her scallops.

Brook covered her French fries and fried chicken with ketchup and didn't hesitate to start eating. With her fingers.

Maggie took a deep breath. This was their first real meal together. Too early to say anything about table manners. And she'd have to remember to put ketchup on her shopping list. She hadn't bought any in years.

They finished eating in silence. Brook finished every scrap of her chicken and fries and mopped up leftover smears of ketchup on her plate with her fingers, which she then sucked.

Maggie bit her tongue. Brook was skinny. Maybe she was starved.

Brook started in on her Whoopie pie, dribbling the filling down her red-and-white striped T-shirt. She wiped up the escaped filling with her fingers.

She really was hungry. Maggie mentally doubled her food budget.

"Okay," said Brook. "Now I want to see my red room."

"It's waiting for you."

They washed up in the ladies' room, and headed for downtown Waymouth.

"That's the church, and the library," pointed Maggie. "Do you like to read? We could get you a library card."

"Books are boring."

Maggie flinched. "And this is Main Street. It has some fun little shops."

"Ice cream!" Brook pointed out.

"Yes. That's where I got the ice cream we had when you were in the hospital. The next time you come we'll have to stop there," agreed Maggie. "They make it themselves. It's really good. And here's the Madoc River." She drove slowly along Water Street as Brook looked out the window at the boats and wharves.

"Wait! Stop!"

Maggie stepped on the brakes and pulled her van to the side of the street. "What is it? Are you all right?"

"I think I saw a seal," said Brook. "I want to get out and look."

"All right," said Maggie. "If you can walk a little."

Brook had already thrown open the door on her side of the van. By the time Maggie got to her side Brook and her crutches were on the sidewalk. She'd left her stuffed seal in the van, Maggie noted.

"Where'd you see it?" All Maggie could think of was the dead seal she'd seen Monday. It was proof seals were in the Madoc River, but she'd never seen one that was alive. "Are you sure you saw a seal?"

"Come," said Brook, moving faster on her crutches than Maggie anticipated, and heading for the wide town wharf.

The wharf was quiet. Lobstermen who'd left at dawn, like Eric, were still out working their traps, and only a few recreational boats were moored so far. Most people, summer and winter, put their sail and motor boats in the water during Memorial Day weekend.

Brook hobbled quickly down toward the water, Maggie following her. What had the girl seen?

Then she stopped and pointed. "See? There!"

Brook was right. A large gray seal was stretched out, sunning him- or herself on the float. "There's one swimming, too. See?" Brook pointed.

Maggie could see a dark spot in the waters. As she looked, the spot disappeared, and, a few moments later, reappeared nearer to the wharf. This time the seal's head was clearly visible.

"How wonderful," she said. "I'm so glad you saw that. I would have missed it."

Brook just stood, her eyes fixed on the seals.

"Have you seen seals before?" Maggie asked.

"A long time ago. When I was little. Seals lived in the harbor near our house." She looked up at Maggie. "My mother—my real mother—and I watched them. I remember. She liked seals, too."

Maggie didn't say anything. But when she put her hand gently on Brook's shoulder, the girl didn't turn away.

A few minutes later the seal on the float wriggled off and into the water. Maggie and Brook watched for several minutes, but no dark heads appeared above the waters.

"They must be catching fish, under the water," said Maggie.

Brook turned to Maggie. "Can I see my red room now?"

13. Seaside Vacation

A.B. Frost (1851–1928) black-and-white lithograph of vacationers in a small sailboat. Six men are fishing (one of them pulling in a small fish) in a harbor, while the one woman in the boat watches.

9 x 13 inches. Price: $60.

S O, WHAT DID Brook think of her room?" Aunt Nettie leaned toward Maggie, eager to hear.

"She loved it, thank goodness! And she agreed two red walls were enough. The other two are staying the pale peach I'd first painted them. The combination sounds weird, but somehow it works."

"Rhubarb red, and peach. It's a healthy room," Aunt Nettie said, her eyes sparkling. "So how do you think it's going? Is she going to be moving to Waymouth?"

"We have a long way to go, but tonight I'm optimistic," answered Maggie. "I wasn't so sure when we were eating lunch—she wasn't adventurous in her choices, and her table manners leave a lot to be desired. But she certainly ate as if she were comfortable with me, and of all the stores in town we drove by, the ice cream shop was the one she pointed to."

"Just as it should be. She's nine, after all. Table manners and adventurous tastes will come in time." Aunt Nettie was excited. "She probably hasn't had a chance to eat a wide variety of foods in the past. She'll learn, though."

"What she was excited about was seeing two seals in the harbor, down by the town wharf. She told me she used to watch seals with her mother. And she carries an old stuffed toy—a seal—around with her. I wonder whether her mother gave it to her." Maggie couldn't help smiling. "I can't tell what she'll say or do the next time we meet. But I suspect we'll be looking for seals again."

"Don't tell the lobstermen you love those seals," said Will, coming in from the kitchen. "Seals steal fish from fishermen, get caught in fishing nets and lobster rigs, and are generally a nuisance for men working the waters."

"But they're so cute," said Maggie. "I'd never paid much attention to seals before, but now I'm a fan. Those whiskers, and those big eyes."

"Those big appetites," Will added. "And speaking of appetites, while you ladies were chattering I fried haddock for our dinner." He walked over to Aunt Nettie and steered her wheelchair toward the kitchen. "Dinner is now served."

Will had fried the haddock in panko crumbs ("Some people use crackers, but these are lighter, and have less fat") and served the fish with homemade tartar sauce ("It's simple to make, and tastes much better than the bottled kind"). He'd also grated carrots and cabbage for coleslaw and made biscuits.

"You're even baking now," Maggie said, sitting down and admiring the meal. "This all looks delicious. A simple dinner, but very New England. And delicious!"

"Much appreciated," said Will. "And Aunt Nettie, I made enough so there'll be some left over for you tomorrow night," Will added as he helped his aunt to sit at the table.

"You won't be joining me then?" Aunt Nettie asked.

"Sorry. It's a special day. Maggie, I assume you haven't made any other plans for your birthday?"

"You remembered." Maggie hadn't thought anyone would remember this year, which was all right. Adult birthdays hadn't been major causes for celebration in her life.

"How could I forget May twenty-third was the day my lady was born?" Will sat down and served all three of them generous pieces of haddock. "I thought we'd go out for a special dinner. Besides, it's our anniversary."

"Anniversary?" Maggie asked.

"This is Memorial Day weekend. Two years ago we met on Memorial Day weekend at the Rensselaer County Antiques Show in New York."

"So we did," Maggie agreed. "I hadn't thought of it as an anniversary."

"I believe in celebrating the good things in life," Will said, raising his glass of white wine. Maggie and Aunt Nettie did the same. "To us, Maggie. To your new life in Maine, and to Victorian House. And to one of the best parts of my life…you."

"And to Brook," Aunt Nettie added. "To the young lady who may soon be a part of our family."

14. Nightmare

Dark scene of trees blowing in heavy winds. An ugly goblin clings to one of the branches, glaring down at something the viewer can only imagine. Lithograph for *Comus*, a masque by John Milton (1608–1674) in honor of chastity, first performed in 1634. Illustration for the 1921 edition by noted early twentieth-century illustrator Arthur Rackham (1867–1939), master of drawing fantastic and strange creatures.

5 x 7 inches. Price: $65.

MAY TWENTY-THIRD dawned warm and bright. Maggie stretched and smiled. Forty. So this was what being forty years old was like.

Pretty darn good.

She'd been focused on her future, not her past. But Will had reminded her it was only two years since they'd met, two dealers at an antiques show.

She'd been a new widow then, putting her life back together. He'd been a widower for several years, who'd just quit his job teaching woodworking in a Buffalo high school to make a living selling antique kitchen and fireplace wares.

She'd lived in New Jersey, where she taught American Studies at Somerset Community College and sold antique prints at shows on weekends and in the summer.

They'd both been alone.

Their lives had changed so much since then. Will had sold his home in Buffalo and moved to Maine after Aunt Nettie's stroke last summer.

She'd decided to adopt an older child. And now she wore the green tourmaline ring Will had given her last Christmas on the fourth finger of her left hand, and was on sabbatical, living in

Maine, helping him establish Victorian House, and she'd met Brook Deschaine, who, she hoped, would soon be her daughter.

Life was good.

Despite their work schedule, Will had suggested she take her birthday off, but Maggie planned to paint the walls of her print room anyway. She'd already finished sanding them in spare moments, and wanted to prove she had time for Will and Victorian House as well as for Brook.

Tonight he'd promised they'd feast on lobster and other seafood on a wharf overlooking Boothbay Harbor. Maybe he'd even find a way to spend the night.

As she pinned up her long hair and covered it, unromantically, in a shower cap to protect it from stray paint, she smiled to herself. Sounded like a pretty great birthday.

But an hour later, as she carefully painted the walls and tables of the room that soon would be full of her prints, Maggie couldn't help thinking about that dead seal. Two weeks ago she would have been saddened to know someone had shot a seal. Anyone cruel enough to shoot a defenseless animal deserved to be fined, at the least.

But now that Brook had shared her fascination with seals, the senseless killing of that seal infuriated her.

What if there were no more seals in Waymouth? What if Brook heard someone in town had shot one?

Brook's joy at seeing the seal had been a step toward focusing on the good in life. Remembering happier times. And, maybe, beginning to believe future moments could also be full of joy and love.

Maggie shifted the roller she was using. Beige paint splattered beyond the newspapers she'd put down, leaving dots of beige on the pine floor. She'd clean it up later. Right now she was so angry it was hard to control the paint.

"Happy birthday, lady!" Will hugged her from behind, and she jumped, dripping more paint onto the floor.

"I thought you were taking Aunt Nettie to Clip 'n' Curl today," Maggie said, moving out of Will's arms and away from the wet paint on the floor. "Damn. What a mess."

"Aunt Nettie's appointments take a couple of hours. She's having a perm," said Will, trying not to laugh at the mess Maggie was making.

"I didn't know women still got perms."

"Aunt Nettie does," said Will. He looked around the room. "If you have to work on your birthday, you might try not to paint the floor. It's the walls that need paint."

"I *am* trying," said Maggie testily. "The newspapers on the floor slipped."

"I see. Was that after you got out of bed on the wrong side this morning?"

"Oh, Will." Maggie put down her roller, carefully. "I keep thinking about that seal someone shot, right here in Waymouth Harbor. I hope they catch whoever did it."

Will tilted his head slightly. "I know you've been involved in solving shootings before. But those other times people were involved."

"You know it's illegal to kill a marine mammal," Maggie informed him, ignoring the reference to her involvement in previous murders, which Will had never approved of. "Who would do that?"

Will shook his head. "I don't know. But don't worry. You can count on the clam cops finding out. They don't take crimes like that lightly." He reached over and touched the shower cap on her head. "You look particularly glamorous today, I must say."

"I hate people who hurt animals," Maggie answered, ignoring him. "And, on top of that, Brook loves seals. When she was here yesterday she saw two. She was so excited. She couldn't stop talking about them all the way back to Augusta."

"So it's Brook who's crazy about seals." Will's hand dropped. "Well, just don't tell her what happened. Lots of Mainers love seals."

"That isn't what I was hearing down at the wharf."

"Let me guess. Lobstermen and fishermen were not exactly upset that it had been shot."

"Exactly."

"Seals mess up their businesses, Maggie. It used to be legal to shoot seals. But ever since the Marine Mammal Protection Act, no one's been allowed to touch them, so now more and more are on the coast of Maine. Most hang out closer to the ocean than Waymouth, but they do swim up here occasionally."

"Which is why Brook saw them here," said Maggie. "For the first time since I'd met her she seemed relaxed. Almost delighted!"

"Just forget about the dead seal. It happened once; it won't happen again. I'm looking forward to our dinner tonight." He looked around at the room and at Maggie. "Will you and the room be cleaned up enough so we could leave about three-thirty? I thought we'd walk around Boothbay Harbor for a while, play tourist, and then eat before all the summer folks get there. It's still early in the season, but I don't want us to have to hurry."

"I'll be ready," said Maggie. "And Aunt Nettie?"

"She'll eat some of our haddock from last night, and I've promised to bring her some fried clams. She loves those, even if I have to heat them up later."

So Will would be going home after they had dinner.

Maggie hid her disappointment. "I'm looking forward to some quiet together-time. The evening sounds perfect."

"Good." Will looked at his watch. "Time to pick up Aunt Nettie. I did a little grocery shopping before I stopped here. I'm going to go over the accounts while she's napping this afternoon. We're getting down to the end of both our time and money. I want to make sure we're still on track with everything."

"I'm going to finish up here, and then take a long bath."

"Sounds like a good idea. You need to relax a little." Will shook his head as he walked out. "Getting that upset about a seal. Crazy."

She wasn't crazy, Maggie told herself. She was concerned. About the seal, yes. But, especially, about Brook's reaction to senseless cruelty. Brook had seen and felt enough violence in her life. She needed time to heal before confronting it again, in any form.

And, Maggie thought, as she added more paint to her paint tray, she needed time, too. Time to feel at home in Maine, and in this house. Time to feel like a mother.

And time with Will. This afternoon and evening would be special. It was a crazy period in their lives; they both had so much on their minds.

But they loved each other. They needed to focus on that, too.

And, she admitted to herself, during the past couple of weeks she'd been spending more time thinking about herself and Brook than she had about Will or Aunt Nettie.

He had obligations. Aunt Nettie was sweet, but caring for her was a major responsibility.

She should help Will more with Aunt Nettie. And it would be good for Brook to meet her, too. She was the closest thing to a grandmother Brook would have, since both Will's and her parents were dead.

One more wall to paint, and then she'd touch up a few print racks to go on the tables. She'd be finished in time to take that long warm bath. With bubbles.

After all—it was her birthday.

15. Galleon being tossed in a stormy sea in a lightning storm

Illustration by Edmund Dulac (1882–1953) for 1908 edition of William Shakespeare's *The Tempest*, published by Hodder and Stoughton, New York and London. Dulac was born in France, but moved to England, where he became one of the most famous "Golden Age" illustrators of magazine stories and books. His work was heavily influenced by romanticism and Persian art.

4.5 x 6.5 inches. Price: $60.

*W*ILL AND MAGGIE didn't talk a lot as they drove down Route 27 toward Boothbay, passing women working in their gardens and farmers preparing fields for planting. A couple of men were mowing their yards with tractors. Cows and calves, goats of all sizes, horses, and even llamas, were in fenced-off fields munching on the new grasses and yellow dandelions that colored the landscape.

"I love fields of dandelions. In New Jersey, people consider them weeds."

"In Maine, people eat them," Will pointed out. "Along with fiddleheads, they're our spring tonic. And in a couple of weeks the lupine will be in bloom."

Maggie nodded. "I love lupine. Purple, pink, yellow, white, and growing wild."

"Sometimes people plant lupine seeds," Will said, "but the seeds only seem to germinate when and where they please. Lupine is independent."

"Like Mainers," they chorused together.

Maggie thought of the birthdays she'd spent in New Jersey. Of the birthday parties her mother had organized when she was little, and which few children had come to, because her birthday so often fell on Memorial Day weekend. She remembered forcing herself to smile instead of cry when her father had given her a doll for her thirteenth birthday, when she'd been wishing and hoping and hinting for a pair of low heels, like those other girls wore. Adult birthdays when Michael'd forgotten the date, or called her from out-of-state conferences and told her to buy herself flowers.

She glanced over at Will. Theirs might not be a perfect relationship, but he was kind and honest, and Maine was a beautiful place to be.

As they pulled into the parking lot near the footbridge across Boothbay Harbor she decided this birthday was her best one yet. The future, and changes, were approaching like a freight train, but this was a day to relax and enjoy the moment.

She breathed in the ocean air as Will took her hand and they walked down to the commercial wharves. Boothbay Harbor had been home to lobstermen and fishermen since the seventeenth century, but today the wharves were covered with restaurants, gift shops, and booths where you could reserve seats on boats that made sightseeing trips to islands off the coast, and took tourists on excursions to watch whales.

They watched several large boats pull in and deposit their afternoon cargoes of sun-burned families wearing souvenir sweatshirts.

"It's still early in the season," said Will. "I'm surprised so many tour boats are here. Most of them head for Florida in the winter. Maybe they're just doing pre-season shakedowns."

A good-sized boat pulled into its dock past Fisherman's Wharf Inn. "That's the boat that goes to Monhegan Island," he pointed out. "Goes out in the morning, and comes back in the late afternoon. Generally people who live on the island have their own boats. But visitors take that boat out on day trips, or to stay at one of the inns there. Abenakis and early European fishermen had shelters on Monhegan back in the sixteen-hundreds and before. Pilgrims traded there."

"And later the artists came," Maggie added. "Someday I want to visit Monhegan. I've heard and read so much about it."

"We'll put that on the list," Will agreed. "After we're sure

Victorian House can run without us for a couple of days we'll go out and stay overnight at the inn there."

And Brook? And Aunt Nettie? Maggie thought, but didn't say. Somehow it would all work out. It had to. Other people had elderly relatives and children. They managed.

They sat quietly on a bench on the pier, watching children chase each other, parents cautioning them, teenagers holding hands, and older couples sitting companionably, facing the harbor.

Generations of people, from Maine and from away, enjoying this bright May afternoon. Would she and Will be like one of those old couples someday, helping each other over the uneven boards on the wharf and sitting and looking out at the boats in the harbor?

Will held out his hand. "Lobster time?"

The lobster wharf Will had chosen was on the east side of the harbor. They crossed the footbridge together, enjoying the sea air and each other's company and anticipating their meal.

They both ordered "shore dinners": one steamed lobster plus corn and steamed clams and plenty of butter. Will added a pint of fried clams to their order for them to share, and another pint for Aunt Nettie.

They sat at one of the picnic benches, sipped wine, and looked out at the harbor, waiting for their dinners to be cooked.

It didn't take long. Then they concentrated on cracking their lobsters and dipping sweet meat from both their lobsters and clams into melted butter.

The corn might be from away—May was early for Maine—but it was traditionally served with lobsters and clams, and tasted better than Maggie'd anticipated.

As they ate, lobstermen unloaded their day's catch at the wharf below them.

"What a perfect evening," Maggie said, leaning back for a moment before starting on her lobster's tail. "Thank you for bringing me here."

"Thank you for being born," said Will, his blue eyes looking deep into hers. "And thank you for being part of my life."

They finished their food, and used the little wipes supplied by the restaurant to clean themselves up. "Eating lobsters and clams is pretty messy, but that's part of the fun," Maggie declared, before they walked slowly up the hill and back across the footbridge to where they'd parked.

She hated that the evening would end. It had been perfect.

In the car, Will opened the glove compartment and handed Maggie a small box. "Happy birthday, Maggie. With love from Maine."

She opened it carefully. Would it be another piece of tourmaline jewelry? Last year Will had given her a pair of green tourmaline earrings for her birthday. She'd worn them today, to his approving look. And for Christmas he'd given her the tourmaline ring she wore on her left hand.

Inside the box was a bracelet. It wasn't tourmaline.

Maggie looked questioningly at Will.

"It's made from small sea-smoothed pieces of Maine stones, set in silver. To remind you that you're a Mainer now. Tough, and beautiful."

She leaned over and kissed him. Then they kissed again, lingering a little longer the second time. "It's perfect. Thank you."

"We're just beginning, Maggie," said Will. "You and I and Maine."

And Brook, Maggie added silently to herself as Will fastened the bracelet around her wrist.

And Brook.

16. Chipmunks Playing

Brightly colored print by Jackson Miles Abbott (1920–1988), printed in 1948, showing several chipmunks running in and out of a stone wall. Abbott grew up in New England and California, and was known for his natural history paintings and prints, especially those of birds.

9.5 x 12 inches. Price: $50.

*B*Y SUNDAY MORNING Maggie was glad she'd gotten to bed (and to sleep) earlier than she'd hoped.

Church bells were calling people to worship. What, if any, religion had been part of Brook's life? Maggie hadn't attended church regularly since her mother'd insisted on it when she was a child, but spirituality was a part of her life, and always would be. She wanted the same for her daughter. She made a mental note to ask Sandy Sechrest about Brook's religious background.

So many things she didn't know about this child who might soon be her daughter.

Will planned to work with Giles and Brian today clearing out the kitchen and pantry so space would be ready for the elevator installers.

The bookcases and lights in the front room were set for Joe Cousins. He planned to arrive Tuesday with his antiquarian books. Maggie looked forward to seeing her old friend, although her day was already looking full.

Annie was scheduled to start working on the website and setting up the software for their inventory and accounting then. Maggie'd promised she'd be available to answer questions. Work would begin on the elevator on Tuesday. And, most important, Maggie had promised to pick Brook up in Augusta after school and bring her to Waymouth for dinner. This time the social worker'd agreed she could introduce Brook to Will and Aunt Nettie.

She was already nervous at that prospect. How would Will react? Brook had trust issues with men. Will hadn't wanted to be a father. It might take a while for them to accept each other. And Aunt Nettie was so excited about being an "almost-grandmother." Would that excitement be too overwhelming? Would Brook be comfortable with her?

Keeping busy helped keep Maggie from worrying. Saturday's paint in her print room was now dry, although she didn't dare put anything heavy on the tables yet. But she could finally empty her van, bring in her portfolios and framed prints, and hang a few prints on the walls and in the main hallway. Her room at the mall wasn't the largest one, but she'd chosen it because it included a deep closet (now equipped with shelves) where she planned to store prints she wasn't featuring. That way it would be easy to pack her van if she did an antique show.

In New Jersey she'd had a large workroom in her home where she could store her inventory and do matting and simple framing. Her new apartment was small in comparison, especially since (she kept hoping) she'd soon be sharing it.

Just one of the differences between her life in New Jersey and her new life in Maine.

She looked down at the stones in the bracelet on her wrist. Granite. Hard, but beautiful. Like life. And not just life in Maine.

She moved her van near the side entrance closest to her print room.

"Morning, Maggie." Brian tossed part of one of the old wooden cabinets from the pantry into the Dumpster. "Moving in? Thought we'd helped you with that a couple of weeks ago!" He grinned.

"Moving my prints in," Maggie answered.

"Need help?"

She was tempted. But, "No—you need to get that pantry cleared out today. I've carted these prints in and out of antiques shows for years. I'm good."

He nodded. "Will said you were bringing your daughter here Tuesday. When do I get to meet my new cousin?"

Sweet. Brian's father was Will's cousin, and if she and Will ever married, Brian and Brook would be…second cousins? Third? "Soon, Brian. One step at a time. She and I are still getting to know each other. But I'm hoping she'll meet Will and Aunt Nettie this week."

Brian grinned and gave her a thumbs-up.

"Oh, Brian? When Brook was here the last time she saw a couple of seals down at the town dock—near where your friend Eric's boat is tied up. And then last week a dead seal was on the mudflats. Are there many seals around here?"

He shrugged. "Hard to say. They come and go, up and down the river. Eric, or one of the fishermen, would have a better handle on how many there are. They're the ones out on the river every day."

"Thanks. Next time I see Eric I'll ask him." Seals sunned themselves on river or ocean ledges. If they had a favorite spot near Waymouth she wanted to take Brook to see them.

Maggie pulled her large portfolios full of Winslow Homer wood engravings out of the van and headed for her print room. It wasn't good for the prints to stay in the van for long; even though they were in portfolios, they still reacted to the weather. Dampness and heat were enemies of old paper. Victorian House wasn't climate-controlled, but it was better than the van.

She focused on moving the prints inside, and arranging her portfolios on the shelves. She had more prints than shelves, but as soon as her tables were dry she could start arranging stands or stacks of prints there. She'd decided to display prints of New England, except for her Massachusetts prints, which were already in Gussie's shop on Cape Cod. Then she'd choose a few birds, fish, trees, and other natural history subjects. Military prints; a lot of people were Civil War buffs. And, of course, a few Winslow Homer wood engravings.

Working with her prints was comfortable. Relaxing. She'd examined and sorted through them so often they were like old friends.

She shook her head as she realized what she'd just thought. It was definitely time to have a family if she thought of pieces of old paper as friends.

Brook had said she didn't like "old things," but she'd probably never seen prints like these. Maggie hesitated at the "marine mammals" portfolio, and then decided to display them. Brook might like to see the seals and whales, and other people loved them, too.

"Setting up on a Sunday?"

Maggie looked up. "Nick! What're you doing here on this beautiful day? Hasn't anyone been murdered recently?" she teased.

Nick Strait made a face. "No murders today. And besides, it's Memorial Day weekend. Even detectives get time off. At least officially. Thought I'd stop down and see what you and Will were doing. I figured you guys wouldn't be taking the weekend off." He looked around the room. "I was right. Will's done a great job with this place. Hard to believe it was a dark Victorian house with crumbling walls and almost no light a few months ago."

"He's been working long hours, seven days a week, since January," Maggie agreed. "He'd finished most of my apartment before I moved here. And the display spaces on the first floor are close to being done. There's still work to do on the second floor, but we're not looking to fill those rooms with dealers right away. By the middle of the summer, though, I hope we can add people. The wiring and security systems are already finished."

Nick walked over to look at one of the framed Winslow Homers she'd hung on the wall. "I like this. Homer?" He read the tag. "When I think of Homer I remember his sea scenes. The stuff he painted down at Prouts Neck. This isn't like those at all."

"No. I can't afford his paintings! This is his early work—1858 to 1874—when he worked as an illustrator for several of the major newspapers in the north. That one you're looking at is 'Dad's Coming.' It's one of a series he did in Gloucester, Massachusetts."

"I like it. The simplicity of the boy and his mother standing on the beach near the overturned skiff, looking out to sea. Waiting."

"Your father was a lobsterman, right?"

"He was." Nick hesitated. "Lived and died a lobsterman."

"You've never said much about him."

"He was lost at sea when I was twelve."

"I'm sorry!" Maggie reached out and touched Nick's arm. "I had no idea."

"Seas were rough that day. Dad caught his foot in the line as he was throwing a trap over. The trap pulled him down."

"How awful."

Nick ignored her hand and stared at the Homer engraving. "Accidents like that shouldn't happen. It was a freak thing. Even if the rope pulled his leg, it should have just pulled his boot off—left him on board and angry as a squabble of gulls fighting over bait. But that day I was his sternman. He'd given me his boots." Nick's voice was low. "I couldn't pull him back. He was gone so fast. It was my fault he didn't come home that day."

"Oh, Nick. You were only twelve."

"Old enough. Some kids lobster when they're eight or nine. I knew better. I should've been able to save him." Nick turned toward Maggie. "It was a long time ago. Mom was a nurse. She sold his boat, and she kept working. We managed. She never blamed me. But I blame myself. Kept those boots of my dad's, the ones I was wearing that day, all these years, to remind me of how I failed that day. I see them whenever I open my bedroom closet. Not that I need anything to remind me."

"I didn't know."

"No reason you should," said Nick. "Not sure why I told you now. Except you're going to adopt a young lady who's lost her mom and her dad. Not the same way I did, but still, I'd bet she has memories."

"She saw her dad kill her mom," Maggie said quietly. "Four years ago."

Nick didn't look surprised. "I see a lot in my job. Kids like that are survivors, sure. Tough. They've got to be. But don't be surprised if she feels her mother's death was somehow her fault. That she should have protected her mom."

"She was only five when it happened!"

Nick shook his head. "Doesn't matter. Take my word for it."

"Hey! It's happened again!" Brian burst into the room. "Hi, Nick. Maggie, there's another dead seal. This one's down on the wharf."

"Another dead seal?" Nick repeated. "Are they sick?"

"Not unless being shot in the head counts as sickness," said Brian. "Eric just called to tell me. He's upset; couldn't reach Deputy Trask."

"A dead seal's not the problem of the local police," Nick said. "I suspect he's off getting ready for the Memorial Day parade tomorrow."

"Eric's yelling. He said a crowd is gathering," said Brian.

"Lots of folks on the waterfront this weekend. I'll go down and see if I can help." Nick headed for the door.

"I'm going with you." Maggie put down the portfolio she was holding. All she could think about was another poor seal with big innocent eyes being murdered. And how she'd explain it to Brook, if she found out.

17. The Fisherman's Family

Black-and-white steel engraving from *Peterson's Magazine*, 1866, depicting small boy and girl leaning on a bench on the shore. The bow of a skiff is on their right. On the bench are several fish, including a flounder, squid, several oysters and mussels. Another small fish hangs from one of the fishing poles leaning against the bench, next to a wooden bucket. Stacks of fishing creels and baskets are also on the shore, with the ocean in the background, and several small sailboats in the distance.

4.5 x 6.5 inches. Price: $50.

*B*RIAN WAS RIGHT. An increasingly aggressive crowd had gathered on the town dock, surrounding the body of a dead gray seal on the float. Eric and Annie were both there.

"No way did I shoot that seal," Eric was yelling. Annie stood next to him, ready to defend him. "I'd never hurt a seal. Not like some of you guys, who're always saying seals mess up your lines."

"So why is there a second dead seal right close to the *Lucy II?*" another lobsterman called out.

"We were just out on the river. That seal was here when we got back," Annie retorted. "Don't blame Eric!"

Jill Pendleton ran up and hugged Annie, and then Eric. "Oh, how awful!" she said, looking down at the seal. "To be out for a romantic boat ride, and come back to this."

Eric patted her back and then gently pushed her away. "Don't see you down here on the waterfront during the day too often, Jill."

"I'm on my break from the restaurant. Just went for a walk. It's a gorgeous day."

"It was a great day, until we came in and found that poor seal," said Annie, holding tight to Eric's arm.

"It's near where you tie up. And this is the second time in a week someone's shot a seal around here," an older man Maggie didn't recognize yelled. "Hey, Sirois, you sure you didn't have anything to do with this? What're we supposed to think?"

"You can think I'm not stupid enough to shoot a seal," Eric answered.

"Don't you keep a gun on your boat?" asked Jill.

"Shush!" Annie said, glancing around to see if anyone had overheard Jill's comment.

Eric's voice lowered. "You know I do. It's safe. Hidden. If everyone who had a gun was accused, there'd be no one left."

"Seals and fishermen don't mix," said Abe Palmer, who'd joined the crowd. He shook his head. The top of a flask was sticking out of his back pocket. Maggie could smell the whiskey on his breath. Abe had been grieving for veterans a little early on this Memorial Day weekend. And was that a gun holster under his loose shirt? "Don't matter what those conservation people say." She tried to see, but Abe moved away.

Why would Abe be carrying?

Nick stepped into the middle of the group. "Calm down, everyone! Nothing's going to be accomplished by blaming each other."

"What're you here for, Strait? Investigating seal homicides these days?" Abe called out.

"I might do that," said Nick, bending down to look at the seal. "This animal's been shot."

He stood up. "Who here doesn't know killing seals is against the Marine Mammal Protection Act?"

No one answered, but the small crowd quieted down. "That's a federal law, if any of you don't remember. NOAA doesn't take kindly to anyone messing with seals or any other marine mammal. Killing seals isn't sport. It's illegal. So if any of you know who did this, report it to the Marine Patrol. They're the ones investigating. Yelling at each other's not going to solve anything." He looked around. "Abe, go home. Drinking and wharves don't go together. I have no desire to jump into forty-degree water to save anyone today." He turned to Eric. "Any idea who did this?"

Eric shook his head. "Abe and I pulled traps this morning. Then I cleaned up the *Lucy II*, as usual, and took Annie down river for a bit this afternoon. That seal wasn't there when we left. Got back, and there it was, with Abe yammering about it, and a couple of other folks poking the thing."

"Eric didn't do it," said Annie, taking his arm. "Eric wouldn't hurt a seal. He wouldn't hurt anyone."

"Hope not," said Nick. "I'd hope nobody would. Looks to me like someone was target shooting. And that's just plain wrong." He looked around. "Not to mention anyone aiming at a seal could hit someone out on the water. Okay, folks. Show's over. I'm calling the Marine Patrol, and staying until they arrive. Everyone, go home. Go barbecue some hot dogs or work on your floats for tomorrow's parade. This isn't a sideshow."

"You guys, come on down to The Great Blue. You both could use a beer. My treat." Jill walked off with Annie and Eric, heading down Water Street toward the restaurant.

One at a time everyone but Nick and Maggie left the dock. "You don't need to stay around for this, Maggie," said Nick. "Holiday weekend, Marine Patrol is busy."

"It's your weekend, too," she pointed out.

He shrugged. "Law enforcement doesn't take holidays. Seals aren't my bailiwick, but those guys looked pretty angry. Wouldn't want to see a dead seal causing a fight. Or worse."

Maggie looked down at the seal. Blood was clotted around the bullet hole, and its large eyes stared at a world it could no longer see. "Why would anyone kill a seal? You said target practice. Would someone really do that?"

"It's happened before. Kids, usually, practicing with rifles. Or with their parents' handguns."

"Kids, with guns?"

"This isn't New Jersey, Maggie. Most folks in town grew up with guns. I'd wager ninety percent of the homes in Waymouth have at least one firearm. Kids hunt with their moms and dads. It's sport, sometimes. A rite of passage. And a way of filling the freezer for winter."

Maggie shook her head. "My dad was a hunter. I hated it. He'd get a deer, take it to be hung and butchered, and my mom would cook it. But I never ate it. I always hated the idea of eating deer." She looked down at the dead seal. Flies were beginning to buzz around the body. "I guess I fell prey to the Bambi syndrome." Maggie was sure of one thing. Her home in Waymouth was going to be one of the ten percent without guns.

Nick smiled down at her. "You weren't hungry. A lot of Maine families need venison to keep their families fed in winter. Moose and turkey meat, too."

"But no one here eats seals," Maggie added.

"Not seals. But if it wasn't some dumb kid showing off, the shooter could have been any of the fishermen or lobstermen in town. A seal can eat twenty or thirty pounds of fish a day. Fish that won't end up on anyone's table. Most of the time seals eat fish people don't care about, like sand eels. But sometimes they get caught in fishing nets, or steal fish from fishermen. I once saw a seal jump up and take a fish right off a fisherman's hook. They may be cute, but they're not popular with guys trying to pull a living from the water. Seals are competition."

He looked around. "This poor guy was probably just taking a sunbath, right here on the float. Made itself an easy target for some idiot."

"Last week Brook and I saw a seal sunning itself here," Maggie said. "Maybe it was this seal."

"Could be," agreed Nick. "Seals are like people. They hang out with the same other seals, and they have favorite places."

"It's big."

"Seals aren't lightweights. They can weigh up to eight hundred pounds. This one's probably only half that." He looked around. "None of those looky-loos admitted to seeing it happen, so whoever shot it must have done it quickly. And recently."

"Maybe to send a message?"

"A message? The only message here is that some stupid guy shot a seal. Marine Patrol will be asking around town. I hope someone'll admit to seeing the shooting. Or hearing someone brag about doing it. If that doesn't work, they'll talk with the local fishermen, and anyone else who was out on the water today. On a holiday weekend, with so many people using the town boat ramp to put their boats in for the summer, that'll take a while. But someone should have seen something."

The two stood together, quietly.

"Thank you, again, for what you told me earlier, about your dad. It's important for me to understand as much as I can about Brook."

"Brook? That's her name?"

"Brooklin Deschaine."

"Oh, shit." Nick looked out over the Madoc River, and then turned to Maggie. "I remember her. I was on that case, four, five years ago. Scared skinny kid, trying to protect her little brother. Her dad was Ernie Deschaine. Serial abuser, but his wife wouldn't get an order of protection. Said they loved each other. Until the night he proved he didn't. Nasty case. Nasty man."

"He's in prison now."

"Yup. I hope forever. Must have had rights to your Brook taken away. What about her brother? You're not adopting both of them?"

"Another family adopted her brother. They didn't want Brook."

"A shame, that. Brothers and sisters shouldn't be separated." He put his hand on Maggie's shoulder. "You take good care of that little girl, Maggie. She deserves someone like you. If I can ever help with anything, you let me know."

18. Godey's Fashions for May

Five elegantly attired women and a little girl dressed
in green, standing on a balcony overlooking mountain
views. From *Godey's Lady's Book*, May 1870. Hand-
colored steel engraving.

8 x 10 inches. Price: $65.

*B*ROOK WAS WEARING a red T-shirt and holding tightly
to her stuffed seal when she climbed into Maggie's van
Tuesday afternoon. She was only using one crutch.

"How's your ankle?" Maggie asked.

"Okay. The same," said Brook. She held out her leg. "One of the
little kids scribbled on my cast when I was asleep."

Sure enough, black crayoned scribbles covered the red cast.
Maggie'd hoped some of Brook's friends would have signed it.
She remembered that happening when she'd broken her left arm
roller-skating in the third grade. Centuries ago.

"Good day at school?" Maggie asked.

Brook shook her head. "I don't like school."

"I remember. You told me," Maggie said, hoping somehow she
could change how Brook felt about school. But that would take time.
She couldn't do it right now. "Do you have many friends there?"

"No." Brook looked at her as though she'd asked a stupid question. "I'm still the new foster kid."

"Maybe you'll find friends in Waymouth," Maggie said optimistically as they got into her van. "If we're a family, we'll be together
for always. You could make friends and keep them. You won't have
to leave."

"You could die," said Brook.

Maggie swallowed hard. "I hope not for a long time."

"You can't tell. Sometimes people just die," said Brook. "Sometimes they get murdered or killed in a car crash or burned up in

a fire or they get cancer." She looked seriously at Maggie. "I watch TV."

"Those things don't happen often. That's why they're on television. Most people live pretty long lives."

Brook looked out the window. "If you say so."

Wonderful conversation to begin their time together. Maggie tried to change the subject. "Today I'd like you to meet two people very important to me."

"Why?"

"Because when you come to live with me, I hope they'll be important to you, too."

"*If* I come to live with you," corrected Brook.

"I hope you do," said Maggie.

"Are we going to see any seals today?"

"I don't know," Maggie answered, hoping nowhere they went anyone would mention the two dead seals. "We're going to my friends' house to have supper. My friend Will is going to cook for us. I think it'll be spaghetti. That's his favorite."

"Spaghetti's all right," Brook acknowledged. "But not if there's a lot of stuff in it. I like plain spaghetti."

Stuff? Could she mean meatballs? Or onions and tomatoes? Maggie couldn't imagine.

"I hope you'll like the spaghetti. Will's making it especially for you."

"And you, too?"

"And me. And his Aunt Nettie." Maggie paused. "Aunt Nettie's an old lady. She uses a wheelchair. She's looking forward to meeting you."

Brook perked up. "My grandma used a walker sometimes and a wheelchair sometimes. She died."

Back to the death conversation.

"Aunt Nettie's healthy now. But old people do die."

"I hope the old lady doesn't die tonight."

"I don't think she will," said Maggie. How could she talk to Brook and be honest, but not depressing? "She just has a little trouble walking."

"I want to see the seals again," said Brook.

"Let's drive down by the pier, to see if any are there," Maggie agreed, mentally crossing her fingers that Sunday's scene wouldn't be repeated. "Then we'll go to see Will and Aunt Nettie for dinner."

"Okay."

The rest of the drive was quiet, Maggie hoping Brook would eat Will's spaghetti, and their drive by the harbor wouldn't reveal any dead seals. She and Brook were just beginning to know each other. Was it was too early for her to meet new people?

"No seals today," said Brook, sadly scanning the river as Maggie drove slowly down Water Street. "Just boats. And mud."

"Maybe the next time you come we'll see some," said Maggie. "It's mid-tide. The seals are probably all under the deep part of the water now, catching fish for their dinners."

Will and Aunt Nettie were waiting for them. The aroma of spicy tomato sauce filled the kitchen, and the little house seemed warm and cozy.

"This is Brook," Maggie said, lightly putting her arm around Brook's shoulder and pushing her forward a bit. "My daughter, Brook."

"Not your daughter yet," Brook said softly. But she smiled.

"This is Aunt Nettie, and this is my friend Will." Aunt Nettie was wearing a blue sweater set over gray wool slacks. She'd obviously dressed up for the evening.

"I'm so glad to meet you," said Aunt Nettie. "Maggie's told us a lot of things about you."

"She has?" Brook glanced at Maggie.

"All good things," Aunt Nettie answered. "And I see you've brought your seal for supper. Does he like spaghetti?"

Brook shook her head. "He doesn't eat. Except fish sometimes."

Aunt Nettie nodded. "He's very smart. But I like spaghetti. Do you?"

"One of my foster brothers eats it with his fingers. That's gross."

"Is he a little boy?"

"He's four."

"Well, then. He hasn't learned how to use a fork yet, I guess. He sounds pretty messy."

"He is. He's a total mess," declared Brook. She looked at Aunt Nettie's wheelchair. "Could I push you in your wheelchair? I know how. I used to push my grandmother."

"I'd love you to do that. Could you push me into the living room now? We could talk a little before dinner is ready."

To Maggie's surprise, Brook handed her the precious seal, put her crutch under her arm, and carefully turned Aunt Nettie's wheelchair toward the living room. As the two of them left the room she turned to Will. "Aunt Nettie seems to have made a new friend."

"Would you set the table while I mix the salad?" said Will, working at the counter.

"Of course." Maggie set the kitchen table for four. How often she'd dreamed of doing this: having dinner with Will and Aunt Nettie and her daughter. And so far Brook seemed to be holding her own with Aunt Nettie. Or maybe it was the other way around. "Your spaghetti smells wonderful."

"Thank you." Will reached down and kissed Maggie's forehead. "So, she's here." He paused. "She looks as though she could use a mother."

"One step at a time. And so far, so good."

"You could still change your mind," Will said softly.

Maggie backed away from him. "No, Will, I can't. I won't. This is what I want to do. If she accepts me, then I'm her mother."

"Is the table set? Because dinner is ready."

Maggie reached to kiss him, but he moved away.

19. The Helping Hand

A young girl in a pink gingham dress and white pinafore holds onto one oar of a skiff as an older man, complete with yellow sou'wester, white beard, and pipe, holds the end of the oar. A fishnet lies on the floor of the boat, and a gaff is balanced on the seats. The second oar is not visible. Lithograph, published by The W.C. Co., Inc., Tyrone, Pennsylvania, circa 1925.

8.5 x 10.5 inches. Price: $20.

*S*UPPER WENT QUIETLY. Brook was surprisingly polite. She ate her spaghetti, and even asked for seconds, although she carefully removed every tiny piece of chopped onion and green pepper in her serving of sauce and put them on the side of the plate.

No one mentioned that, thank goodness, Maggie thought, although she noted Aunt Nettie trying not to smile, and Will trying not to watch.

One step, one meal, at a time.

"Will is fixing up Victorian House. He built our apartment for us," Maggie said, trying to bring Will into the conversation.

"Did he paint my walls red?"

"No. I did."

Brook turned back to Aunt Nettie. Maggie's fear that Brook wouldn't be interested in someone who was ninety-one seemed totally unfounded.

"When you were nine, were there seals in the river?"

"Lots of seals," Aunt Nettie said. "And then for a while there weren't as many. Seals and fishermen both catch fish. Some people thought there weren't enough fish for all of them."

"And now there are?"

"Now there are laws to protect seals," Aunt Nettie explained.

"When I was little, seals took naps on ledges near my house," Brook chattered on.

Maggie'd never seen her so relaxed.

"That's where I got my name. When I was little I lived in Brooklin."

Aunt Nettie nodded. "I like your name."

"What kind of name is 'Nettie'?" asked Brook.

"My real name is Jeannette," said Aunt Nettie. "But no one's ever called me that."

"I could call you Jeannette," said Brook. "I like 'Jeannette.' It's fancy."

"Too fancy for me. I'll just be Aunt Nettie. I've been Nettie for ninety-one years, and that name feels right to me now."

"But you're not my aunt."

"Doesn't matter. Everyone in town calls me Aunt Nettie."

"I never had an aunt before."

"So now you do," Aunt Nettie declared.

"Will," Maggie asked quietly, "do you have anything for dessert?"

"No. I didn't think about it," he said, beginning to clear the dishes from the table.

"I'd like dessert. I'd like ice cream," said Brook. "Strawberry ice cream."

Everyone looked at Maggie. "There's an ice cream shop a few blocks from here," she said. "We could get dessert there."

Brook looked at Aunt Nettie. "Could Aunt Nettie and I get it? I could push her chair."

Maggie thought of Brook, with her crutch, pushing Aunt Nettie's chair on the uneven sidewalk. "I'm not sure," she started to say.

"That's a splendid idea," said Aunt Nettie. "Why don't Brook and I go for ice cream while you and Will clean up the kitchen."

Maggie felt trapped. "Okay. But, Aunt Nettie, take your cell phone, in case you have any problems. And, Brook, be careful crossing the streets."

Brook gave her a withering look. "I've known about streets since I was a child."

"I don't need any help with the kitchen," said Will. "Maggie could go with you."

"No. I just want to go with Aunt Nettie," said Brook. "The two of us can get the ice cream. Right, Aunt Nettie?"

"We can," agreed Aunt Nettie. She looked delighted that Brook wanted to be with her. "Brook, you go bring me my pocketbook. It's next to my bed. And then we'll go." As Brook went in search of the pocketbook, Aunt Nettie looked at Will and Maggie. "You two should have a little time together. Brook and I will be fine. She'll have a little responsibility, taking me." Aunt Nettie's eyes twinkled. "Besides, it'll be fun!"

Will opened the door to the ramp in back of the house and Brook carefully wheeled Aunt Nettie down it.

Maggie waved.

"I hope they'll be all right," she said.

"If not, Aunt Nettie has her cell phone," said Will. "Why didn't you tell me Brook wouldn't eat onions or peppers?"

"I didn't know. There are a lot of things I don't know about her yet," said Maggie. "And she doesn't know a lot about me. But we have the rest of our lives to learn."

"She could use a haircut. And some new clothes," he pointed out.

"After she moves in," said Maggie.

"*If* she moves in," Will added. "She seemed to connect more with Aunt Nettie than she did with you."

"I know," said Maggie, a little hurt that Will had not only noticed, but was pointing it out. "But I'm glad they were comfortable with each other. She and I are doing fine. She's had an assortment of foster moms as well as a biological mom. Right now I suspect she thinks of me as just the latest in the line. But I think we'll make it."

Together Maggie and Will washed and dried the dishes and sat on the small front porch overlooking the river and the sidewalk leading to Main Street. Brook and Aunt Nettie should be coming back any time. They kept glancing in that direction, hoping to see the couple heading home.

Then Will's phone rang.

20. Plate XXV: Carnivora

Lithograph by Henry J. Johnson, 1880, showing "True Seal, Walrus, Crested Seal, and Harp Seal" lounging on ice floes.

8.25 x 6 inches. Price: $40.

*A*UNT NETTIE! WHERE ARE YOU?" Will held his cell close to his head as Maggie moved closer, trying to hear. "Are you all right? Okay. Hold on. We'll be there in a couple of minutes."

"What is it? What happened?" Visions of overturned wheelchairs and hit-and-run drivers streamed through Maggie's head. "Where are they?"

"Aunt Nettie's fine. She's just stranded," said Will, not looking at Maggie as he headed down the porch steps. "Thank goodness I gave her that cell phone a few weeks ago."

"Stranded? Where's Brook?"

"Brook took off," Will said, striding ahead as Maggie tried to keep up.

"Took off? Then where is she?" Maggie panicked. She'd let Brook go off without her. Brook had run away. The agency would never let her adopt Brook if she couldn't even keep track of her. She'd been stupid to let Brook and Aunt Nettie go off together.

She wasn't responsible. She didn't deserve to be a mother.

Why had Brook left? Where had she gone?

What if someone picked her up? What if she got lost?

Disastrous pictures filled Maggie's head.

Aunt Nettie was only four blocks away, on Main Street. But she was close to the river on Main Street—the opposite direction from the ice cream parlor.

She seemed fine; her wheels were locked, and she wasn't in any danger.

But where was Brook? Maggie looked up and down the street, toward the river, and then toward the town. "What happened? Where did she go?"

"It was all my fault," Aunt Nettie said. "We were getting along so well. She wanted to know if we could go down toward the river, so she could look for seals. She asked very politely, so I didn't see the harm in it."

"Blasted seals," said Will. "And then she just left you here? Alone?"

"No! First of all, I agreed. I thought going an extra block or two wouldn't hurt anything. So we headed down there." Aunt Nettie pointed to where Main Street met the bridge over the Madoc River. "The tide is going out. Brook got all excited. She said she saw a seal near the edge of the marsh grasses, on the mud, and asked if she could go closer to see it." Aunt Nettie looked at Maggie. "She said 'please.' I didn't see any reason why not. I told her not to go too close, and I'd lock my chair and watch her."

"And?" Maggie kept looking around, hoping she'd see Brook hobbling down the street or coming out of one of the stores.

"She went down the bank to the edge of the flats, just as she said she would. And then she started screaming. I didn't know what to do. I called to her, and finally she came back. She was upset, Maggie. She said the seal she'd seen was dead."

"Oh, no."

"I tried to get her to calm down. She seemed to be doing all right, and she wheeled me this far up the street from the river. She kept saying, 'I hate seals,' over and over."

"Sounds like she went crazy," said Will.

"Seals are more than animals to her," Maggie explained. "That stuffed seal she carries everywhere? Her mother gave it to her. Not one of her foster mothers. Her real mother."

"She started crying, and I told her to stop pushing me. We could talk for a few minutes, and then get the ice cream." Aunt Nettie shook her head. "That's when she ran off. She headed up Main Street."

Maggie started running.

"Maggie! I'm sorry!" Aunt Nettie called after her as Will turned the wheelchair toward home.

Maggie looked in shop windows and down side streets.

"Have you seen a brown-haired girl with a crutch?" she asked clerks in the bookstore (they had stuffed seals in the window, she winced to see) and the gift shop. Most of the shops on Main Street were closed. It was after six o'clock.

No one'd seen Brook. Where had she gone?

She'd headed away from the river.

How far could she get, hobbling with a cast and one crutch?

Maggie'd never felt so alone, and so panicked. She looked back. Will and Aunt Nettie were gone. He'd taken her home. She was his responsibility. Brook was hers.

What if she couldn't find Brook before night fell? May days were long, but it was almost seven-thirty. Only half an hour of light was left.

Maggie forced herself to calm down. Take a deep breath.

Brook had only been in Waymouth once before. She didn't know the town; she didn't know anyone here except for Maggie. Would she remember how to get to Victorian House?

Will had put a sign on the corner of Main Street—VICTORIAN HOUSE — ANTIQUES MALL, OPENING JULY FOURTH. Maybe Brook had seen the sign.

Maggie half walked, half ran toward home.

The street was empty. Early on a Tuesday evening people were probably having quiet suppers with their families. Why had she let Brook take Aunt Nettie out on her own?

And why was another seal dead in Waymouth Harbor?

Victorian House was locked, just as Will must have left it when he went home to prepare dinner. Maggie walked around the house, checking everywhere. Around piles of construction materials. In the Dumpster. The small barn was locked. No windows were open.

Brook wasn't there.

Maggie sat on the front steps and wiped tears of frustration from her eyes. Where could she be?

She couldn't check every street and lot in town.

What could she do?

She pulled out her cell and dialed Nick's number.

He picked up immediately. "Maggie?"

"Nick, you told me to let you know if I needed help. I do. Brook's run away. She's somewhere in downtown Waymouth."

"I'm at home. It'll take me ten minutes to get downtown. Where are you?"

"At Victorian House."

"Did she leave from there?"

"No. She was on Main Street, near the river, with Aunt Nettie. Nick, she found another dead seal."

"Shit. I'm on my way. Walk toward the center of town, and then up the hill toward the church. I'll meet you there. From that hill we can see a lot."

"Hurry, Nick."

"I will. We'll find her, Maggie. I promise."

21. The Haunted House

1891 black-and-white steel engraving by Illman Brothers for *The Lady's Friend*, a British magazine for women first published in 1880, and still published today. Large ivy-covered turreted house, with sections of roof missing and broken windows, on a dark hill above a wall topped by gargoyles. A dry marble fountain is surrounded by uncut grass and untrimmed bushes. A dead tree rises above everything else, its branches seeming to touch the full moon.

5 x 7 inches, with rounded top corners. Price: $60.

*T*HE SUN WAS SETTING. Would Brook be scared to be in the dark, in a strange place?

Maggie did as Nick had told her: she walked back toward Main Street and headed up the hill toward the Congregational church. Nick's church, she remembered. She and Will had attended a candlelight service there last Christmas Eve.

So much had changed since then.

She passed the Waymouth Inn, where couples were dining next to candlelit windows. Brook wouldn't have gone in there, she was sure.

The Waymouth Library might have offered sanctuary, but it was now closed.

Maggie looked down every side street. Every few minutes she called, "Brook! Brook!"

She'd reached the Green below the church when Nick found her. "There you are! Any sign of her?"

Maggie shook her head. "Nothing."

"Did I understand you? Brook and Aunt Nettie were in town by themselves?"

Maggie nodded miserably. "They went out to get ice cream.

Brook saw a dead seal near the marsh grasses down on the flats, and was very upset. They turned back toward town, but then Brook ran."

"Aunt Nettie had a cell phone?"

"Yes, thank goodness. She called Will."

"Where's Nettie now?"

"Will took her home."

"And you've been out looking."

"I checked the couple of shops still open, and Victorian House, but I haven't found her, or found anyone who's seen her. She has a cast on her ankle, Nick, and a crutch. I wouldn't think she could go too far or too fast."

"Is there any place she's been with you where she might feel safe?"

"Only Victorian House, and she's not there. She loves seals, so she likes to look at the harbor, but Aunt Nettie said she ran away from the river."

"She was upset, seeing the dead seal."

"Yes."

"I called the Marine Patrol on my way here. They're on their way. They're up in arms that three seals have died here in the last nine days."

"Two were shot."

"Yes. Of course, we don't know about this latest sighting. Sometimes seals die on their own."

Death seemed to be the theme of the evening.

"This time of night there aren't many places she could be, unless she's found an open barn or house," said Nick. "Have you checked the Sunken Garden?"

The Waymouth Garden Club had designed a garden in the stone-lined cellar of a nineteenth-century Waymouth tavern that burned to the ground years before. Lush plants and flowers surrounded a brick path through the cellar, and several granite benches provided resting places.

The sunken garden was also the place, Maggie knew, where an unknown girl's body had been found, years before. The case Nick had become a cop to solve, but, so far, never had.

She shuddered. "No. I didn't check the garden."

"Let's both go. She knows you. An unknown man might frighten her."

The garden was now dark. Nick had a small flashlight, and reached for Maggie's hand as they went down the uneven granite steps from the sidewalk into the old cellar. His hand was warm and comforting. "Brook? Brook? It's Maggie," she called.

A bat flew over their heads, and a small creature rustled in the foliage.

Brook wasn't there.

Maggie was relieved to be back at street level again, where street lights and passing cars gave some illumination. And no girls had been found murdered.

"Let's check the church," Nick suggested. "You haven't been up there yet, right?"

"No," said Maggie. "Will it be open?"

"Always," said Nick, as they headed up the steep hill.

The large pine doors to the sanctuary were closed, but opened easily with a push. Inside, low electric lights on the sides of the large room lit the white-painted pews and chancel of the room. "Brook?" Maggie called. "Brook? Are you in here? It's Maggie. I'm not angry. I just want to know you're safe."

Nick nodded at her approvingly. He pointed at one of the two side aisles in the old church. Maggie started down it, as Nick went down the other side.

Halfway down Maggie heard a soft sob. She stopped.

Brook was sitting on the floor between two of the pews, tears streaming down her face.

"Brook! Are you all right?"

"The seal was dead, New Mom. All alone on the mud. It was dead." She sniffed. "And my ankle hurts. It hurts bad. I hate this town. I never want to come back here."

22. Lilies

Five white lilies on a tan background, framed in red. Lithograph from *My Lady's Casket: Jewels and Flowers for Her Adorning*, illustrated by Eleanor W. Talbot. Verse on lithograph: "Here one may place the woman's name / Held dearer than aught other. / Of sister; lover; friend or wife; / Or write as I do, Mother. December 31, 1883." Lee and Shepard Publishers, Boston, 1885.

8.25 x 5.25 inches. Price: $60.

N ICK PICKED BROOK UP, carried her to his car, and drove them all to Aunt Nettie's house.

"I need my seal," Brook said, softly.

"She left her stuffed seal in the kitchen," Maggie explained.

"I'll get it for you," said Nick. "You get in Maggie's van and rest that ankle. I'll tell Will and Aunt Nettie you're all right."

"Thank you, Nick," said Maggie.

"Not a problem. Glad I was home and could help," Nick answered. "Hold on, and let me get the seal."

He took the front steps of the small house two at a time and Maggie watched as the door opened and Nick and Will talked briefly. Then Will disappeared for a moment. When he reappeared he handed the seal to Nick.

"Here's your seal," Nick said, handing it through the van window to Brook. "You take good care of him, okay? And rest that ankle. No running around for a while."

Brook nodded as she took her seal.

"Should I take her to an emergency room, do you think?" Maggie thought out loud.

"I suspect she's fine. But she shouldn't put much weight on her ankle. If you were taking her to your home, I'd suggest calling her orthopedist. But since you're taking her back to Augusta...it's up to them. The doctor there will probably say to stay off it for a day or two."

"Thank you, Nick."

"Glad everything turned out all right."

"Let me know what the Marine Patrol finds out," Maggie said, turning the key in the van.

"Will do. You ladies both stay in touch, all right?" Nick said, loud enough to include Brook in his words. "Take care of yourselves tonight."

Maggie headed toward Augusta. Brook was asleep, her head on her seal, before they left Waymouth.

Glancing over at the sleeping child, Maggie allowed herself her first deep breath in more than an hour.

Parenting wasn't going to be easy.

But Brook had called her "New Mom."

No one had ever called her "Mom" before.

It sounded right.

But Brook had also said she never wanted to come back to Waymouth.

23. The Seashore

Hand-colored steel engraving, fashion print, from 1859 *Godey's Lady's Book*. Four elegantly dressed women wearing hooped skirts and beribboned bonnets standing on the beach, as a boy, perhaps twelve years old, rows his skiff close to shore and tips his hat to them. A large hotel is in the background. As with many prints of this period, some colors in the ladies' dresses (red, sage, lavender, and blue) are water-colored, but the rest of the print is black-and-white.

5.25 x 8.5 inches. Price: $50.

*M*AGGIE WAITED for Will to call, but her phone never rang. Should she call him? Certainly he'd want to know how she was, how Brook was.

But Nick had told him they were all right. Will was probably busy taking care of Aunt Nettie. She'd certainly been upset that Brook had run away while in her care. But what could she have done? She was ninety-one, and in a wheelchair.

The fault was all Maggie's, she knew. She should have gone with them.

And what would Sandy say? The third time Brook and Maggie had met, Brook had run away. Thank goodness for Nick's help. She'd never even thought of looking inside the church. What if she hadn't found Brook? What if Brook's ankle was worse than she and Nick had assumed?

Maggie poured herself a small glass of sherry and treated Winslow to two sardines.

What would the consequences of tonight be?

She paced her apartment, and then Winslow followed her up the narrow staircase to the small enclosed cupola above. That tiny room had convinced her that, yes, Will should buy this old house and convert it into an antiques mall and apartment.

He'd promised to build a window seat around the outside wall, but it was one of his unfinished projects. His current priority was getting the mall open. The work on the house so far had cost as much as its initial price.

Will had been able to do a lot himself. But no one could do everything. This house, and caring for Aunt Nettie, had been his life since January.

She'd only been in Maine…was it three weeks now? Not long, anyway.

And her priorities hadn't been the same as Will's. She'd wanted to settle herself in the apartment and make it seem like her new home. Make Brook feel part of her family.

She and Will had been on parallel paths. In a month the mall should be open, and she'd know about Brook. Life, her new life, would settle down. She hoped she could spend more time with both Will and Brook then.

Unless she'd ruined everything tonight.

Maggie sipped her sherry and looked down at the town and river where she'd cast her future. It was late; Mainers, especially those working on the river, went to bed early, and got up before sunrise. Lights in most houses were out by now. The river was dark. Winslow chased a moth from one window to another.

Maybe Brook's finding the dead seal was an omen. Or a test.

If it was a test, who had passed or failed?

Maggie smiled to herself. She was still a teacher, thinking of life in terms of grades. Outside the classroom, life wasn't that simple.

Up here, above Waymouth, the world seemed peaceful. But who knew what was happening in all those dark houses below? Or in the minds of those who lived there?

Being this high above the problems below might be peaceful, but it was also lonely. Tonight she needed a hug, and a shoulder.

Even just a hand to hold.

She missed Will.

Nick's hand, helping her down the steps in the Sunken Garden, had been warm and steady.

He was a good friend. But Will was more than a friend.

Sherry finished, Maggie went back down to her apartment and went to bed. Winslow followed her and curled up by her feet, as though knowing she needed company.

Maggie slept lightly. Her dreams were filled with confused images of lost children with large dark eyes.

24. The National Home for Disabled Soldiers...Togus, Maine

Wood engraving, black-and-white, of large Victorian-era building with several wings and many turrets. Man with crutch, and several other people not visibly disabled, are walking on the large lawn surrounding the building.
4.5 x 8 inches. Price: $35.

*M*AGGIE CALLED SANDY Sechrest a little after eight in the morning to tell her what had happened the night before. Sandy was out on a home visit; her secretary said she'd call back.

More hours to be nervous about that conversation.

She jumped when her telephone rang a few minutes later.

"Maggie? It's Nick. Last night was scary. I wanted to check in and see how you and Brook were doing."

"Thank you. Yes, last night was a nightmare. But I'm all right, and Brook seemed back to herself when I dropped her off at the agency last night. I've called my social worker to tell her what happened. I'm nervous about what she'll say."

"You did fine. Kids do unpredictable things. Nothing bad happened."

"Thank goodness. And thanks to you guessing she went into the church."

"I've been looking for runaways since I was a beat cop. I knew the church was open. It's one of the first places to look."

"Still, I hadn't thought of it."

"I'm glad you called and asked for help. If you ever want to talk, pick up the phone. If I don't answer right away, I'll get back to you as soon as I can." He paused. "I've been a single parent, Maggie. Sometimes you just need to talk with someone. I was lucky; Zelda and I lived with my mom. You're alone."

"I have Will," Maggie said. She remembered Zelda hadn't been an easy teenager to parent. And Nick hadn't always coped well. She couldn't forget seeing Zelda's black eye during the Christmas holidays. "I'll be okay, Nick."

"Yes, of course. You have Will."

Right. She had Will. But Nick, not Will, had been the one who'd called to see how she was. "Did you find out what happened to that seal Brook saw?"

"That's one reason I called. I just heard. The seal was shot, like the other two. The Marine Patrol is zeroing in on Waymouth. I suspect you'll see them around town today, especially down by the river, talking to everyone they can. No one can shoot seals and get away with it."

"I'm glad. I don't know if Brook will want to come back to Waymouth. But I want to be able to assure her that if she does she won't see anything like that dead seal again." Maggie could still close her eyes and see the seal on the wharf covered with flies.

"I agree. She's seen enough horror in her life. She needs to feel secure and safe, for at least the rest of her childhood, before she has to deal with more violence."

"I hope she never has to deal with violence."

"Violence is part of life, Maggie. Your Brook learned that when she was very young. You can't pretend what happened to her mother didn't happen. Or even what happened to that seal."

"I know," Maggie said sadly.

"If I hear anything I'll let you know. In the meantime, take care of yourself."

He hung up.

Maggie busied herself around her apartment for half an hour or so. Annie would be coming in at nine o'clock. She wanted to be downstairs by then. She could already hear the loud whirring sounds of drills, and the voices of the men preparing the space for the elevator. A wide hole in the floor near her apartment door now marked where it would soon be.

When the phone rang again it was Sandy Sechrest.

"Maggie, thank you for calling me first thing. Last night must have been frightening."

"It was, Sandy. I'm so sorry. I never should have let Brook and Aunt Nettie go out together, without me."

"I talked with Brook's foster mom after I got your message. She says Brook's fine. Her ankle hurt last night because she'd run on her cast, which she knows she's not supposed to do. Her mom is keeping her home from school and making her keep her foot up on a stool. No permanent damage was done."

"Thank goodness."

"As you said, Brook is nervous about coming back to Waymouth. She's not angry with you, but she is upset about what happened to the seal."

"I know."

"I think it would be wise to skip your next scheduled visit with her. You and Brook both need to think a little more about this. I don't want to pressure her to go back to Waymouth before she's ready. So instead of your coming to get her Friday, I'd rather you visit next Sunday."

Maggie was silent.

"It's not a big delay. But maybe we've pushed this placement a bit."

"So you're not pulling back the referral?"

Sandy laughed. "No, no. Believe me, I've had worse situations. You learned something about Brook last night, and Brook learned about you, too. She was scared, Maggie. She didn't know where to go. And you found and rescued her."

"The Marine Patrol is investigating. They hope to find whoever is killing the seals here."

"Good. Let's hope they find the person responsible soon. Being able to tell Brook no seals in Waymouth will be hurt again will reinforce her trust in you, and in law enforcement. She's had some issues with the police in the past. Maybe it was chance that you called a state trooper to help, but Brook liked him. That was important, too."

"I was so scared. And I called the trooper because he was a friend, not because he was with the state police."

"Of course you were scared. Any parent would have been. So… you'll pick Brook up next Sunday, about noon? My office."

"I'll be there."

Maggie slumped into a chair, relief flooding over her. It would be all right. She'd see Brook again on Sunday. Five days from now.

Maybe the seal killer would be found by then.

And Brook had liked Nick. Good. But how did she feel about Will?

25. Herring Gull

Hand-colored steel engraving by William Home Lizars (1788–1859) from *Illustrations of British Ornithology*, 1834, Edinburgh. Scottish painter and engraver Lizars specialized in natural history subjects. A gull is on a beach, standing in front of a rock. Other gulls are in the background, both on the beach and in the air. Central gull is painted with water-colors; other gulls and background are not.

6.5 x 4 inches. Price: $45.

*H*OW DOES THE WEBSITE look now?" Annie Bryant turned the computer screen so Maggie could see. She'd changed the home page she'd designed the day before to "antique" it, using a nineteenth-century type font above a sepia'd photograph of Victorian House that almost looked like a daguerreotype.

"I love it," said Maggie. "You only need to add the address and hours. And then links to pages of the dealers who'll be exhibiting here."

"No problem." Annie nodded. "Will all the dealers be supplying photographs of their inventory, or will we have to take them? Joe Cousins, the guy with the old books, left me some photos and captions to put on his part of the site before he left last night. I'll set up that section and then you can see what it looks like."

"Good. I have pictures of some of my prints," Maggie said. "I can give those to you. We can't picture everything in the mall. We'd have hundreds of pictures on the site. I'll check to see if Will has any other ideas, or has promised a certain amount of space to anyone."

Maggie suspected providing inventory photographs was not in the dealer contracts. Will had been focusing on the house itself, and on filling the first-floor rooms. He hadn't thought a lot about marketing.

By default, that would be her job. But she'd rather write press releases and invitations to the Victorian House opening than do more shellacking. Plus, she could work on publicity in her apartment, where it was quieter than in the main hall, near the elevator construction. Her head was already pounding and it was only midmorning.

"Maggie! There you are." Will's head appeared above the remaining part of the wall that had been removed for the elevator. "Checking in. Last night turned out all right?"

"Brook's fine. Nick probably told you we found her at the church."

"Good. Aunt Nettie was worried. Listen, we haven't had much chance to talk since your birthday. And I have tons of spaghetti left from last night I can heat up for Aunt Nettie. Make it a Great Blue evening?"

"Sounds good," Maggie answered. "Meet you there? I was thinking we needed to talk about advertising, and the opening."

"A little past six would work. It's still early in the season. Shouldn't be a problem getting a table."

Someone in back of him yelled, "Will! Question?"

"Got to go. See you then!"

Annie shook her head. "I swear, that man works as hard as Eric does. And as many hours."

"Eric starts earlier in the morning, though," said Maggie.

"Lobstermen do. Got to get their catch to their dealer or co-op by late morning, if possible."

"I've heard lobsters out of the water for very long don't taste as good."

"That's why the best restaurants outside of Maine pay to have lobsters shipped by air. Trucks take too long." She smiled as though she had a secret. "But even shipping takes away some taste. People say lobsters they eat in Maine taste best. They're right."

"Every hour out of the water must count," said Maggie, looking over the notes Annie'd made for Victorian House's accounting system. "I'll need you to explain this to me when you're finished. You won't be here from nine until six every day, and I'll need to manage it on my own."

Or explain it to someone else, if we can afford another receptionist/cashier, Maggie thought. She wouldn't always be available after Brook moved in. Will would have to take his turn, and they'd need an alternate. She and Will could answer questions about the antiques, but Annie didn't know them. At least not yet. Finding someone who'd want to work at a desk and who understood the inventory wouldn't be easy.

"I'll see you at The Great Blue," Annie continued. "Jill asked me to waitress tonight. Suzy, the other waitress who works with her, has a migraine and they need someone to fill in. And with Hay at the bar, and Jill and I there, I'll bet Eric and Brian show up, too." Annie paused. "They hang out there most nights anyway."

Maggie glanced at Annie's hand. "No ring yet?" she teased.

"Soon, I hope." Annie relaxed. "Eric's been hinting he'll have a surprise for me soon, and the lobstering has been going well for this time of the year. He's been bringing in a lot of hard shells; the ones shipped out-of-state. The ones he gets paid most for."

"I didn't know that. I like the soft shells, myself. Or—'new shells' as people call them now."

"Right. Mainers like those best. Right after they've molted they're sweeter, and easier to take out of their shells. Eric should start pulling in new shells in early July. But hard shells have more meat in them, because the lobsters had more time to grow, and their shells protect the meat so the lobsters can be shipped. People pay more for hard shells."

"Interesting. I thought they cost more because they had more meat, since lobsters are sold by the pound."

"That, too," she agreed. "But soft shells have to be sold locally."

"So, you think Eric is saving for a ring?"

Her smile was wide. "I sure hope so. I'm saving for a wedding."

"The last time I saw Eric you were both down at the dock."

"When we found that seal?" Annie shuddered. "That was awful. Someone found another dead one last night. Eric told me the Marine Patrol guys questioned him this morning, before he and Abe went out. He was furious. He hates that someone killed those seals." Annie smiled. "He's a real softy about animals."

"The Marine Patrol must keep early hours."

"They make sure the lobstermen and fishermen obey rules about what they can bring in and sell, so they drop by at odd times to check on what's happening on each boat. I don't think it bothers Eric—he knows it's their job, and he obeys the rules. But some guys hate having to account for everything in their boats."

"I hope they find out who's killing the seals."

Annie wriggled her nose. "It's awful, isn't it? And wait 'til the tourists come. 'Oooh, those cute little seals. How could anyone hurt them?' I'm surprised it isn't all over the news already."

"Nick Strait said most people in Waymouth have guns."

"Sure," Annie agreed. "I learned to shoot when I was a kid. Jill and I used to go target shooting with her dad when we were in middle school. All the kids went. And their parents, too, of course." She turned back to her computer.

Would Brook expect to learn to shoot? Maggie hoped not. But what if "all the kids" were doing it? Gun ownership wasn't a problem she'd anticipated when she'd thought of adopting, back in the suburbs of New Jersey. From all she'd heard, some people she'd known there had guns. But no one talked about them. They weren't part of the culture.

"Sounds as though you have plenty to do today. If you need me, I'll be working with my prints in the back room. I'll get you a disc with photos by tomorrow. I have to find it."

The print room looked a mess, but it was a manageable mess. She'd hung her SHADOWS ANTIQUE PRINTS sign on Sunday. She'd stored the one she planned to use at shows. Would she have time to do shows now? A question for another day, but an important one for her budget. She was registered for several New England shows this summer, and unless Victorian House became incredibly profitable right away—something she seriously doubted—she'd need to do at least some of them.

She was already feeling pressure. How could she finish her book and be a full-time parent and work here at Victorian House this summer? After school started in September, hours Brook spent in school would have to be writing hours for her. And if not many customers came to the house, she could work on her manuscript at the front desk.

Thank goodness she'd already done her research and outlining.

Maggie tried to focus on her prints. Good; the table tops were now dry enough so she could put her stands and prints on them.

Her small Reverend Morris birds, many of which could be found on the sea and shore, fit nicely in one stand. People looking for souvenirs of the coast of Maine, or decorations for their summer homes, should like those. They were small, as were many prints from the first half of the nineteenth century. Large printing presses were rarities then, especially in the United States. The best printing had been done in England, Scotland, or Germany.

She pulled out prints of eggs and nests, popular with decorators or those with modern homes, and then set up a rack of Gentry birds, checking to make sure she didn't include any duplicates. They were larger and brighter than the Morris birds, giving people a very different selection of ornithological prints. Since most old prints were smaller than paintings, people often hung them in groups. Maggie matted her prints so they'd be protected, but customers could select their favorites to have framed so they'd best fit with decorating plans.

She picked out several groups of framed prints to demonstrate how different arrangements would look. Some she hung on the walls of the print room; others she arranged in the hallway. Victorian botanicals that were French-matted and framed in the elaborate gold frames favored at the end of the nineteenth century looked stunning in a group of four.

A full dozen Denton fish, three high and four across, fit in the hall. They'd go well in a game room or study. Or local fishermen might like them.

She looked at her two Denton lobsters, one male and one female. They were the most valuable Denton prints. She'd framed the pair, thinking they'd be perfect for her print room here in Waymouth. But looking at them again, she decided that for now she'd hang them in her kitchen upstairs. She could always bring them down and put prices on them if she changed her mind.

She also selected four of Winslow Homer's Gloucester series to hang over her couch.

An antique print dealer should be able to enjoy her own inventory, right?

She set aside the prints she planned to take upstairs, and opened the portfolio she'd labelled "creatures of the sea." Whales and porpoises were popular with many people. But today she was looking for seals. She decided to frame all five early, hand-colored prints. They'd fit in Waymouth. And maybe Brook would like to choose one for her room.

If Brook wasn't interested (Maggie still remembered her saying she didn't like "old things") then they'd all be for sale. One of the advantages of being an antiques dealer was that if you tired of something, you could always sell it and buy something else. Someone, she was sure, would like hand-colored prints of seals.

Maggie found herself humming. This was her world. The world she knew best. The world that took her far from runaway children and dead seals.

Today she needed to be with her prints, and not think about anything else.

Except dinner with Will tonight.

Now that she knew soft-shelled lobsters wouldn't be available for another month, she'd have scallops for dinner. Or fried haddock. After all, she'd had lobster twice already this week.

She was in Maine. This was her new life.

Prints, seafood, the man she loved, an almost-daughter.

The next time Brook came to Waymouth the room of prints should be finished and ready for business.

Life was good.

She repeated it, as though reassuring herself.

Yes. Despite its challenges, life was good.

26. Cupid's Friend

Beautiful young woman holding yarn for Cupid to wind into a heart-shaped ball. Lithograph by Harrison Fisher (1877–1934), popular American artist and illustrator who specialized in painting strong, confident, athletic American girls. This picture was published in his *American Beauties* portfolio, 1909. The "Fisher Girl" was the successor to Charles Dana Gibson's "Gibson Girl," and helped shape the world's vision of American women.

8.5 x 11 inches. Price: $75.

*T*HE GREAT BLUE was buzzing when Maggie arrived. Will was already seated. He'd chosen a table for two, she was pleased to note as she answered his wave. She was looking forward to a quiet romantic evening with an attentive beau.

"Evening, Maggie." As promised, Annie was waitressing tonight. She still had on the jeans she'd worn at Victorian House that morning, but she'd added an apron and a Great Blue T-shirt with a line drawing of the Great Blue Herons the restaurant was named for. "Will's over by the window, in the corner." She leaned over and whispered, "After all that construction noise today, I thought you both deserved a quiet table."

So she had Annie to thank for the cozy table, not Will.

"Thank you, Annie." Maggie glanced around. Jill Pendleton was taking an order from an older couple, Haywood Johnson was behind the bar, filling a tray with drinks, and, as Annie had predicted, Eric and Brian were both seated at the end of the bar. It was early. As she walked by on her way to join Will she noted the two at the bar were drinking beer and sharing a large plate of onion rings. She hoped they'd have more to eat than that.

But they were young men, not children. What they chose to eat or not eat was their business. Nutrition wasn't one of their top concerns.

She heard Brian laugh. Tonight he and Eric didn't look as if they had anything to worry about other than paying for their beer.

Brian touched her arm as she passed. "Hi, Maggie! Good to see you out on the town!" She high-fived him and kept going.

Small towns. If you didn't remember what you'd done yesterday, someone else would remind you.

Will stood up as she reached their table. "I ordered you a glass of dry white wine. Hope that was okay."

"More than okay," she said, sitting down. "Beautiful night, isn't it?"

"Tide's coming in," he agreed. "No mudflats in sight." He gestured at their window view of the harbor. "I've been noticing all the boats people put in the water last weekend. Summer is officially here!" He raised his glass of beer to meet her wineglass. "To us, and to Victorian House."

"To us," she added. "Annie made major progress on the website today. Take a look tomorrow and tell her how happy we are that she's working for us. Let's make sure she knows she's appreciated. Joe's room is set up, and I don't need much more time with mine. That leaves the jewelry and silver dealer and the woman with the smalls. They won't move in until the end of June, right?"

Will nodded. "They want to make sure all the construction is over—or at least the major part of it. And the security system has to pass some tests. They're also the most nervous about leaving their inventory with us."

"Rightfully so. Expensive items, and easy to pocket," Maggie agreed. "And you can set up your inventory in the kitchen after the elevator is finished. How *is* that construction going?"

"Clearing out the area last weekend is paying off. With the past two days' work, the space for the elevator is cleared from the first floor to outside your apartment. Tomorrow the crew will begin working on the wiring and the cables. I'm hoping the whole thing will be operational—and even inspected—by next week."

"Great! I'm looking forward to not having to tote groceries up three flights of stairs," said Maggie. "And with Brook on crutches, the elevator will be a big help."

"Ready to order?" Jill was their server. She was dressed the same way Annie was, but her Great Blue shirt was tighter, and she wore heels instead of sneakers.

Sure, she was young. But her feet must hurt by the end of a busy night.

"I'd like the broiled scallops," said Maggie. "And coleslaw."

"No appetizer?" asked Will.

"I'm saving room for dessert."

"What about sharing some mussels steamed in wine?" he asked.

"You talked me into it," Maggie answered.

"Then the mussels to start with," he said to Jill. "And I'd like the Madoc burger—it comes with bacon and blue cheese, right?—and fries."

"Got it," said Jill. "I'll be right back with your mussels."

"Don't rush," said Maggie. "We're enjoying the view." And the conversation, she thought. "Will, I've been thinking about our opening. It's only five weeks off."

"I thought we'd take out ads in the three local papers covering Waymouth," Will said. "The Portland and Lewiston papers, too. And send a notice so the Maine Antiques Dealers Association includes it in their members' bulletin."

"We should have an official opening reception," said Maggie. "Wine, cheese: like the preview for a high-end antiques show. Let people see what Victorian House has to offer the night before the official opening."

"Who would come?"

"The MADA members—and remember, the second floor will have rooms for more dealers soon. We could have contracts available for anyone interested. I could write up a press release about the dealers we represent, with a couple of pictures of the merchandise, to go in those newspapers. Plus, we could invite people we know in Waymouth, and those who've helped get the house set up. It would be a way of celebrating the opening…and thanking everyone for all their work. And we should invite all the Chamber of Commerce folks, and those at nearby Tourist Information booths. And our neighbors, who are probably curious about what the house looks like now. We'll also need to have a postcard or brochure printed up advertising Victorian House for information centers to give out to people looking for antiques."

"That all sounds expensive," Will reminded her. "We don't have much money left, and we still have to finish the second floor. We could invite the antiques dealers and those in town. But I don't think we need to include everyone who worked on the house. They got paid."

"Not everyone did. Nick helped you a lot during the spring, right? And Aunt Nettie has been patient. Not to mention that you're paying Giles and Brian less than they get for their day jobs in construction." She sipped her drink. "And what about other people? Your family alone—don't you have a raft of cousins around here? It would be a way of showing off what you're doing. If we're lucky, there might even be some early sales. And if people are impressed, they'll tell their friends and summer visitors. We want to make Victorian House a destination for people interested in antiques."

"That part of your plan I like," said Will. "Although I'm still worried about how much an opening will cost."

"But it will introduce the town to a new, high-quality venue to buy antiques."

"I already paid for a couple of signs."

"Signs aren't enough to pull people in."

"Okay. I don't have time to think about all those details. If you think an opening is important, go ahead and make a list of people we should invite and write up an ad and an invitation, and start thinking about interviewing our tenants for those articles. And figure out how much it'll all cost. Once you get the whole thing thought out I'll decide."

"*We'll* decide," corrected Maggie. "Partners, remember?"

"Right. But I've been working on the place since January. And since you finally got here three weeks ago you've been fixing up your apartment and thinking about Brook. I've been slaving with wood and paint and contractors."

"And spending my money as well as yours on the improvements," she reminded him. "And I've painted and shellacked and been working with Annie."

"Right," said Will, putting up his hand in a gesture of surrender and taking a long drink of his beer.

Arguing about who'd worked when and how much wasn't what she'd had in mind for the evening. "Leave the opening to me, then. Maybe I could convince one of the local vineyards to give us a special deal on wine for the evening, if we credited them."

"I suppose so," said Will. "Just let me know what you're planning."

"No surprises," Maggie promised as Jill put a large bowl of mussels and an empty bowl for shells between them on the table.

"Extra bread?" Will asked. "To sop up the wine and herbs."

"On its way." Jill bent low over the table to align the bowl of mussels. Low enough to provide a view.

"Thank you, Jill," said Maggie as the young woman walked away. "I don't know much about Jill, other than she's one of Brian's friends. And Annie's."

Will shrugged. "And she's Hay's girlfriend, so far as I know. Been with him a couple of years."

"Annie works so hard, and so does Eric. I'm impressed with both of them," Maggie said, reaching for her second mussel and dunking it in the wine and herb broth. "Brian, too. He told me he's saving so someday he can move into his own place and work independently."

"People in my family are hard workers." Will nodded. "Although Brian has a way to go before he can set up his own business."

"He's young and ambitious and works hard. That's a darn good start," said Maggie. "I see students at the college whose parents are paying their tuition. They treat college as an extension of childhood, and do the minimum to pass. Young people I've gotten to know here are taking life seriously."

"True," said Will. "Some lobstermen start with a few traps when they're about the same age your Brook is. By the time they get out of high school—or drop out—they have a good idea of what it's like to work hard."

Maggie finished her wine.

"Another glass?" Will asked.

"We're both walking, not driving. Sure," said Maggie. They looked around to find Jill, to order refills. She was hanging over the bar, talking and giggling with Hay and Eric.

"So—not every young person in Maine is working hard every minute," said Will. "I'll go to the bar myself." He picked up their glasses.

Jill had taken their earlier orders quickly, but now the quartet at the bar were paying more attention to each other than to customers. Maggie watched them ignore a man at the other end of the bar calling for another refill.

That was no way to earn a generous tip. Maybe the restaurant's owner was away tonight, or doing accounts in his office. His staff wasn't exactly providing great service.

Will interrupted the group, and Hay apologized, as Brian and the others laughed a little too loudly. How long had Brian and Eric been at the bar?

Will returned, putting down their fresh drinks. "If I were the boss here, I'd throw Brian and Eric out. They've already had more than enough to drink. And it's only," Will checked his phone, "six forty-five. The night is young."

"I was thinking the same thing." Maggie twisted around and noticed Hay giving Jill a glass. It wasn't for a customer. Jill took several gulps before Hay put the glass back behind the bar. "So, forget what I said about working hard. I agree. If I were the boss here Hay and Jill would be out, too, for drinking during their shifts. At least we got our appetizer, and it's delicious. I don't mind if we wait a little while for our main course." She helped herself to another mussel. The bowl of empty shells was filling. "It gives me more time to talk with my favorite guy. And I don't see Annie at the bar. She may be in the kitchen, picking up an order."

"In other words, working," said Will.

"Can you keep a secret?" Maggie leaned forward. "Annie's saving every penny she can for her wedding."

"Wedding? I didn't know she was engaged." Will's eyes focused on the ring on Maggie's left hand.

"She isn't. But she thinks Eric will propose any time."

"Seems to me she's putting the cart before the horse," said Will. "I thought proposals normally came before weddings."

"Ah, true. But dreams can come before anything," said Maggie, wiping the mussel broth off her fingers. "Almost every little girl has a bride doll, and dreams of a perfect wedding."

"Did you dream of being a bride?" Will asked. "Because I'll tell you right now: I never dreamed of being a groom."

"Of course I dreamed of being a bride, and having a perfect wedding. And I had one," said Maggie. "The only problem was, I didn't choose the perfect groom. At least not the first time." They didn't talk much about their marriages. "Did you have a beautiful wedding?"

"I don't remember." Will picked up his glass and drank deeply. "It was a long time ago. I'm going to get another beer."

How had they gotten into this subject? They'd never talked about a wedding. They'd promised to love each other. No timetables. Their only plans had been for Maggie's apartment and the antiques mall. And Maggie had planned for Brook.

Why should talking about someone else's wedding be threatening?

But Will looked as though the subject of weddings had caught him totally off guard. He didn't look like a man in love.

He looked like a little boy who'd just wet his pants in front of the whole class.

Unprepared, embarrassed, and ready to run.

27. Weapons

Lithograph by Roberta Samsour from *Czechoslovakian Folk Toys*, printed in Prague, 1941. This print is one in a portfolio picturing simple hand-made wooden toys of various kinds: dolls, cars, folk figures. "Weapons" include a slingshot, handgun, shotgun, and bow & arrow, all made from blocks of wood.

8 x 20 inches. Price: $60.

*M*AGGIE WOKE Thursday morning with a slight headache. A little too much wine, she thought, as she stretched. She and Will had stayed at The Great Blue for a couple of hours. He'd walked her home, kissed her almost chastely, and left.

She'd hoped for a different ending to the evening, but getting to bed early meant she'd had a good rest. Will didn't seem concerned that they were sleeping across town from each other. But she missed their double bed at Aunt Nettie's house.

She glanced at the clock.

It was only five-thirty. Still early, she decided, turning over.

Then she heard the sirens. Close by.

She needed an aspirin, she decided. Plus, she wanted to know what was wrong.

Sirens were rare in Waymouth. Was there a fire? A bad automobile accident? Sirens meant the police or fire department or ambulance squad was coming to help someone. If Brook were here, that's what she'd tell her.

But sirens also meant someone needed help.

She went to the window. Layers of fog wafted across the Madoc River, hiding the water in streaks and swirls of mist. But parts of Water Street were visible.

Despite the early hour, a small group of people had gathered by the town wharf. An ambulance and at least two police cars she could identify were there, too. No fire engines; no smoke, although smoke might have been mixed with the mist.

Had someone hurt another seal? Maggie's heart fell. Why couldn't whoever was targeting those poor animals leave them alone?

But there hadn't been sirens for the first three.

And a seal wouldn't require an ambulance.

Maggie forgot her headache. She pulled on jeans and her old red Somerset County College sweatshirt against the damp morning, and headed downstairs. In a few minutes she was out on Water Street, heading for the spot where she'd seen the crowd.

Voices were low, but she sensed more tension than when Eric had found the dead seal. She glanced down at the float. The *Lucy II* was still docked. This time of morning Eric was usually out on the river. Was the fog too thick for lobstering? No. Fog didn't stop fishermen.

Who did she know here who could tell her what was happening?

Waymouth Deputy Owen Trask was directing people to go back, get off the wharf, back to the parking lot along Water Street.

Maggie maneuvered her way toward Owen.

The tide was high. A skiff under the wharf was so close to its underside she couldn't see who was in it, or what they were doing.

What would someone be doing there that would attract so much attention?

In back of her, a car door slammed. The crowd opened to let someone through.

Nick Strait spoke briefly to several people in the group as he made his way to where Owen was standing.

What was Nick doing here? He'd been here when the second seal was found, but that was because he'd been visiting Victorian House and Brian had heard about the seal. He was on vacation this week. It was chance he'd been the one who'd ended up calling the Marine Patrol about that seal.

Maggie's headache pounded.

Owen must have called him. And there was only one reason for that. Nick was a homicide detective.

As she got closer to Owen she saw Annie, standing near the deputy, but apart from everyone. She was sobbing.

Maggie maneuvered through the crowd, trying to get to her.

She watched Nick and Owen confer briefly, Owen gesturing at the skiff below the wharf. Then Nick went over to talk to Abe Palmer, who was slumped against the pier's railing, near Annie.

Owen held out his arms and walked toward the crowd. "Back up! Onto the street. No one should be on or near the wharf." Another local officer Maggie didn't recognize was also herding bystanders.

"What happened?" she asked the young woman next to her. She'd seen the woman in town, but didn't know her. She hadn't had time to meet her new neighbors. Not yet.

"It's Eric Sirois. Annie Bryant and Abe Palmer found his body floating in the river this morning."

At first Maggie thought she'd misunderstood. "Eric found a body?"

"No. Annie and Abe found the body. Eric Sirois is dead." She shrugged. "Must have drowned."

Maggie crossed her arms and held tight. Eric. Dead. But—how?

She'd seen him at The Great Blue hours before. And if he'd drowned, why were Owen and the other Waymouth policeman now putting crime scene tape across the entrance to the wharf?

Thank goodness Brook wasn't visiting Waymouth today.

28. Crabs, Scavengers of the Sea, Abound in Cracks and Pools

National Geographic lithograph, c. 1910, showing four crabs, rockweed, and barnacles, under the sea.

6.5 x 8 inches. Price: $35.

*A*NNIE, WHAT'S HAPPENED?"
Maggie hadn't totally digested the news about Eric. She kept hoping the young woman who'd told her he was dead had been wrong. Maybe the body they were lifting out of the skiff and onto the float wasn't Eric's.

But Annie's tearstained face brought her back to reality.

"The police took his body out of the water." Annie pointed toward the dock. Luckily, it was far enough away so she couldn't see any details. She hoped Annie couldn't either. "I came down to see him this morning. I brought him coffee." The young woman was holding a Thermos. "I needed to talk to him. I didn't see him right away, so I thought I'd gotten here before he did. Then Abe arrived. He's the one who saw Eric under the water."

Annie was holding onto the Thermos as though it was a lifeline: something that made sense in a world she didn't understand. Tears were running down her face. "At first I hoped it wasn't Eric. But then I knew it was. He was wearing that orange sweatshirt last night."

Annie was staring at Owen and Nick, who were now taking pictures. An EMS team was bringing a stretcher and a body bag down from the ambulance.

Maggie looked again. The body did seem to be wearing something bright orange. Blaze orange. The color hunters wore.

Annie stood, silently sobbing. Maggie put her arm around the young woman and led her over to a bench a little way down the wharf, near the street. If Annie was right, and the body on the pier was Eric's, the body of the man Annie was (almost) engaged to, then she didn't need to see what was happening right now. Or what he looked like. Bodies that had been in the water weren't pleasant sights. But how long could he have been in the water?

"I saw you all last night," Maggie said, still trying to understand what had happened. "You and Jill and Brian and Hay and Eric. At The Great Blue."

"Yes. We were all there. You and Will, too."

"We left at about eight-thirty. How late were you there?"

Annie raised her head, looking toward where the body was being lifted into the bag. Her words were for Maggie, but her eyes were on what was happening on the wharf. "Until about ten-thirty. Closing. Jill and I and Hay were working."

"Of course," said Maggie. "And then you all left?"

"Eric and I left." Annie kept shaking her head. "I was so tired. I'd worked all day, and then waitressed at night, and I had to work again today. The others said they'd have a last drink after the place closed. I hung up my apron, signed out, and Eric said he'd walk me home. I was in bed by eleven or eleven-thirty." She looked at Maggie. "I was surprised Eric'd stayed that late. He gets up at four-thirty to go to work."

Maggie watched as the EMS crew took the body off the wharf and moved it to the ambulance. "The medical examiner will figure out when Eric went into the water. Maybe he fell off his boat this morning."

Annie shook her head. "When it was moored at the dock? The *Lucy II*'s right there. Eric's careful, and he knows every inch of that boat. He grew up on it. He wouldn't fall off. And even if he did, he wasn't like most fishermen. He knew how to swim. The dock is only twenty feet from shore. He wouldn't drown."

Maggie couldn't help asking an obvious question. "Don't fishermen know how to swim? They spend so much of their time on the water."

"Fishermen used to have a joke. 'If you fall overboard, what should you do?'"

Maggie shook her head.

"'Start drinking,'" Annie said, softly. "The water's so cold most of the year you'd die fast of hypothermia. Even if you could swim, you couldn't stay alive long enough to reach the shore. Fishermen believe it would be better to drown quickly."

Maggie shuddered.

"Maggie? Annie?" Nick had come over to them. "Annie, I know Abe called it in, but you were there. You probably know already, but it was Eric. He's gone."

Annie's tears were silent. "What happened?" she asked, as she wiped her face on her sleeve.

"We don't know yet," said Nick. "But we'll find out. Would you come with me for a few minutes? I understand you were with Eric last night. I want you to tell me about that if you can."

Annie held onto Maggie's hand for a moment, but then she stood up and left with Nick.

Maggie sat on the bench, staring at the mists beginning to lift and burn off, revealing the steady flow of the river. The river Eric had known so well, and would never see again.

29. King of Vultures

Hand-colored steel engraving of a vulture standing on its nest from *Natural History of Birds*, 1815 edition, by Georges-Louis Leclerc, Comte de Buffon, whose work dominated zoological illustrations in eighteenth-century France. His birds and animals were often turned into needlepoint designs by women wealthy enough to own a copy of his work. He was appointed director of the Jardin du Roi by Louis XV and, despite changes in the French government, held that post for fifty years, making his zoological gardens the leading biological research center of its time.

5 x 7 inches. Price: $70.

*S*HE COULDN'T HELP ANNIE. The young woman had been crying, but through her tears she'd seemed remarkably calm for someone whose almost-fiancé had just died. Probably she was in shock.

Maggie went back to her apartment, exchanged her sweatshirt for a T-shirt, and drank a can of Diet Pepsi with an aspirin. Caffeine was supposed to be good for headaches, right? If only it would work for heartaches.

A little before eight she unlocked Victorian House for the men working on the elevator. Where was Will? He was usually on site before eight.

She told the men she'd be in the print room if they had any questions, hoping they wouldn't have any. She hadn't been involved in the elevator installation details.

Today her mind was not on antiques. But she needed to do something, and finishing her exhibit area wouldn't require her to think much about what she was doing.

Close to nine o'clock Will stomped in.

"Where's Annie?" he asked. "I need her to check a couple of

things on our website. She's not at the front desk. She should have been here an hour ago!"

"You're late," Maggie said, calmly putting down the stack of Dulac prints she'd been sorting.

"Aunt Nettie had a bad night," said Will. "She kept having night-mares, and then she'd wake up, and need to use her commode. I was up with her most of the night."

"I'm sorry," said Maggie. "Then you haven't heard."

"Heard what?"

"Eric Sirois is dead. Apparently he drowned sometime after we saw him last night. I don't think we can expect Annie to come in today."

Will stopped. "What? Drowned? How?"

Maggie shook her head. "I don't know any details. I heard sirens and went down to the town wharf early this morning. Owen was there, and Nick. From what I could see, Eric's body was caught under the wharf." She paused. "Annie was there, at the wharf."

"Does Brian know?"

"I'm surprised the whole town doesn't by now. You know Way-mouth. Nothing stays secret long."

"Working on the water can be dangerous. But Eric seemed to have a steady head on his shoulders. And his boat was docked?"

"It was. And the river was calm," Maggie said. "I can't imagine what could have happened. I didn't know him well, but I liked him."

Will turned to go toward the room where men were working on the elevator. Then he came back. "Wait. You said Owen and *Nick* were down at the wharf?"

"I thought of that, too. I assume they took Eric to the medical examiner in Augusta. And Nick's on vacation this week, remember? Maybe Owen called him, not knowing that, and he came down to help."

"Maybe," Will agreed, grudgingly. "But Owen wouldn't have called him unless something was suspicious. A body in the river would automatically go to the medical examiner. Nick wouldn't be involved unless…"

"Unless there was a chance it was a homicide. I know."

"What about Annie? Does she understand that?"

"Probably not. But when I left the wharf she was talking to Nick."

They stood, silent, for a minute or two.

Then Will returned to his earlier question. "Do you know what she's doing with the website?"

"We've been working on it together. What do you want to know?"

"The woman with the smalls wanted to know how many pictures of her inventory we could post. I told her she'd have the same opportunity as everyone else. But I don't know what Annie's been doing about pictures." Will followed Maggie to the front hall, running his hand through his hair.

Maggie reached up and plucked a piece of oatmeal out of his beard. "I could guess at the answer, but I'll count. Annie has Joe Cousins's pictures up now, and I was going to give her mine today. You go and work with the guys on the elevator. I'll let you know."

Will turned toward the door to the kitchen. "Don't forget. Find me when you know about the pictures."

"Don't worry," said Maggie. "And while you're thinking about photographs, Annie needs pictures of your inventory, too."

"Right," said Will as he left.

Maggie suspected she'd have to remind him of that later. For now, she checked the computer.

All was in order, as she'd expected. Annie was very competent.

30. Danger Ahead

Winslow Homer wood engraving in *Appleton's Journal*, April 30, 1870, showing a steam engine pulling passenger cars across a curved trestle bridge over water. Two railroad employees in the caboose look over the side of the train to see if the engine has stayed on the tracks.
6.25 x 6.5 inches. Price: $150.

*M*AGGIE COUNTED the pictures on the Victorian House website and reported back to Will that thirty of Joe Cousins's books, a selection of twentieth-century first editions (some signed) and nineteenth-century books with elegant leather bindings, were now up.

After the site was public and functioning they might be able to add more items to each dealer's section. Plus, she reminded Will, Annie was going to link the dealers' own websites to the Victorian House site.

Assignment completed, and print room finished, by late morning Maggie found herself at "sixes and sevens," as Aunt Nettie would say. All she could think about was Eric, and what had happened to him. And how Annie was coping.

"Not well," was the young woman's quiet response when Maggie finally called her.

Maggie checked her watch. "Let me buy you lunch."

Annie was silent for a moment. "If people see me at The Great Blue they'll think I don't care."

"Why don't you leave your phone at home? I'll pick you up and we'll go to Pemaquid. Sit on the beach there, eat a lobster roll or hot dog, and be away from Waymouth for a couple of hours."

"You'd do that for me?" said Annie, choking on sobs.

"What's your address? I'll pick you up in half an hour."

"I'm not far. I'll come to Victorian House," said Annie. "I don't want to talk to anyone but you." She hesitated. "But I'll bring my phone. My friends would think I'd hung myself or something if I didn't answer their texts."

Annie was, what? Seventeen years younger than she was. A member of the cell-phone generation. "See you whenever you can get here." Maggie went upstairs and optimistically put a bathing suit on under her clothes, changed her sandals for sneakers, slathered on sunblock, and finally found a hat in the back of her new closet. She'd lived in Waymouth three weeks now and already seldom-used accessories had accumulated on the floor. Storage was something she definitely needed more of. On the second floor of Victorian House's barn? She made a mental note to ask Will later.

In the meantime, she picked up towels and stuffed her hat and sunglasses in her canvas bag. She was ready for the beach.

She'd thought her first beach trip of the summer would be with Brook.

But today a few hours outside with the ocean as a backdrop sounded soothing.

Annie wasn't the only one who could use a relaxing day.

She couldn't make a difference in Brook's life today, but maybe she could help Annie a little.

Annie arrived at Victorian House a few minutes after Maggie'd gone downstairs to tell Will what they were doing. He'd shrugged and told her to "have a good time on your day off." She hoped he understood what she was doing was important. No way could she or Annie focus on the computer that afternoon.

The two were quiet as Maggie headed up Route 1, through Damariscotta, and then down the peninsula, through Bristol, to Pemaquid. Gardens and fields were being prepared for planting, or showed early signs of young green sprouts emerging from dark soil. The smell of manure permeated the car as they drove past farms. Signs of approaching summer were everywhere. The sign in front of the Bristol Consolidated School announced EIGHTH GRADE GRADUATION JUNE 19. FOURTEEN MORE DAYS OF SCHOOL!!!

A church advertised VACATION BIBLE SCHOOL. A bearded man was painting a weathered ice-cream-and-fresh-vegetables stand.

In front of a large house a handwritten sign announced OPENING JUNE 1! BED AND BREAKFAST. Three open antiques shops tempted Maggie. But today was not an antiques day.

Annie leaned her head against the passenger door, lost in thought. Probably not good thoughts. Once they got to the beach she might be ready to talk a little. In the meantime, Maggie let her be. Twice Annie picked up her phone to answer texts, but responded only briefly.

Maggie almost cried out in delight when she spotted a bald eagle circling above a farm in Bristol, its wide wings lifted by sea breezes.

But eagles were killers. This wasn't a day to call attention to them, even if they were a relative novelty to someone from New Jersey.

Annie was texting someone again.

Maggie suppressed her urge to ask who.

Had Brook ever seen eagles? Did she know how they used to be an endangered species, and had been saved by environmentalists and lovers of birds?

Or did she take birds, of any kind, for granted?

So many things she didn't know about Brook. She looked forward to a summer of their sharing beautiful Maine days.

She'd take Brook to Pemaquid Light, to see the waves breaking over the ledges beneath the lighthouse. The archaeological digs uncovering the remains of colonial settlements. The old fort. Maggie'd seen them all. She especially loved the seventeenth- and eighteenth-century graveyard near the site of the old settlements.

Would Brook share her passion for any of those things? Or would she look away, as Annie was doing now, and stay in her own world?

"Shall we stop at the lighthouse?" Maggie asked.

Annie shrugged. "I don't care."

"Let's make a quick stop," said Maggie. "It's one of my favorite places on the coast, and I haven't been there this year. Looking out at the ocean always makes my problems seem smaller." Would it do the same for Annie?

A few minutes later they'd parked and were walking past the lighthouse to the ledges, where waves were breaking below them.

"That's Monhegan Island, isn't it?" asked Maggie, pointing to a small dark spot near the horizon.

Annie nodded. "I think so."

"I've always wanted to visit Monhegan," Maggie said.

"I've never been, either," said Annie. "I've lived here my whole life, and I've never been."

"I grew up in New Jersey. A lot of people there never visited the Statue of Liberty. We take nearby places for granted. We always think we can visit them any time."

Had Eric ever visited Monhegan? He'd probably been close by, in his boat. This wasn't a day to ask.

"Maybe," said Annie. She sat down on one of the ledges, and Maggie joined her. "When you live here you don't want to go places full of tourists."

Maggie swallowed. Of course. She was from away. Maine was still a novelty to her, a place full of beauty and wonder.

To Eric and Annie and their friends, Maine was just home.

"Being in a place like this reminds me that we people are temporary, but the seas and these rocks we're sitting on go on forever," Maggie said, realizing as soon as she spoke that her words sounded trite. Even professorial.

"I don't care about stupid rocks. When I look at the waves breaking over these ledges," Annie pointed at the long stretches of sharp granite shaped by centuries of pounding surf, "I think about all the ships wrecked here. The people who died trying to make it to land."

Today everything would remind Annie of death

"On the other side of the lighthouse there's a plaque to the first wreck recorded," Annie went on. "Probably hundreds of vessels were destroyed on these rocks before then, when the Abenakis lived here, but no one wrote them down. The first one recorded was in August of 1635."

Annie knew her history. Maggie was surprised. Although, of course, this was Annie's heritage; her local history. "What happened?" She looked out at the point of jagged rocks and imagined what would happen to a ship that hit the point in the dark, or in a storm.

"The ship was the *Angel Gabriel*," said Annie, her voice flat and unemotional, repeating facts she knew well. "It was one of a fleet of five ships headed to the Massachusetts Bay Colony from England. They sailed into a hurricane."

Maggie shuddered slightly, imagining.

"All five ships were driven off course. Three ships outran the storm, but ended up in Newfoundland. The *Angel Gabriel* and the *James* ended up on the coast of Maine. The *James* came close to foundering at the Isles of Shoals, but eventually made it to Boston. The *Angel Gabriel* hit the rocks here at Pemaquid Point and sank."

"And those aboard?"

"Some passengers had gone ashore near the beach where we're going today. They were at the small settlement there when the storm was at its worst. Afterwards, some of them stayed here in Maine. Others found ships to Massachusetts. A few were afraid of the sea, and walked to Massachusetts or New Hampshire. The crew and everyone else who'd stayed on board the *Angel Gabriel* died."

Maggie looked down at the sea. Now she imagined faces in each wave that hit the jagged shore. People struggling for land and safety.

Annie stood up. "Let's go to the beach. History's boring."

Brook had said the same thing about old things. Maggie stood, too. How could something she found so fascinating be boring to others? "I remember Maine was called the wilderness of Massachusetts until it became a state in 1820. And John Adams complained bitterly whenever he had to try a case in Maine. I've read his letters."

Annie looked at her. "Maine's never been an easy state."

31. *Ulva lactuca,* L.

Lithograph of the edible green sea algae commonly
called "sea lettuce," found on many coasts. In the book
Sea Mosses (the nineteenth-century term for seaweeds)
by A.B. Hervey, 1882.

4 x 7 inches. Price: $35.

QUARTER-MILE-LONG Pemaquid Beach was off Snow-
ball Hill Road. In July or August the gravel-and-sand parking
lot would be full. Early on this Thursday afternoon in May
two school buses and a half dozen cars were the only vehicles there
as Maggie pulled her van into one of the spaces.

Brook must have been to a beach at some time, she thought.
Someone else would already have had the thrill of taking her for the
first time.

But, then, there were all those New Jerseyans who'd never been
to the Statue of Liberty. She'd have to ask Brook. A beach trip would
be easiest to arrange after she moved in. Maggie realized she'd
stopped thinking "if she moved in."

She paid the eight dollars admission for the two of them. Annie
didn't seem to notice.

They passed through the building holding the concession
stand, rest rooms and changing rooms and followed the narrow path
through the dunes and grasses to the beach.

The tide was out, so the beach seemed larger than usual. Three
older couples had spread blankets on white sand near the dunes.
One ponytailed man was walking the darker damp sands with a
metal detector, searching for treasures. Further down the beach,
students on a school trip were filling red and blue plastic buckets
with limpet, periwinkle, mussel and clam shells, pieces of driftwood,
sea glass and smooth stones.

"Is this spot okay?" Maggie asked Annie, pointing at dry sand near the center of the beach.

Annie was answering a text. "Sure. Anywhere."

Maggie spread out the towels she'd brought and sat down to renew the sunblock she'd slathered on at home. She'd also put on a bathing suit, but she'd already decided she wouldn't do any more than wade in the shallow water warmed by the sun. Maybe not even that. Annie's problems were more important than getting wet sand between her toes.

The sun was hot on their backs, but sea breezes kept the sand cool. The waves here were low and regular; very different from the breakers they'd seen on the other side of the point.

Annie put her cell in her pocket and joined Maggie on a towel.

"Lots of people are thinking about you today," Maggie commented.

"I don't want to see anyone, or talk to anyone," said Annie. "That state trooper, Nick Strait, asked me all sorts of questions this morning. Personal questions. I told him what I knew. I don't have to tell everyone in town."

"Police are trained to ask questions." What "personal" questions had he asked Annie?

"It's bad enough Eric is dead. Dead!" Annie's eyes started welling up again. "I can't believe it. I almost texted him a few minutes ago to tell him about everyone calling me. But I can't. I can't ever text him or call him or talk to him or hug him or anything. He's gone!" Annie's eyes were red and swollen, and the mascara she'd put on early that morning was badly smudged, making the swollen circles under her eyes even darker.

"Have you been in touch with his family?"

Annie shook her head. "They won't want to hear from me. His mom's probably drunk already. His sister lives in Florida now."

"What about his dad?"

"His dad left when he was a kid. Eric didn't know where he was. His grandfather is the only one who cared about Eric, and he's in Florida now, too."

"Eric was lucky to have you, Annie."

"That's what makes it even worse. He didn't think so. Last night, after I finished at The Great Blue, I asked him to walk me home. I wanted to talk to him." She hugged her knees and put her head down. As the sea breeze moved strands of her loose red hair it shone in the sun. "I'm so stupid, Maggie!"

"You're not stupid. You're smart."

"I was stupid last night. You don't know what happened!"

"Want to tell me?"

Annie wiped her nose with the back of her hand. Maggie handed her a tissue. "I'm so embarrassed. But everyone in town seems to know already. If I don't tell you, someone else will."

"What happened?"

"Eric and I had a fight. That's what happened. I wanted to tell him what the wedding planner said…that if we wanted to get married in October, we had to make plans now. I thought I'd wear a fancy white dress and we'd get married up in the church, and have a reception on the church lawn. Sort of a pot-luck wedding. But she said we'd need to reserve the church, and give the organist a deposit and… Oh, you don't want to hear all that."

"So you and Eric argued about your wedding?"

"Worse." Annie's nose was beginning to drip again. She dabbed at it with her tissue, and then gave it a good blow. "He said he wasn't ready to talk about a wedding. He didn't want to get married for years. He wanted to enjoy life, and make things comfortable for himself and take care of his mother. He wasn't ready to think about weddings, or wives, or babies."

"How did you feel about that?"

"I told him to go to hell. Sorry, Maggie. But I did. I love—loved—him, and we'd been together since we were kids. Everyone expects us to get married. How could I show my face in town if we broke up?"

"What did Eric say?"

"He said, 'Live with it. I never promised we would get married,' and he went off to have another beer with Hay and Brian."

"I thought Hay and Brian were only having one more beer after the bar at The Great Blue was closed." If Annie and Eric had had a serious argument, the other guys would have left the bar by the time Eric got back there.

"They'd left the bar by then, sure. But Brian had bought some beer earlier. It was in his truck. They planned to go somewhere to drink it. Usually they went to the town wharf."

"And you?"

"What do you think I did? I went home and hid under my blankets and cried all night.

"After a few hours I thought, Eric had been drinking too much last night. Maybe he meant October wouldn't be a good time for the wedding. He's loved me forever. At least he said he loved me. I came on too strong. He hadn't meant to break up with me. He just wasn't ready for a wedding." She sniffed again. "I could live with waiting a while longer. I could. But I can't live without him!" Her tears started again.

Maggie handed her more tissues.

"I decided to go down to see him before he took the *Lucy II* out. I made coffee for him, as a peace-offering. When I got to the *Lucy II* I didn't see him, so I waited. I checked the boat. Sometimes he sleeps there. I figured he'd been up so late last night he'd overslept. Then Abe showed up. He saw Eric first." Annie wiped her nose again. "It was my fault he died! And now my whole life is ruined!"

"You feel that way now, Annie. It's a shock that Eric's gone. But it wasn't your fault. And although you're hurting now, hurting badly, your life isn't over."

"But if I'd gone with him last night, maybe he wouldn't have had as much to drink, and he wouldn't have drowned. That's what everyone says!"

"You can't believe you were responsible, Annie."

"Then why have Hay and Brian and Jill been texting me all day saying I put too much pressure on Eric, and if I hadn't gone home last night…if I'd come with them…then he'd be alive now."

Annie's and Maggie's phones buzzed at the same time. They both looked down.

"Oh, no. No!" said Annie.

She looked over at Maggie. "Did you get the same message I did?"

Maggie took a deep breath. "Mine was from Will. Who was yours from?"

"That state trooper. Nick Strait. He says to come back to Waymouth. He needs to ask me more questions."

Maggie picked up the towel she'd been sitting on. "You're right. That's what Will said, too. We need to get back."

32. Common Dandelion

Brilliant chromolithograph of yellow flowers by Anne Pratt (1806–1893), a self-taught English botanist and illustrator. Her twenty books, written in nonscientific terms, were accurate, and helped make botany a popular hobby during the second half of the nineteenth century. From her *Wild Flowers*, 1852.

6 x 9 inches. Price: $35.

*T*HEY HADN'T HAD anything to eat, Maggie realized as she and Annie passed the beach's concession stand. And, after all, she'd invited Annie for lunch.

"What would you like? We can eat on our way back to Waymouth." Annie shook her head. She was too distracted to eat anything.

Maggie, on the other hand, was suddenly starving. She bought a hot dog and ate most of it before she started driving.

The bright sun had turned cloudy. It hadn't turned out to be a good beach day.

"Could you drop me at the Waymouth Sheriff's Office?" asked Annie. "Detective Strait said he had an office there."

Maggie's stomach dropped. Nick had planned to be on vacation this week. He only had an adjunct office in Waymouth when he was investigating a local murder.

In Maine, state police investigate all homicides outside of Portland or Bangor. Nick was assigned those in the town where he'd grown up, and still lived. His bosses figured he'd know the hidden agendas and backgrounds of the people there. He'd once told Maggie that made his job more difficult, since it meant he had to assume the worst of his neighbors, but it also meant he almost always got his man. Or woman.

Will's message to Maggie had been simple. "Bring Annie home. Nick's looking for her."

Last night Eric had been at The Great Blue with Hay, Jill, Brian, and Annie. Brian and Eric had been drinking at the bar; Hay, Jill, and Annie had been working. But she'd seen Hay and Jill drinking, too, despite being on duty. Had Annie been drinking?

Right now it seemed like an unimportant detail.

Annie said the guys had continued drinking after she'd gone home. Had Jill gone with the men, or had she gone home?

Did any of that matter? When did Eric die?

Nick might know by now, Maggie thought, as she drove, but the medical examiner probably wouldn't finish examining Eric's body until later today, at the earliest. Whatever Nick thought was an educated guess.

During the past two years she'd been connected to enough investigations to know his first step would be to establish where Eric had been between the time he left The Great Blue last night, and when Annie and Abe discovered his body early this morning. No doubt that was why Nick wanted to talk with Annie. She'd been one of the last people to see Eric last night.

"Don't worry," Maggie said to Annie, who'd stopped talking again and was slumped against the passenger door. She hadn't even picked up her phone the last few times it had buzzed. "Nick's trying to figure out where Eric went last night after he left you. Lots of people saw you all at The Great Blue. Nick will want to know where Eric went after that." And what happened, wherever he went, Maggie added to herself.

"I don't know anything!" Annie said. "All I know is, Eric told me he was going to drink more beer. He drank too much. Maybe he stayed out all night. I don't know. I only know for sure he wasn't with me."

"Nick will talk to Brian and Hay," Maggie reassured her. "Tell him what you told me. The facts. You don't have to tell him all the details. Keep it simple. You and Eric had an argument and then you went home. He'll ask what direction Eric was heading when you last saw him."

"The last time I saw him…" Annie's voice was strained. "I still can't believe I'll never see him again." She turned to Maggie. "Will you go with me? When I talk with Nick? Please? I can't do this by myself."

Nick would want to talk with Annie alone, Maggie was sure. But Annie was shaking. She was only twenty-three. This had been the worst day of her life. "I'll go in with you," Maggie promised.

"Thank you." Annie sat up and pulled down the car's sun visor to look at herself in the mirror. "I look awful." She ran her hand through hair that was the worse for sea breezes, wiped the mascara off her face with a tissue, and reapplied lipstick. Then she sat back in the seat. "I'm okay. I can do this."

Maggie reached out and touched her hand. "I know you can. You'll be fine."

33. *"And sometimes voices"*

Clouds full of faces framed with long hair hover above a barren landscape. Illustration by Arthur Rackham for William Shakespeare's *The Tempest*, edition published in 1926.

5 x 6.5 inches. Price: $60.

*B*UT I WANT Maggie with me!" Annie protested.

"Maggie can wait here for you," said Nick. He opened the door of his temporary office at the Waymouth Sheriff's Department. Deputy Owen Trask followed the two of them in, and closed the door. A witness.

Cozy, Maggie thought. If Eric had been drunk and slipped on the deck of the *Lucy II* and fallen into the water, Nick wouldn't be questioning Annie.

But she might not know that.

Maggie sat in the reception area and picked up a local newspaper. But she couldn't concentrate on stories about car accidents and fires and Rotary Club meetings.

What had happened to Eric? If Nick and Owen knew, the whole town would know soon enough. Some murder investigations were closed quickly, focusing on the obviously guilty party. Other investigations were never closed.

But the case wouldn't have been opened if Eric's death hadn't been determined a homicide.

Her phone rang. "Hi, Will."

"Where are you? I've been looking all over. The police are trying to find Annie."

"I brought her straight to the sheriff's office. She's talking to Nick and Owen now. She was nervous, so I came with her. I told you I was taking her to Pemaquid for lunch." Maggie's stomach was telling her how small her lunch had turned out to be.

"You don't need to get mixed up in whatever happened to Eric. You're new in town. You have responsibilities here at Victorian House."

Maggie'd been involved (indirectly) in several murders before this. Not that she'd intended to play amateur sleuth, but there always seemed to be a reason for her to be consulted. Or, she'd admitted to herself more than a few times, she'd been smart enough to figure out what had happened before the police had. It wasn't a part of her life Will was fond of.

"You talked to Nick. Do you know what happened to Eric? I'm assuming he didn't simply drown." Maggie kept her voice soft.

Will sighed, audibly. "When Nick was here looking for Annie he didn't say exactly what had happened. But the word around town is Eric was shot."

Shot! Like the seals had been? "It's easy to tell whether he drowned or not. The medical examiner would know if there was water in his lungs."

"Nick didn't tell me. We're old friends. But despite some of the conversations you've had with him in the past, an antiques dealer isn't normally someone a homicide detective would confide details to," said Will drily.

"I've only helped Nick out when he asked me," said Maggie. She didn't mention that in the past Owen had told her more about investigations than Nick had. "I'm curious. I can't imagine why anyone would want to kill Eric."

"That's Nick's problem. So when are you coming home?"

Home. To Victorian House.

"I promised Annie I'd wait for her. When Nick and Owen are finished questioning her I'll drop her off at her place, and then come home. I can't imagine they'll keep her here long. She's—she was— Eric's girlfriend. Not his killer."

Will didn't answer for a moment. Then, "People are saying Annie and Eric had a major fight last night. Several people heard them yelling. They say Eric broke up with Annie, and she didn't take it well. That she's the number-one suspect."

"No!" said Maggie. "I don't believe it."

"Believe it, Maggie. And don't get involved." He hung up.

"That's all that happened. I told you." Annie's weepy voice came from the door of Nick's office, which had just opened.

"Thank you for coming in." Owen was following Annie into the reception area. "If you think of anything else we should know, call Detective Strait or me."

"I don't know anything else. I told you everything." Annie's voice was high and strained. "We argued, and I went home last night. I didn't leave my house again until early this morning. And I don't know where Eric went after he left me. I just know he planned to hang with Brian and Jill and Hay."

"We'll be talking to all of them, I assure you. And we may have other questions for you when we know more."

Annie ran over to Maggie. "It's awful, Maggie. They think someone killed Eric. Killed him! Why would anyone want to kill him?"

"That's what we need to find out," said Owen. "Good to see you again, Maggie. I saw you down at the wharf. Welcome to Waymouth."

"Thank you. Good to see you, too, Owen."

"Why don't you take Annie home? She needs to rest."

"I will." Maggie put her arm around Annie. "Come on. See if you can get some sleep."

Annie'd said she hadn't been able to sleep after arguing with Eric, and she'd left home early this morning to talk to him before he went out lobstering. Had she wanted to confront him? She'd brought him coffee. That sounded more like an apology than the beginning of another argument.

"I'm going to turn off my phone," declared Annie. Her voice was shaking, and her cheeks and eyes were swollen and red. "I don't care what anyone wants to say. I don't want to hear it. I don't want to talk to anyone, or text anyone. I just want to be alone."

She climbed into Maggie's van. "Thank you for waiting for me. My house is down there."

Annie pointed, and Maggie followed her directions. Brian had said all his friends lived in town. Annie's house was only four or five blocks from The Great Blue, perhaps six blocks from the river.

Six blocks from where Eric's body had been found.

34. Fashion Print

From *The Gentleman's Monthly Magazine of Fashion and Costumes de Paris*, May, 1853, edited by Louis Devere, London, and J.H. Chappell, Philadelphia. Hand-colored steel engraving of three boys and one girl standing on a footbridge, dressed in elegant attire. Two boys wear navy blue jackets and checked trousers; one is dressed in black. The girl is wearing a purple-and-black dress over white pantaloons. Black and purple were colors of mourning. Fashion prints of men and children are rarer, and therefore more desirable, than women's fashion prints.

6.5 x 9 inches. Price: $85.

*M*AGGIE PARKED HER CAR by the Victorian House barn. It was only midafternoon, but it had already been a long day. Will's car, which had been Aunt Nettie's before her stroke last August, was there, and so was Brian's pickup and his dad's jeep.

The elevator installers must have left for the day. At least the noise level would be down.

She went in the side door, near her print room, and absent-mindedly straightened two of the framed seal prints and one of the Denton fish that had gone awry, probably a result of vibrations from the elevator construction. She liked the way the room looked. Familiar prints, emphasizing themes in northern New England and history. When she had a chance she'd add some prints for children's rooms...nursery rhymes, Beatrix Potter, Jessie Willcox Smith. Grandparents shopped at antiques malls, and young children with Grandma or Aunt Stacy might be drawn to those prints.

Her children's prints were too young for Brook.

By adopting a nine-year-old, a child adoption agencies classified as "older," she'd missed the fun of decorating a nursery or toddler's room.

But Brook still had plenty of growing up to do.

Maggie stared at the seal prints she'd liked so much. She'd wait to show them to Brook until she was sure Waymouth's seal killer had been caught. Brook didn't need to be reminded of what she'd seen on the high-tide mark.

"Maggie! There you are." Will stood in the doorway, a little sawdust sprinkled in his gray beard, and a hammer in his hand. "I thought you'd never get here. You took Annie home?"

"I did. She was upset, of course. She lost the man she loved, and then was cross-examined by the police."

"Did she admit killing Eric?"

"No! And I don't think she did." Maggie shook her head. "Her story made sense to me. She said she didn't see him alive after he walked her home last night."

"A woman scorned...you never know," said Will. "But I hope she didn't do it. We need her finishing up the website and working here, not in jail."

Maggie stared at him. Then she changed the subject. "I saw Brian's and Giles's cars outside. They're not working for Brent Construction today?"

"Nah. Brian was a little freaked out this morning. And, I strongly suspect, hung over. Giles didn't want him going to work that way. So he declared today a family emergency day for both of them. They've been taking wallpaper off the front room on the second floor. If they finish today, tomorrow we can start patching the horse-hair plaster underneath."

"How's Brian doing?"

Will shrugged. "He seems okay."

"I'd like to talk to him," said Maggie, moving toward the door.

Will blocked her way. "Don't get him all upset, now. He's been doing fine all day."

"One of his best friends died last night. If he's working, he's holding his emotions in."

"So, let him."

"Nick is going to talk with him, Will. Assuming what Annie told me was true, Brian was one of the last people to see Eric last night."

"Don't get involved, Maggie. I told you. Eric's death is a police matter. Nick will take care of it."

"I know he will." She reached up and brushed some of the sawdust out of his beard. "But I want Brian to know what's happening. He deserves to be warned Nick's going to call him. I don't want him to be freaked out."

"Are you sure that's the only reason you want to talk to him? He's my cousin. I don't want him upset."

"I want to tell him I'm sorry his friend is dead," said Maggie. "He lost Crystal two years ago, and I don't think he's ever totally gotten over that. Now to lose one of his best friends? It has to be hitting him hard, Will."

"He's a man now. He needs to pull himself together."

"He's twenty-one. How did you feel when your wife died?"

Will stepped back. "That wasn't the same thing, and you know it, Maggie. Keep my wife out of this. Brian wasn't married to Eric. Or to Crystal, for that matter."

"No, he wasn't."

Will had turned slightly away. Maggie could see the pain in his eyes. "You're right. I shouldn't have mentioned your wife."

"Just because you didn't love Michael, doesn't mean I wasn't devastated when my wife died," Will said. "You've known me for two years. You knew that."

"I did, Will. I'm sorry."

Maggie moved past Will and headed for the staircase to the second floor. "I'll be brief. But I'm going to talk to Brian."

35. Bald Eagle

Chromolithograph of bald eagle sitting on its nest with two hungry eagle chicks. From *Birds of North America: One Hundred and Nineteen Artistic Colored Plates Representing Different Species and Varieties*, by Jacob Henry Studer (1840–1904,) a printer, lithographer, artist, and ornithologist from Columbus, Ohio. 1903.

9 x 12.25 inches. Price: $80

*B*RIAN LEARY AND HIS DAD, Giles, were scraping red-and-green striped wallpaper, and the five layers of other papers below it, off what had once been someone's bedroom walls. They'd used water, a chemical spray that should have loosened the papers, and several sizes of scrapers and putty knives. Although they'd covered the floor with drop cloths and newspapers, now piles of small torn pieces of wet wallpaper were on the floor, stuck to each other, to the cloths and papers, and to the men's shoes.

Victorians put wallpaper on with strong paste. They intended it to last. In a house this old, those layers of paper often were holding up the plaster. When the paper came down, so did a good part of the wall.

This room would need a lot of new plastering.

"Maggie," said Giles. "Come to inspect our work?"

"I'm impressed. What a mess this is! But, no. I came to talk to Brian."

Giles nodded, and Brian turned away from the wall. "What d'you want?"

His eyes were swollen. Had he been crying? Or maybe his eyes were reacting to the chemicals he'd been using. The windows were open for ventilation, but the room stank.

"I wanted to tell you how sorry I am about Eric."

"Yeah. Wicked crazy," said Brian.

"Annie and I spent some time together today. Then Nick Strait questioned her at the sheriff's office."

"Annie? Why?" said Brian.

Hadn't he heard the rumors about Eric's death? Or maybe he didn't want her to know about them.

"She and Eric were close. And she was one of the last people to see Eric alive." Maggie hesitated. "Nick said he was going to talk with you and Hay and Jill. I thought you should know."

"I've got nothing to say to him."

"Son, you have nothing to hide. If Nick Strait wants to talk with you, you do it. Don't fool around with a state trooper's investigation," Giles put in.

"So, what? He's investigating Eric's being stupid enough to drown?"

Brian had been working all day. He hadn't heard Eric had been murdered. Maggie didn't want to be the one to tell him. But Brian needed to be prepared before he talked with Nick and Owen. "I don't think he has the medical examiner's report yet. But he's making sure Eric's death was accidental. It was an unattended death."

Brian paled. "He thinks someone murdered Eric?"

Maggie didn't reply. "You were with him last night at The Great Blue."

"No secret about that. Half the town was there."

"What happened after the restaurant closed?"

Brian dropped the plastic bag he'd been filling with pieces of wallpaper. "Nothing! Nothing happened! Do you want me to say I killed Eric? I knocked him out, carried him down to the river and pushed him under. Is that what you want me to say?"

"Whoa, Brian," said his father. "Calm down. Maggie asked you what happened last night. Should be a simple question to answer, right, son?"

Giles was frowning. What was he thinking?

"Okay. Hay and Eric and me were at the Great Blue bar, drinking. Beer, mostly. Jill had beer, too."

"Was that before or after the bar closed?" Maggie asked.

"Both." Brian looked over at his father, who was shaking his head in disapproval. "Hay let us keep drinking while he was cleaning up. Then Annie came over. She hadn't been drinking, and she made some comments. You know. Nasty stuff. Said we were drinking away our futures or something. She was always harping on us, especially on Eric. Just because she didn't drink and we did."

"What happened then?"

"She said she was tired; she was going home. Eric said that was fine with him; she wasn't any fun when she was in a mood."

"So she left?"

"Yeah. She left. But a few minutes later Eric finished his beer and went after her. Jill told him he was a wimp; he didn't need..." Brian glanced at Maggie. "He didn't need someone like Annie."

"But he left anyway."

Brian nodded.

"What about the rest of you?"

"Hay finished cleaning up and Jill and I finished our drinks. I had some beer in my truck. It was a comfortable night, not cold for May. I said we could go down and sit on the town wharf and have a nightcap."

"And Jill and Hay agreed?"

"Sure. They always agreed."

"So it was something you guys did often."

Brian glared at his father and shrugged. "Often enough."

"And Eric?"

"He wasn't there. Not yet. We didn't think much about it. Sometimes he joined us and sometimes not. He got up early in the morning. We got the beer and headed down to the wharf."

"And?"

"I don't exactly remember what happened next." Brian glanced at his dad. "I'd been drinking for five or six hours by then. I remember Jill and Hay arguing about something. Nothing new. They always argue. And then Eric was there, too, I'm pretty sure."

"So he joined you after you'd been at the wharf for a while."

"I don't know how long we'd been there. But he got into it with Hay and Jill."

"You weren't involved in the argument?"

"Hell, no. I haven't even got a girlfriend."

"They were arguing about girls?"

"Eric said he and Annie had a fight, and Hay told him to forget her." Brian was quiet. "I remember saying we'd all been friends for years. We should stay friends, even if we didn't always agree."

"And?" his father asked.

"They laughed at me," Brian said sheepishly. "I'm the youngest, you know, and they don't take me seriously. I don't remember much more."

"Did you drive?"

"Nope. Walked. Figured I needed fresh air. And our house is only three blocks from the wharf. I left the truck on Water Street. Figured I'd get it in the morning. I do remember thinking that."

"When you left, Hay and Eric and Jill were still on the wharf?"

"I'm pretty sure."

"And did you go home?" Maggie asked.

"Must have. I was in bed this morning when Hay called me to tell me about Eric." Brian shook his head. "I thought he was kidding. But I guess he wasn't." His eyes filled. "Eric is really dead."

Maggie turned to leave. Then she stopped. "Brian, do you have a gun?"

"Sure." He looked at his father. "We both have guns. They're locked up, at home."

"What about your friends? Do they have guns?"

He scratched his head. "Eric did, I'm sure. And Jill. And Hay." He frowned. "Don't know about Annie. We don't exactly walk around town with guns. Some folks have concealed carry permits, but I don't think any of us do. No need."

"I saw Abe Palmer with a gun last week."

"He has a permit," Giles pointed out. "Don't know why Abe would have a gun with him. But getting a concealed carry permit is simple. And some folks don't even bother with that." He looked at Brian. "Most of our guns are rifles. Only time we have 'em with us is during hunting season. Waymouth isn't like Portland, where the police sometimes seize guns and melt 'em down for anchors."

"Why are you asking?" said Brian.

"Because I heard Eric was shot," Maggie answered.

"Like those seals," Giles said, under his breath. "It's bad enough to shoot seals. Why would anyone shoot a kid like Eric?"

36. The Atlantic Salmon— Salmo Salar

Chromolithograph by naturalist Sherman Foote Denton (1856–1937). Denton's fish, sought after as among the best prints of fish ever produced in the United States, were published in the State of New York Fisheries, Game and Forest Commission's annual reports from 1895 to 1909 and, later, in a separate folio.

8 x 11 inches. Price: $80.

MAGGIE WENT DOWNSTAIRS slowly. Will was sweeping up sawdust in Victorian House's kitchen. "You're back. Talk to Brian?" he asked.

"His story agrees with Annie's," said Maggie.

"Neither of them would have hurt Eric. They were close friends!"

"He says he left Hay and Jill and Eric on the town wharf. They'd all been drinking, and the three others were arguing. Sounds like he had the sense to leave and go home."

"Good," said Will. "I'd be surprised if he'd done anything else."

"Will, I hate when we argue," said Maggie. "It's been an awful day for everyone. Brian and Giles are finishing up. Why don't you take a break? Come upstairs, have a glass of wine with me, and relax. I have cheese and crackers. Or we could order a pizza." Maggie still regretted only having one hot dog for lunch.

Will leaned his broom against the wall and went over to Maggie and held her for a few minutes. "You're right. It's not only been an awful day, it's been an awful week. Seals killed, Brook running away, and now Eric dead." He looked at her. "Pizza sounds good, but I can't stay for dinner. I have to be home for Aunt Nettie. But I'd like that glass of wine."

"Good," Maggie said. "Give me a few minutes upstairs, and come on up after Giles and Brian have left."

"I will." He blew her a kiss as she headed for the staircase.

Upstairs, Maggie quickly changed out of the bathing suit she'd been wearing under her clothes since morning. Had she really thought she'd swim at a Maine beach in May? She put on clean slacks and a loose shirt and then made up a tray of cheeses and crackers, and added a bowl of the garlic-stuffed green olives she and Will both loved. Scrounging in her kitchen she also found half a can of cashews and some leftover Maine smoked salmon she'd treated herself to a few days before.

"A veritable feast," Will said as he walked in a few minutes later and spotted the food on the coffee table.

"Red or white wine?" Maggie asked. "I have both."

"I'm not surprised. I remember carrying those liquor cartons up three flights of stairs when you moved in," he pointed out.

"Just taking your suggestion that wine and liquor cost less in New Hampshire," said Maggie, "and stopping on my way up from New Jersey."

"Red, I think tonight," said Will.

"You open," she said, handing him the corkscrew and a bottle of merlot. "I'll have white, and there's already a bottle of that open in the refrigerator." Thinking of Eric, Maggie couldn't face sipping red wine. Tonight it looked too much like blood.

Settled cozily on the couch Will had found at an auction earlier that spring, Maggie raised her glass. "To us! And to friends and family. No matter what happens."

They clinked glasses.

"This is nice," said Will, popping an olive in his mouth and cutting a piece of cheese. "We should enjoy the peace and quiet while we can. When is Brook coming again?"

"If all works out, her next visit is scheduled for Sunday."

"'If all works out'?"

"Brook was angry about the seal being killed. She said she never wanted to come back to Waymouth."

"I didn't know that." Will reached over and touched her hand for a moment. Then he reached for the bowl of cashews. "She and Aunt Nettie seemed to get along. Until she ran off, anyway."

"Aunt Nettie reminded Brook of her grandmother. But when she left here she was sad and angry, and afraid. Seeing that dead seal reminded her of bad times in her life. I'm hoping she's old enough not to let one horrible incident influence her too much. She and I both have to agree to the adoption before it goes forward."

"She won't move in until almost July, right?"

"If it all works out, that's the plan." Maggie put some herbed goat cheese and lox on a cracker. "I hope those 'clam cops,' as Eric called them, will find whoever shot the seals soon. Preferably before Sunday, when Brook might visit here again."

"They're just seals, after all," said Will. "But now that Eric's been shot… I don't like coincidences when it comes to guns."

"Neither do I. I'm upset about Eric, and I'm concerned about Brook. Seals were important to her, because of her childhood."

"Like she felt comfortable with Aunt Nettie because of her grandmother."

"Exactly. She has a history."

"But once you adopt her, that history will be in the past. You can start from scratch," Will pointed out.

"Her history will always be her history," said Maggie. "She may understand it better as she gets older, but she was born into a violent home. I'm sure she loved her parents. Children do, no matter what happens. But horrible things happened in that home. I don't think she'll forget easily."

"But here she'll be safe."

"I hope so. But life happens. Look what happened to Eric."

Will shook his head. "I keep hoping Nick was wrong about his being shot. Let's hope he drowned. That his death was an accident. Horrible, but no one's fault."

Maggie doubted that. "I hope you're right. But I'm hearing practically everyone in town has a gun."

"True," said Will. "Guns are a part of Maine's culture."

"Do you have one?" Maggie'd never thought to ask.

"I had a rifle," Will said. "But I sold it before I left Buffalo. Didn't figure I'd be doing much hunting."

Maggie relaxed. She wouldn't have to worry about Brook finding a gun at Will's house.

"You told me Brook's father killed her mother."

"Yes. And she's had a couple of bad experiences with men in her foster homes. That's one reason the state thought a single woman would be a good placement for her. Let her trust one person at a time, and start with a woman." Maggie looked at Will. "But of course you'll be part of her life, too."

Will ate three olives in a row, and poured himself some more wine. "Maggie, you know this adoption's always been your dream, not mine."

"We talked about that the first time I came to Maine, in August, two years ago. You explained why you didn't want to be a father."

"I told you about my wife bleeding to death from an ectopic pregnancy."

"It must have been a nightmare." Maggie reached out to hold Will's hand, but he moved away.

"It was. I couldn't face going through the hopes and fears and possible disasters of anyone else I loved being pregnant."

"I never talked about getting pregnant. I wanted to adopt an older child."

"I know."

"Then…"

Will got up off the couch and walked to the window overlooking the river. "I should have told you this a long time ago. I know I haven't been as excited as you'd like about Brook, about her coming to live with you." He turned toward Maggie. "Part of it I'll admit is jealousy. I want to be with you. I want us to run Victorian House together, and drink wine like this together, and sleep together."

"But, Will—"

He put his hand up. "No. You need to hear this. Those reasons are selfish. And I've told myself they're why I haven't been as supportive of adoption as you would've liked. But there's another reason. A reason you don't know."

Maggie was silent as Will poured himself a third glass of wine.

"You know I taught woodworking at a high school in Buffalo before I met you."

"Of course. You've talked about how much you loved teaching. But you left teaching to try to make a living selling your antique brass and iron." Maggie focused on Will. "You never said, but I always thought it was because your wife had died. You didn't want to stay in your house in Buffalo alone, so you went on the road."

Will nodded. "That's partially true. I saw her in every room, and nights without her were so empty…plus, I'd been doing antiques shows in western New York for a while, and thought filling my RV with my inventory and going from show to show would keep me from thinking about the past. I'd thought about doing it for a while. But that wasn't why I left teaching."

"So, why?"

"Maggie, I want you to know I did nothing wrong. But one of my students, a sophomore, was going through a difficult time. Her parents were getting divorced. It was a nasty breakup. They each told Kate—that was her name, Kate—how awful the other one was. Kate was in the middle. She'd been in the college track, but she started failing her courses, so the guidance counselor suggested she take a lighter load at school. She transferred to one of my woodworking classes. And she started staying after school, hanging around my classroom. She confided in me. Told me how awful her life was. Told me she'd been thinking of killing herself."

"Oh, no!" said Maggie.

"Of course, I talked with her, and I told the guidance counselor, and she called Kate's parents and told them Kate needed to be in counseling. But they didn't see it. They said she was fine; she was just trying to get attention."

"She was, in a way," said Maggie quietly. "An awful way. So what happened?"

"She hanged herself in her closet one weekend."

"Oh, no! You must have been devastated."

"I was, of course. But that was only the beginning. Her mother found her diary, and Kate had been writing about…me. About 'our relationship.' She'd written that I was the only one she trusted, and about what I looked like and…Maggie, the way she wrote, it could have meant we were having an affair."

"No!"

"We weren't! I swear, Maggie, I never suspected she was having those thoughts. But her parents took the diary to the school board and said I had unduly influenced their daughter and that was why she'd killed herself."

"What happened?"

"I resigned. If I hadn't, her parents were going to sue, and I would never have been able to get another teaching job. Any hint of sexual…indiscretions…between a teacher and a student is a guarantee of unemployment. So I left on my own. The school worked something out with Kate's parents. It was all kept quiet, and I went on the road."

Maggie was silent. Then, "Why haven't you ever told me this?"

"Because I was embarrassed, and humiliated, and you wanted to be a mother. And if an agency ever investigated me the way they investigated you, then my history could keep you—or us—from adopting."

"Oh, Will."

"And before I finish, I have to admit I'm nervous about Brook. I didn't mean to give Kate any mistaken ideas about how I felt about her. But I don't know what I did wrong. I don't want to mess up any other girls."

"Will, I'm sure you won't."

"I wish I were that sure. You need to think about this, Maggie," Will said, putting his empty glass on the table. "I don't know if you can trust me. I don't know if I can trust me. I don't know what to do, or what not to do. And until I do, I don't want to get close to Brook."

Maggie stood up and went to him. "Will. I…"

He pushed her away. "No. I want you to take time to think about what I've said. It's important. Right now I have to get home to Aunt Nettie. Home to someone who needs me, and who won't misinterpret anything I do."

The door to her apartment slammed shut.

Will was gone.

37. Angora Cats

1867 hand-colored lithograph of three cats (black, white
and tiger) in an elegant Victorian boudoir from W.H.
Freeman and Company, 1880.

5.5 x 8 inches. Price: $70.

*M*AGGIE DIDN'T MOVE. She didn't go after Will.
She'd thought she'd known everything about him.
Everything important, anyway. She'd never dreamed
he had a secret like the nightmare he'd just told her.

She went over every word he'd said. He'd been accused of unduly
influencing, perhaps even seducing, a high school sophomore.

Maggie was a teacher. Will was right when he'd said an accusation like that would end his teaching career.

Was it true? Had he been sleeping with a high school student?

No. Definitely not. She couldn't believe that of Will.

But he'd been lonely after his wife's death. He'd tried to help a
young woman in distress. Had he paid more attention to her than
he should?

It would have been simple for him to do that, to try to help. And
teenagers' emotions are strong, whether they're real or fantasies.

Maggie knew she'd gotten more involved than she should have
in the lives and problems of her students a couple of times.

But she taught at a community college. Her students were
college-aged or older.

She'd never imagined she was crossing the professor/student
line with any of her students.

What had her students thought?

Will hadn't felt he'd done anything wrong. His student was going
through a hard time. He'd talked with the guidance counselor. The
guidance counselor had talked to Kate's parents.

Everything by the book.

But the incident had ended his career, and clearly still haunted him. Could change their future together.

Winslow Homer jumped onto Maggie's lap and reached for the plate of cheese. She gave him the last speck of lox, to his delight, and a small bite of cheese. Cheese wasn't supposed to be good for cats, but Winslow loved it and he'd never complained of stomach pains.

When he reached for more, though, she picked up the tray and took it back to the kitchen. Olives and cashews could stay on the table. Winslow wasn't interested in those. Still numb, she slipped the leftover cheeses into sandwich bags and put them back in the refrigerator. She'd accumulated enough small amounts of cheese to make macaroni and cheese soon. Kids liked mac-and-cheese, right? Maybe she'd make it for Brook Sunday. If Brook came Sunday.

She poured herself another glass of wine. Should she order pizza for herself? She'd been starving half an hour ago. Now she wasn't hungry.

She ate a stuffed olive and a few cashews.

She had raspberry truffle ice cream in the freezer. Grown-up ice cream she'd bought when she got the strawberry and vanilla for Brook. She'd thought she and Will could share it.

Would he come back? Was he, like Eric, breaking off their relationship?

She didn't know.

Tonight ice cream looked tempting.

Why hadn't Will told her about the incident in Buffalo before this? In the past he'd said she'd have to choose between adoption and him. Recently he'd been more understanding. At Christmas time he'd finally said he'd try to love her child.

She'd believed there was hope for their future, together.

Tonight he'd even admitted jealousy was part of why he hadn't wanted her to adopt. But why hadn't he explained what he was really scared about? Shouldn't people who loved each other share everything?

But, then, she'd never told Will about Joe.

Will knew she had a brother somewhere. She'd told him she didn't know where Joe was. That was the truth.

What she hadn't told him was that Joe was crazy. Sick. That she was twelve years younger than Joe because her parents hadn't planned to have another child. That Joe had taken her favorite doll, and drawn anatomical details on it and hidden it under her pillow, for her to find. That he'd walked around their house naked when her friends had come to play. That when her kitten had disappeared, she'd been told not to cry, and not to ask about it.

She'd told Will that Joe left home when she was six and he was eighteen. She hadn't told him Joe left to live in a psychiatric hospital, and then, when he'd been released, he'd taken off.

She hadn't mentioned that she hadn't looked for Joe because she was afraid of him. Or that one of the reasons she and Michael never had children was her fear of a baby being born with Joe's problems.

Joe was a secret of her childhood. Unless he showed up, which he hadn't done since her parents' funeral over ten years ago, Will didn't need to know about him. That's how she'd justified not mentioning him.

Will's secret, on the other hand, affected Maggie's life, and Brook's, right now.

Was the adoption going to work out?

Will had been right. The past week had been horrible. Dead seals. Brook running away.

Eric murdered.

And now learning Will had once been called a sexual predator. He hadn't used those words, but probably others had.

Maggie leaned back on the couch, trying to absorb what was happening.

Why had she felt safe because she was in love with Will?

Her own childhood hadn't been perfect, but she'd thought her experiences growing up would help her be a good mother. Help her understand a child who'd had rough early years. She was educated. She was sane. She could raise a healthy child. A child who wouldn't have to lock the door of her bedroom at night because she was afraid. And she could do those things without help.

Part of her had always hoped that after she adopted a child, Will would relax. He'd accept her child. She and Will would get married. Maybe they'd even adopt other children.

In her adoptive parent group in New Jersey she'd met fathers who were as committed to adoption as mothers.

Now that wouldn't happen. Not because of how she and Will felt about each other, but because of something he'd been accused of in the past.

She'd left her job and her home in New Jersey. She'd moved to Maine and invested her money and love in an unsolvable situation.

No wonder Will had never mentioned marriage. Love, yes. Commitment, yes. But never marriage.

He'd been protecting her. Or he'd been protecting himself.

She'd risked everything she'd worked for because she loved Will.

Could she continue, knowing as long as she wanted to be a parent their relationship couldn't go further?

On the other hand, could she give up her hope for a life with Brook?

Maggie's eyes welled up. Why shouldn't she cry?

She'd cry. And then she'd eat ice cream. Maybe the whole pint.

And maybe, somehow, a miracle would happen. Maybe it would all work out.

Or maybe it wouldn't.

38. Sea Stars, like Sky Stars, Vary in Size and Brilliancy...

Undersea scene of kelp, anemones, sea urchins, and several varieties of starfish. *National Geographic* lithograph, c. 1910.

6.5 x 8 inches. Price: $35.

*M*AGGIE DELAYED going downstairs in the morning. She wasn't ready to face Will.

She'd spent most of the night trying to figure out what she should do. What she would do. She'd told herself over and over that she had to be supportive of Will. She should thank him for being honest; for telling her what had happened. Assure him she still loved him, no matter what.

But could she do that? Her dreams felt like water balloons that had burst, spilling her future all over the rocky Maine coast.

When she finally did get up enough nerve to find him, Will was deep in conversation with the elevator construction crew. Giles and Brian hadn't shown up. Because of Eric? Or maybe today they were working for Johnny Brent. Not surprisingly, Annie didn't come to work either.

Maggie waved at Will, who nodded back. Immediately relieved that she hadn't had to talk with him, she headed for the sanctuary of her print room. All she had to do there was add the prints for children she'd thought of the day before. She arranged them on one corner of a table, near prints of dogs and other animals that also appealed to children.

Then she decided to go for a walk.

For at least a couple of hours, she needed to get out of Victorian House and everything it represented.

Eric's *Lucy II* was still docked at the wharf. Had anyone pulled his traps yesterday or today? She'd heard the fishing and lobstering community took care of their own. Maybe someone, even Abe, if he were sober enough, had done that.

Who would inherit the *Lucy II* and all Eric's gear? He and Annie hadn't been married, and she suspected someone as young as Eric hadn't drawn up a will. His parents? But Annie had said his father was gone and his mother drank.

Probably his mother would sell the whole rig. Another young lobsterman could use the *Lucy II* and her equipment.

Maggie watched from Water Street as several official-looking men with notebooks questioned owners of both commercial and recreational boats. The Marine Patrol, she suspected. Trying to find out who'd shot the seals.

While Nick Strait and Owen Trask were at the sheriff's office, talking to people about Eric Sirois.

Had the medical examiner's report come in? How was Annie coping today? Had the police questioned Brian yet?

Maggie said a silent prayer that whoever shot the seals would be identified and caught soon, and so would whoever'd killed Eric. Preferably before Sunday, when Brook was scheduled to visit Waymouth again. If she chose to.

Maggie walked slowly, every step an effort. The past month had been physically and emotionally exhausting, from packing up in New Jersey and moving to Maine, to setting up her apartment and Victorian House, to meeting Brook.

Not to mention the events of the past few days.

Until now, the excitement of her new life had kept her energy high. But now she was weary of violence. Weary of emotional complications. Weary of broken dreams.

She stood and watched a pair of goldfinches flitting back and forth to a bird feeder in someone's yard. Further down the street a cormorant was drying his wings on a rock near the shore while a Great Blue Heron, stepping carefully in shallow water, hunted small fish.

She'd only had a few pieces of cheese and a bowl of ice cream for dinner the night before, and suddenly she was ravenous.

The Great Blue opened at ten o'clock for late breakfast or early lunch. Food might help her bring the world back into focus.

Hay was behind the bar. She slipped onto a bar stool and watched him mix three Bloody Marys for a table of women wearing sparkly T-shirts. People from away were easy to pick out, Maggie thought, not for the first time. Of course, she was also from away. But at least she didn't dress as though she was.

But the Bloody Marys looked good. "A Bloody Mary," she told Hay. "And can I order food here at the bar?"

"No problem," he said, handing her a menu.

While he was mixing her drink she decided. "Eggs Benedict with crabmeat," she told him when he put her drink in front of her.

"Good choice. One of my favorites," he said approvingly.

She looked around. Only a half dozen tables were occupied. But it was early in the season, midmorning on a Friday in May. By July the room would be full.

Hay returned after putting her order in. "You heard about Eric."

"Something new?" For a moment Maggie hoped it was good news.

"Nick Strait called me in for questioning first thing this morning, before I went on duty. Seems the medical examiner has officially ruled Eric's death a homicide."

Maggie inhaled. She'd suspected as much. But that didn't make hearing it confirmed any easier. "Did he say what happened?"

Hay shook his head. "Nope. He wanted to know what Eric was doing the night before Abe and Annie found him."

"He was here, at the bar. Sitting right over there," Maggie pointed to a seat that was now empty.

"He was," agreed Hay. "He and Brian came in about six o'clock and stayed until closing."

"What happened then?" She'd heard Annie's and Brian's versions. Would Hay's be any different?

"Annie wanted to leave when her shift was over. She kept telling Eric it was time to go. He'd had too much to drink, he had to be up early in the morning, and he should walk her home and then get to bed." Hay grinned. "She wasn't in the best of moods."

"So did Eric go?"

"Finally. He was a little pissed, to tell the truth. But Jill got down from his lap and he followed Annie."

Had she missed something? "Jill was sitting on Eric's lap?"

"Yeah. She'd had a few in between customers, and she was being obnoxious." He flicked his towel along the counter. "A real pain, actually. And Eric was encouraging her."

"Jill's your girl, right?"

"So everyone says," said Hay. "But Jill's Jill."

"Eric and Jill had both been drinking."

"We all had. No secret about that. The boss lets the staff sip as long as it doesn't show. But Jill passed that border the other night."

Maggie remembered Jill bending over the table when she was serving. She'd been flirting with Will. Her T-shirt had revealed more than Annie's, for sure.

Of course, Jill had more…to show.

Maggie didn't remember Jill's seeming drunk. But she'd seen Jill early in the evening.

Hay went to draw a Pemaquid Ale for Abe Palmer, who was sitting by himself at the end of the bar. The space where Brian and Eric had been sitting two days before. Abe must not be planning to pull Eric's traps today.

What had Hay meant by "Jill's Jill"?

He didn't come back until he put Maggie's Eggs Benedict in front of her. "Enjoy," he said, smiling.

She did. The eggs and crabmeat disappeared more quickly than she'd anticipated. She started to put money on the bar and then decided to talk to Abe. He hadn't been with Eric that last night, but he'd been here at the bar for a while, and he worked with Eric. Maybe he had an idea about what had happened. And, of course, he and Annie had found Eric's body.

She slid off her bar stool and walked to where Abe was sitting, staring into his beer. "Hi, Abe! Maggie Summer. Mind if I join you?"

He looked at her. "Not if you buy me a drink."

Maggie sat down, signaled to Hay, and ordered a diet soda for herself and another ale for Abe. If she'd known how ripe he smelled, a mixture of stale sweat and lobster bait and beer, she would have left a seat between them.

"You're not drinking," he pointed out, draining his first glass and starting on the one Maggie had ordered for him.

"Had a Bloody Mary. It's still early."

"Never too early to drink," Abe declared seriously.

"I'm sorry about Eric. You worked with him."

"Worked with his granddad, and then with him. Spent a lot of years groundfishing, but lost my own boat, so been working the *Lucy II* for a while now."

"Groundfishing?" Maggie didn't recognize the term.

"Fishing for haddock, flounder, cod, halibut…fish folks want to eat."

"What will you do now?"

"Don't rightly know. Whoever ends up with *Lucy II* will need someone to stern for 'em. Hope so. It's one of the best boats in the harbor. Wood. Young folks nowadays look for fiberglass. Give me a solid wood boat any day. If God wanted us to have fiberglass boats he'd have made fiberglass trees."

She suspected he'd perfected that line a long time ago, but it was a good one. She couldn't help smiling. "So she's a good boat."

"Solid. The best." Abe managed to get a few words out between gulps. "Used to be, everyone had a wooden boat. Fishermen, lobstermen, even folks who'd have conniptions if a seagull shit on their mahogany steering wheel. Today, all that's changed."

"So life used to be better."

"Boats sure were. And parts of life, no doubt. Used to be a man could make a good living groundfishing. Today, not so much. Water's warmer, so aren't as many around. Plus, shrimp's disappearing. Fishermen and seals are competing for fewer fish." He took a drink. "Lobstering's doing okay, though."

Maggie'd sat down to find out about Eric, but seals had also been on her mind. "So in the old days seals weren't a problem?"

"Not so much. Beginning way back in 1888 Maine and Massachusetts had bounties on seals. They got to be a problem, people could get rid of 'em. No questions. Now everybody's talking about saving the cute little seals. Those clam cops are all over anyone who touches one." He took another deep swallow. "Talked to 'em this morning. Don't think they have a clue who killed those seals around here. Ask me, those seals know they're protected. Napping on a float! Taunting fishermen, that's what they're doing."

"Can't they identify the gun from the bullets?"

"You're from away, right?" He shook his head. "Maine don't register guns. You want one, you buy one. No records, no problems. Rifle shot those seals, I bet. Most folks in town have rifles." He leaned over toward her. "Not as many of us have handguns. But there's a fair number of those around."

"You have a handgun?"

"Did, anyway. Must've left it somewheres. Still got a couple of rifles under my bed, though."

Maggie went back to what he'd said earlier. "So there used to be a bounty on seals. When did that end?"

"Not long ago. I think about 1962."

Not long ago? Over fifty years ago.

"You were a boy then," Maggie guessed.

"Was," Abe agreed. "Just startin' out to make my living on the waters. Had my own skiff by the time I was eight. Dad was a fisherman. Never thought much about being anything else."

"Like Eric. He said he'd always wanted to be a lobsterman."

"Yup. His dad vamoosed, but he and Luther, his granddad, got along. When Luther retired to Florida he gave the *Lucy II* to Eric. Good boat. It'll keep going for years more, if someone keeps it up."

"What do you think'll happen to it?"

"That mother of Eric's will sell it. Or call Luther in Florida and tell him to come get it. Wish I had the money to buy it."

"You and Eric got along."

"Had disagreements. Men do. But on the water, we worked well together. Eric was smart. Smart about almost everything. And he knew the waters."

"Almost everything? What wasn't he smart about?"

"Same thing most young men are foolish about. Women."

"Annie was his girl, right?"

"You'd have to ask her. I'm no gossip." Abe leaned closer. His breath was putrid. "Young fellows should sow a few wild oats before they settle down. Girls, they ain't like that. Just want that white dress and a crib or two." Abe leaned back again. "That's all I'm sayin'. Want to buy me another ale?"

Maggie was about to say "no," when Will walked in with Nick. They didn't look at the bar. The hostess on duty, not Jill, showed them to a table in the far corner of the room. Nick sat as usual, with his back to the wall. He'd be the one to notice Maggie if either of them did.

Will didn't usually go out for lunch on a working day. And in the past months almost every day had been a working day.

Why was he making an exception now?

"You buyin' another, or is it up to me?" Abe asked again. "You want to go talk to your guy, there?"

"One more," Maggie agreed. She signaled to Hay. "Another ale for Abe, and an Indian pudding for me. Dessert sounds good."

"Coming up," replied Hay.

Abe looked hard at Maggie. "Heard you were thinkin' of taking in a tough kid."

"I've applied to adopt a little girl," said Maggie. "Yes."

Abe leaned closer to her. She had all she could do not to lean back to stay away from the fumes on his breath. "You and Will Brewer have a good thing going. Why mess it up?" Abe shook his head. "That's all I have to say on the matter. Life's hard enough without taking on others' troubles."

Maggie didn't answer.

The lunch crowd was filling up tables. The Marine Patrol guys she'd seen at the town wharf earlier were sitting at a table near a window. Most of the people she didn't know. She was a newcomer, from away. Nick probably knew everyone in the room; Will knew most of them.

Growing up in a town and continuing to live there as an adult was an experience Maggie couldn't imagine. Where she'd grown up in New Jersey people came and went, as corporations transferred families from place to place. Only about half of the students in her high school class had been together since seventh grade. Fewer had known each other before that. And after graduation they'd scattered to different colleges or the military. She wasn't in touch with anyone from her high school, and only a few friends from college.

In Waymouth, at least traditionally, people stayed. Aunt Nettie had lived here all her life. So had Nick. Sounded as though Abe had, too. One older woman she'd met on a previous visit had said she had seven brothers and sisters. Six of them married people from Waymouth, and still lived here. "What happened to the seventh?" Maggie'd asked. "Oh, he married a girl from down Boothbay way," was the answer. "Moved down there. Don't see him much." Boothbay was about twenty-five miles away.

Maine was a different world. People now used cell phones and had computers and watched cable TV, just as they did in other places. And some young people left Maine for college or jobs or the military. But a lot of them never left, or ended up back in town as soon as they could manage it.

Community ties here were strong.

"So, are you gonna eat that pudding you ordered, or shall I do it for you?"

Maggie looked down. Her Indian pudding had been delivered, and she'd been so involved with her own thoughts she hadn't even noticed. "I'm going to eat it, Abe," she answered, digging her spoon in.

Why were Will and Nick having lunch together? Will should be supervising the elevator guys, and Nick had a death to investigate.

On the other hand, she was eating Indian pudding next to Abe Palmer.

On a day like this, anything could happen.

39. Untitled

Black-and-white wood engraving of small sailboat in
the midst of a thunder-and-lightning storm. Seas are
rough; the boat is about to be capsized. From Lynd
Ward's *Gods' Man: A Novel in Woodcuts.* 1929.

4.5 x 6.5 inches. Price: $40.

*M*AGGIE PAID FOR her lunch plus Abe's drinks and
left Hay a decent tip. After all, he was working the
day after one of his best friends had been murdered.

She should call Annie, see how she was doing.

Her mind on Annie, Maggie walked out of The Great Blue and
right into Deputy Owen Trask.

"Whoa, lady!" Owen grinned down at her. She hadn't remembered he was that tall. "How're you doing? Thank you for watching
out for Annie Bryant yesterday. If anyone needed a friend, it was
Annie."

"Hay Johnson told me Eric's death was a homicide."

"No secrets in this town, are there," Owen replied calmly. "Yup.
Nick got the medical examiner's report late last night. We suspected
Eric hadn't drowned on his own. ME confirmed it."

"How did it happen?"

Owen glanced around. "You know I'm not supposed to tell
anyone details connected to an investigation, Maggie."

"No details, then. In general. Was he drugged? Shot? Hit over
the head?"

Owen shook his head. "You were a big help in that nasty case
last Christmas, Maggie, so I'll tell you. Eric was shot."

"In the head?" Maggie kept thinking of the seals Eric had loved.

Owen hesitated, and then nodded. "And then either left so the
tide would pick him up, or dumped in the river."

"What kind of a gun?"

"Can't tell you that."

"Come on, Owen. You know you can trust me."

"It's not that, Maggie. We don't know exactly yet. The ME and the crime lab are conferring."

"And is Annie still a suspect?"

He hesitated. "She is. But she's not alone. Eric was with that gang of his—Brian Leary, Hay Johnson, and Jill Pendleton—that night. We're questioning all of them. Their stories don't all jibe. Although they all agree they drank a little, and then everyone headed, safe and sound and alive, to their own beds for the night."

"Witnesses?"

"Not many people wander down near the Madoc River in the middle of the night. In April, after the prom, there're always a few kids down there watching the submarine races. In July, to see fireworks. Or in August, for the meteor showers. But Wednesday night was chilly. So far we haven't found anyone who admits to seeing anything. The clam cops have kept their eyes and ears open for something not quite right, too. But, so far, nothing."

"Do they know who shot the seals?"

"If they do, they're keeping it to themselves. No witnesses, no suspects."

Maggie sighed. "What a mess. I think I'll stop in to see Annie. See how she's coping."

"Good idea. We haven't called her today, and won't contact her again unless more questions come up."

Maggie turned to go, and then retraced her steps. "What about their families? Except for Jill, none of the young people you mentioned live alone. Wouldn't their families know when they came in that night, and whether they went out again?"

"They're all pretty independent. Eric's mom didn't know he was missing until Nick and I went to tell her what had happened. She said he didn't always come home at night. The others? Either their families are covering for them, or were asleep by the time their kids got home. Waymouth folks aren't night hawks, for the most part."

Owen started to open the door of The Great Blue.

"Nick and Will are in there. Will isn't a suspect, is he?" asked Maggie.

"If he is, I haven't heard it," said Owen. "Don't you worry. Your man's in the clear. No motive, and he was probably home taking Aunt Nettie to the bathroom when Eric was killed."

"Then why…"

"He called Nick this morning. Said he needed to talk to him." Owen shrugged. "That's all I know. They've been friends for years. I didn't question why Nick left to meet him. But we're interviewing Brian and Giles Leary early this afternoon. I came down to get a bite to eat and make sure Nick makes it back to the office by one o'clock." Owen glanced at his watch. "Which means I've got to eat fast. Good seeing you, Maggie. And thanks for being a friend to Annie. She needs one."

Maggie stood for a moment, thinking through everything he'd said.

Eric had been shot.

From what she'd been told, practically anyone in town could have done that. Guns weren't a rarity in Waymouth. But who *would* have done it? Who had a motive?

Had he fought with anyone? He'd argued with Annie. Exactly when he'd left the restaurant and whether he'd been with Annie or he'd followed her didn't seem important.

What was important was who'd killed him. He'd been with Brian and Hay and Jill. He'd just left Annie. Would any of them have had guns with them that night? It seemed unlikely.

Maybe Eric's death had been a totally random killing. But that seemed even less likely.

Eric was probably shot by someone he'd grown up with. By one of his closest friends.

Nick would figure it out, Maggie thought. Of course he would. It was his job.

But why had Will needed to see Nick today?

That was another mystery she'd like to know the answer to.

40. American Elm

An elm tree with wide spreading branches, dark green leaves, and an iron bench beneath it. Caption: "American Elm. Well-known as our native forest tree. Adapted to planting on lawns and streets where there is room for it to unfold its graceful, spreading and drooping branches." From a garden catalog, 1881. Dutch Elm disease killed over seventy-five percent of American Elms in North America between 1927 and 1989. Today disease-resistant elms have been developed.

5.5 x 8.5 inches. Price: $40.

*M*AGGIE WALKED up Main Street toward the side street where Annie lived.

The street was busy; cars and trucks passed by, shop doors stood open, and new spring leaves covered the young trees Waymouth had planted to replace the American Elms Maggie'd only seen in early-twentieth-century postcards of Waymouth. Once they'd lined Main Street, their branches arching over the town as if to protect it. Dutch Elm disease had taken them down, and their replacements couldn't replicate their majesty.

A gray squirrel ran down the sidewalk ahead of Maggie, stopped to pick up a crust of bread someone had dropped outside the sandwich shop, and scurried away. The eighteenth-century church where Brook had hidden stood on the hill above the little town, reminding its residents of how important religion had been to the earliest residents of Waymouth.

People had been born here, lived full lives, and died, but the town still looked much as it had in the early twentieth century. Or earlier. As in many Maine towns visitors called "quaint," some Waymouth homes had been built in the late eighteenth century, and many in the nineteenth century.

Looking at them now, centrally heated and equipped with

bathrooms instead of privies, she wondered whether the new homes being built in New Jersey now would be as serviceable in two hundred years. Or would they be deemed disposable, like last year's electronics, and torn down to make way for still newer ones?

A sad commentary on today's culture.

She turned at the corner where the Waymouth Post Office had always stood, and walked the few blocks past houses and galleries to the house where she'd dropped Annie on Wednesday afternoon.

Annie, like her friends, lived with her family. Their home was a small colonial, with two or three bedrooms on the second floor, above a kitchen, living room, and dining room. A swing set was in the side yard, and Annie's car was in the driveway. She was home.

At first no one answered Maggie's knock. Maybe she should have called first.

Then the door opened just wide enough for a little girl, about six years old, to see out. "Who are you?" said the child. Her blond hair was thin, she had enormous blue eyes, and she was wearing a princess dress and tiara.

"I'm Maggie, your majesty. I came to see Annie."

The little girl giggled. "I'm not your majesty. I'm Jenny."

"Is Annie at home?"

Jenny nodded, but didn't move.

"Would you tell Annie she has company?"

"She already has company." Jenny closed the door, and disappeared. A few minutes later Annie, hair disheveled and wearing a long T-shirt over black yoga pants, came to the door. "Maggie!" She opened the door. "Jenny said there was a funny lady at the door. I didn't think it would be you!"

What funny lady had she thought would be there?

"Is the little princess your sister?" Maggie asked.

"She is. The youngest of the Bryant girls," said Annie, gesturing that Maggie should go into the living room.

"How many are there?" Maggie asked. "Bryant girls, I mean."

"Five. I'm the oldest. Charity and Hope are the twins, and then Michelle, and then Jenny." She reached down to adjust Jenny's tiara covered with glitter. "Mom calls Jenny the 'much-loved afterthought.' She's fifteen years younger than Michelle."

"You have a full house."

"Not now. Charity and Hope are working in Boston this summer, near where they go to school. And Michelle lives in Portland. It's just Jenny and I and Mom and Dad right now. Jenny goes to school during the day, but I told her she could stay home today, to keep me company."

Annie followed Maggie into the living room.

Jill Pendleton was already sitting on the couch, a glass of wine in her hand. "Hi, Maggie."

"Jill!" Maggie turned to Annie. "I should have called. You already have company."

"Not a problem. Jill's more family than company. She and I've been friends for years. She took the day off to be with me." Annie smiled at Jill and then turned back to Maggie. "Can I get you something to drink? Jill's drinking wine; I'm having iced tea."

"Iced tea would be fine," said Maggie.

Annie headed toward what Maggie assumed was the kitchen. Jenny sat on the floor, spreading her wide pink ruffled skirt around her, like petals on a flower.

"I had lunch down at The Great Blue, Jill. I wondered where you were."

"Hay's working today. But I couldn't, knowing what Annie was going through. Maybe what happened to Eric doesn't mean as much to a guy. But he was close to all of us. I can't imagine the rest of my life without him."

Annie had said almost those identical words the day before.

"Here's your iced tea," said Annie, coming back in. "I put a little sweetener in it. Hope that's okay."

"Perfect," said Maggie. "How are you doing, Annie? I've been worried about you."

"What is that thing doctors always say? 'As well as can be expected,'" said Annie. "The good news is, I've stopped crying all the time." As she said the words, tears started up again. "Hay called. He talked to the detectives this morning. Now they're saying Eric was murdered." Annie looked over at Jill. "Who would have hurt him? Eric was everyone's friend. He drank a little too much, sometimes." She glanced again at Jill, who put her glass down. "But a lot of people do. Eric worked hard. Harder than any of the rest of us. He always has, ever since he was a kid. And he wasn't mean to anyone."

"He didn't have any enemies?"

"Enemies? Maggie, this isn't New York or New Jersey. No one has enemies in Maine."

Maggie tried not to smile. Annie was still young. "Anyone he'd argued with recently?"

"Me!" said Annie. "That's why the detective talked to me first yesterday. Everyone in the world seems to know Eric and I were fighting. But I wouldn't kill him! I loved him. And, even though we argued about the future, he loved me. I was wrong. I put pressure on him. I shouldn't have. That's what I was going to tell him when I went down to the wharf yesterday morning." Annie's voice faded. "What I never got to tell him."

Jenny got up from the floor where she'd been following the conversation. She climbed up on Annie's lap and hugged her. "Don't be sad, Annie. I love you."

"I know you do, honey." Annie sniffed.

"Have you talked to the police yet?" Maggie asked Jill.

"Nope. I'll probably get a call later today. They're talking to Brian," she glanced at the phone on the table next to her, "right now. He texted us that they'd called him in." She wrinkled her nose. "His dad's going with him."

"They won't let his dad stay with him," said Annie, holding Jenny on her lap. "They wouldn't let Maggie stay with me yesterday."

"When they call me I won't need anyone with me," Jill said. "There's nothing I have to say that all you guys haven't already told the cops. If they're looking for someone who was drunk, they can have Brian. He was soused Wednesday night."

"So was Eric," Annie said. "That's one reason we argued. I told him drinking so much wasn't good for him, and wasted money he should be saving for our future. And he should be getting more sleep since he had to go out early in the morning."

"You weren't his mother," Jill said. "He was old enough to know what to do. Just because you don't drink doesn't mean he couldn't."

"He shouldn't have been drinking so much," said Annie, her voice growing stronger. "Almost everyone around here drinks. But I don't have to like it."

Jill sighed. "It's life, Annie. And Hay and I didn't have that much to drink Wednesday night. We were working."

"Working between drinks," said Annie. "You called me in to help out because Suzy was sick, and I ended up with most of the tables. You were too busy flirting and chugging beer."

"You must have had a good night. You got all the best tips," said Jill. "You're always saving up for living room furniture or something. I figured I'd help you earn a few extra dollars. Next time Suzy's sick I'll call someone else."

"You do that."

Jill got up. "I'm going home to freshen my makeup in case the detectives want to talk to me. That Owen Trask is pretty cute. And I heard he and his wife were splitting up."

Annie put Jenny down and stood up. "I know you're kidding, but don't let Hay hear you talking like that, Jill. He doesn't like seeing you cozying up to all the Great Blue customers."

Jill shrugged. "Hay'll have to cope. He doesn't own me. Flirting gets me bigger tips. I can say anything I want. You or Hay or anyone else can't stop me." Jill flounced toward the door. "Don't bother seeing me to the door I've used hundreds of times. Go upstairs and cry about your Eric. I'm going to focus on people who are still alive."

"Wow," said Maggie after Jill had slammed the door. "Does she always talk like that?"

"Not always. She's upset about Eric, but no one's paying attention to her. Jill likes to be the center of attention." Annie shrugged. "We've been best friends forever. In high school we pooled our clothes money and shared outfits. I'm used to the way she is. She'll forget what she said and call later to tell me how her interview with the cops was, and ask how I am. That's just Jill."

Maggie shook her head. "She doesn't seem like an easy friend."

"When you live in a small town there aren't many people your age around. Jill and I went to kindergarten together."

Maggie thought of Aunt Nettie's friends, who were still close after knowing each other since elementary school. And Aunt Nettie was ninety-one.

In Waymouth, "best friends forever" seemed to be the norm.

Would Brook have friends like Jill? She hoped not. Forever was fine, if it was a caring forever. Forever abusive was something else.

"Is there anything I can do to help?" Maggie asked.

Annie shook her head. "I'll be okay. I will. I'm tougher than I look." She smiled feebly. "Sometimes tougher than I feel. I'll be fine as soon as they figure out who killed Eric. Jill makes fun of me, but Eric *was* the love of my life." She looked down at Jenny, who'd resumed her position on the floor. "My life won't be the same without him. I hope they find the person who killed him. And take my name off their list of suspects."

"I'm glad you and Jenny have each other." Maggie looked down at the little princess. Brook had watched her father kill her mother when she was Jenny's age. She'd probably never had a sparkling tiara.

"Jenny and I are good friends, aren't we, Jenny?"

"Best friends," Jenny declared, climbing back into her sister's lap.

"I have a room of my own, since I'm the oldest," said Annie. "Jenny shares with Michelle. But if she has any nightmares, or there's a thunderstorm, Jenny climbs into my bed to sleep with me."

"I snuggle," Jenny said seriously. "I'm brave most times. But I like company in the dark."

She wasn't the only one who felt that way.

"I understand," said Maggie. "You're lucky to have a sister like Annie."

Jenny nodded. "She's lucky to have me, too."

They were both right.

41. Building the House for Maimie

Dozens of elves and strange little people constructing a small house in the woods. Arthur Rackham illustration for *Peter Pan in Kensington Gardens*, by J.M. Barrie. Published by Charles Scribner's Sons in 1940.

5.5 x 8 inches. Price: $70.

MAGGIE KEPT THINKING of Annie and Jenny as she walked back to Victorian House. They were close friends as well as sisters, despite the difference in their ages. She'd never had a sister. One reason she'd always thought of adopting more than one child was because so many people she knew were close to their brothers or sisters.

She hadn't had that experience. She'd hoped her children would.

But brothers and sisters weren't always close. What could parents do to ensure that?

She didn't know. Jenny seemed closer to Annie than to her sisters closer to her in age. Annie was the one she went to for comfort. And on a day when Annie was dealing with a horrible situation, she'd chosen to keep Jenny with her.

Maggie envied their relationship.

Whatever Will and Nick had been talking about during their lunch together, it hadn't taken long. Will was back at Victorian House working with the supervisor of the elevator crew.

Maggie peeked into the kitchen. The electrical work looked complete, and the actual elevator itself was (in several pieces) inside the room. Would it be installed by Sunday?

Brook could walk up three flights with her crutch, but an elevator would make her ascent a lot easier.

As soon as the elevator was working, Maggie planned to do a big grocery shopping. She wanted to have a full supply of staples—baking supplies, herbs, cereals, potatoes, canned goods—in her kitchen before Brook moved in, but she didn't want to have to carry all those grocery bags up three flights of stairs. Walk-up apartments were common in cities, but she was a suburban Jersey girl at heart. She'd rather use an elevator.

Will didn't notice her glancing into the kitchen.

Just as well, Maggie thought. She hadn't decided what she should say after their conversation the night before.

Annie was convinced her life ended with Eric's death. Maggie didn't feel that dramatic. But she was honest with herself. She was forty. If Will wasn't the man for her, it wouldn't be easy to find someone else.

Not that she couldn't live without a man, she assured herself as she headed upstairs.

But she didn't want to.

Someone was working in the second floor room. She detoured to see what was happening.

Brian was there, alone, filling in the sections of wall where taking off the old wallpaper had also taken off the plaster.

"You're back!"

Brian turned. "Yup. Dad and I went to talk to that homicide detective. Then he went back to work with Brent Construction. He told me to take the day off. But sitting at home and thinking about Eric was driving me crazy. So I came here." He finishing smoothing the patch he'd been filling in. "I thought working would keep me from thinking. But it hasn't."

"How'd it go at the police station?"

He shrugged. "I'm pretty sure they think one of us killed Eric. That complicates everything."

"Why?" asked Maggie. "All you have to do is tell them the truth." She paused. "You didn't kill Eric."

"No! I'm sure I didn't kill him." Brian looked at Maggie as though she was crazy. "I didn't lie to anyone about what happened Wednesday night. Trouble is, I don't remember much after we left The Great Blue. I sure don't remember anyone killing Eric. I don't even remember Annie and Eric arguing, which everyone seems to be talking about."

"So what was complicated?"

"Hay and Jill and Annie are my best friends. Eric, too. I can't imagine any of us killing someone, much less one of our friends. But that detective—Nick Strait—he asked a lot of hard questions."

"Like?"

Brian hesitated. "He wanted to know about the relationship between Eric and Annie."

"Was that a problem?"

"Not a problem exactly. But…Annie was in love with Eric. She always has been, since back in middle school. But Eric wasn't ready to tie himself down."

"That didn't mean Annie would kill him! Did he tell you he wasn't ready for marriage?"

Brian focused for a long minute on stirring the heavy plastic bucket filled with plaster. Then he looked up. "He never said much. I just figured he wasn't ready because of what I saw."

"You saw?"

"Eric and Jill were awfully cozy. I mean, I saw them together on her breaks, a few times, out in back of The Great Blue. They said they were going out for cigarettes. But once Hay asked me to go remind Jill her break was over, and another time I went to find her to tell her one of her girlfriends was asking for her." Brian looked embarrassed. "She and Eric weren't smoking. They weren't even talking, either time. They were…entangled."

"Had that been going on for a while?"

"I asked Eric, after I saw them the second time. He said not to tell anyone, especially Annie. He said they'd been hooking up for months, but he hadn't gotten up the nerve to tell her."

"What about Hay? I thought Jill was supposed to be his girl?"

"You mean, did he know Eric and Jill had…been together? I don't know. But for sure he knew Jill flirted with every guy who came into the restaurant. He saw that every night, and he didn't like it. I heard 'em arguing more than a few times." Brian's eyes pleaded for understanding. "What they were doing didn't have anything to do with me. And they were my friends. I didn't want anything to change."

"Did you tell Nick Strait what you just told me?"

Brian nodded. "Then he asked whether Annie had a temper; whether she was possessive. He wanted to know whether I thought she'd kill Eric if she found out he was cheating on her. I told him Annie could never hurt Eric. But, yes. She did get angry sometimes. She yelled a lot, and cried. But it never came to anything! She'd never hurt anyone. Especially not Eric."

"What about Hay? If Jill was cheating, I'd think he'd be angry."

"Sure. He would. But I don't know for sure whether Annie or Hay knew what was happening. Maybe I was the only one who knew."

"Maybe," said Maggie. She doubted it, though. Jill wasn't the subtle type. She might even have told Annie or Hay herself if she was in the right—or wrong—mood.

"And you told Nick all that."

"I didn't want to. They'll never speak to me again if they find out I told. But I couldn't lie to the police, could I? I kept thinking about when Crystal was killed. You figured out who'd killed her, even though it was one of your friends."

"It wasn't easy," Maggie said, remembering.

"But you did the right thing. The right thing for Crystal. I had to tell what I'd seen. For Eric." Brian's eyes filled. "I just hope *I* did the right thing. I hope Annie and Hay and Jill weren't involved. It's horrible enough to lose Eric. I don't want to lose any more friends."

He turned toward the wall, ostensibly to put on more plaster. But his shaking shoulders said he was crying.

Maggie started to go to him, and then stopped.

Brian wasn't a little boy. He'd made a major decision. No matter what happened, now he'd have to live with the consequences.

"You did the right thing, Brian. You did," she said, and then she left the room.

He needed time alone.

42. Heaven

Tipped-in 1906 lithograph by Arthur Rackham (1867–1939). Small naked baby is being pulled upwards into the clouds by the strings on a kite. A murder of crows flies beneath the infant.

6 x 5 inches. $75.

*B*ACK IN HER APARTMENT, Maggie couldn't decide what to do next. She didn't want to start on a new Victorian House room. She and Will were on uncomfortable terms. For now, she wanted to keep some distance from him. Besides, he was downstairs with the elevator installation crew.

Brook might visit in two days, but it was too soon to cook anything for Sunday, especially since Brook could change her mind and not come.

Maggie wandered into her study and wrote an e-mail to her best friend, Gussie, down on Cape Cod. Most days they exchanged e-mail notes, but since Eric's body had been found she hadn't even checked for new messages.

Gussie sounded fine. She loved being married, loved her new house, and her earlier health problems seemed to have stabilized. Maggie didn't want to sound depressing, but her own life didn't look rosy right now. She turned off her computer. She'd write to Gussie again after Brook visited. *If* Brook visited. By then her world might seem brighter.

She walked into her kitchen. She'd hardly turned on her new stove. Maybe she'd make cookies filled with raspberry jam to share with Aunt Nettie. She loved cookies, and used to bake almost every day. Now she couldn't do it without a lot of help, and although Will could cook, his baking skills were minimal.

He liked Maggie's cookies, too. Was she ready to pretend nothing had happened? That he hadn't told her anything?

She pulled out the small supplies of sugar and flour and baking powder she'd bought, and checked to see that she had enough butter.

Her supply of butter was fine. But she hadn't remembered to buy vanilla.

She couldn't make cookies.

Part of her felt sorry. Another part was relieved.

She put the ingredients away.

Maybe she'd make the macaroni and cheese she'd thought of the night before. She had macaroni, and enough cheese and milk for her own dinner. Comfort food sounded good right now.

She was taking cheese out of her refrigerator when her cell rang.

"Maggie, sorry to bother you so soon. But that detective I talked to yesterday just came to my house." Annie's voice got lower. Maggie could hardly hear her. "He says I have to go back to the sheriff's department to answer more questions. My parents won't be home for a couple of hours. I'm sorry to bother you, but could you come over and watch Jenny? I don't want to take her with me."

Maggie was already putting the cheeses away. "I'll be right there. Let me talk to the detective."

She recognized the next voice she heard.

"Nick! This is Maggie. Can you wait to take Annie in until I get there? She can't leave her sister alone."

"How fast can you be here?"

"I'll drive. Five minutes?"

"We'll wait."

Maggie grabbed her pocketbook and keys and headed out. Hay and Brian had talked to Nick earlier. Probably Owen and Nick had already talked with Jill. What had she said? Had she verified what Brian had confided this afternoon?

If so, then no wonder Nick had more questions for Annie.

It took longer to maneuver her van out of the driveway filled with construction trucks than it did to drive the few streets to the Bryants' house. Nick's car was parked in front.

When Maggie opened the door he and Annie were sitting opposite each other in large chairs in the living room.

"Thanks, Maggie," said Annie, getting up. "I hope I won't be long." She glanced at Nick, but Nick was silent. "If Jenny gets hungry, there's some microwave popcorn in the kitchen. She can show you. Mom and Dad work in Portland. They'll be home by six-thirty and get supper then. But I hope I'll be back before that."

Nick didn't volunteer any estimates on the time he'd need with Annie.

"Don't worry about Jenny and me," said Maggie. "You do what you have to do." She looked at Nick. "I'm sure Detective Strait won't keep you any longer than necessary."

Nick didn't answer her unspoken question. "Thanks for getting here so fast," he said. "Annie, come on. We need to go now."

Annie reached down to where Jenny was sitting on the floor, listening to what was happening. "You be good, now. Maggie will be here. I'll be back soon."

Jenny nodded, as Annie and Nick left.

As soon as they'd left the house Jenny jumped up. "Annie said we could make popcorn."

"She did," Maggie agreed. "Could you show me where it is?"

"Come on," Jenny said, and Maggie followed her to the kitchen. A few minutes later Jenny and Maggie were sitting at the Bryants' round pine kitchen table, sharing a large bowl of popcorn.

"Why did the policeman have to talk to Annie again?" asked Jenny.

"He must have had more questions," said Maggie. She wasn't sure how much Jenny knew about what was happening.

"Annie's sad now," said Jenny. "Eric's dead."

"Yes," said Maggie.

"He died Wednesday night," said Jenny. "I know. I had bad dreams. I went to find Annie. She wasn't in her room."

Maggie listened. "Annie was working Wednesday night at The Great Blue. Maybe she wasn't home yet," she said. Had the little girl gotten days mixed up?

"But all the lights were out," said Jenny.

"Maybe she wasn't home from work yet," said Maggie.

"I can tell time. I woke up at three forty-seven. The restaurant isn't open then."

"No," said Maggie. Annie had said she'd gone home after The Great Blue closed. Yes, she'd argued with Eric then, but she'd gone home. She'd cried; she hadn't been able to sleep. Then she'd gotten up early and gone to find Eric. Had she left that early?

Why hadn't she been home at 3:47?

"Maybe Annie was in the living room, or the kitchen." She'd said she'd made coffee for Eric.

Jenny shook her head. "She wasn't home. Annie gave me a little flashlight to use if I get scared at night. I looked for her everywhere. But then I went back to bed." Jenny took some more popcorn. "She was still gone when I woke up in the morning."

"When do you leave for school in the morning?"

"Mom takes me. We have to leave by seven-thirty."

Annie had definitely been down at the wharf then. Maggie tried to remember when she'd heard the sirens and gone down to the harbor. Sometime between five-thirty and six, she thought. And Annie was talking with Nick when she left. She wasn't surprised Jenny hadn't seen Annie that morning. But how early had Annie left the house?

Maggie looked at the little girl happily filling her cheeks with popcorn. Jenny might not have read the clock correctly. After all, she was only six.

"Look at me," Jenny mumbled happily. "I'm a chipmunk!"

"So you are," said Maggie, nibbling a little more popcorn. "A very cute chipmunk."

Could Annie have lied about what she'd done that night?

Did she know more about Eric's death than she'd said?

According to Brian, Eric hadn't been faithful. If Annie'd known that, she would have had a motive to kill him.

"I think we've had enough popcorn, chipmunk," she said, getting up and taking the unfinished bowl of popcorn with her. "You'll spoil your dinner. Do you have any games we could play?"

"Lots," said Jenny, taking Maggie's hand and leading her to the toy box in the corner of the living room. "I have lots of games!"

Too many people in Waymouth seemed to have lots of games.

43. The Playmates

Wood engraving by Winslow Homer. Illustration for
John Greenleaf Whittier's *Ballads of New England*,
excerpted in *Our Young Folks* magazine, 1869. Boy and
girl, each about twelve years old, standing in a meadow.
The boy is handing a single flower to the girl.

4 x 4 inches. Price: $125.

*A*FTER SEVERAL ROUSING GAMES of Candy-
land, Maggie was relieved when Jenny's mom and dad
arrived home.

She explained who she was, and why she, and not Annie, was
with Jenny.

"Thank you for helping out," said Mrs. Bryant. "We came home
earlier than usual because we were worried about Annie. Such awful
news about Eric. He and Annie have been dating so long it's as
though our own son died." Her eyes filled with tears.

"Why do you think the police needed to talk with Annie again?"
asked her father. "She was at the station yesterday afternoon."

Maggie didn't volunteer any thoughts. The Bryants probably didn't know Eric's death had been ruled a homicide, and she
shouldn't be the one to tell them.

"Nick Strait's a friend," she told them. "I'm sure he'll send her
home as soon as he can."

Which could be any time today or even tomorrow, Maggie
thought. Annie could be his prime suspect.

"I'm glad to have had a chance to get to know another of your
daughters," said Maggie. "I live down at Victorian House, not far
away. If I can help in any way in the future, do let me know." She left
her telephone number, and headed home.

Will was standing on the porch, waiting for her. "Where have you been?" he asked, as she got out of her van. "You've been gone all day. I was worried!"

"I haven't been gone all day," said Maggie. "Everything here was quiet, and I needed a little time for myself. I went out for lunch and then stopped to see Annie. I was home after that, but you were involved with the elevator guys, and then Annie called to ask me to watch her little sister."

"I was worried. After last night..."

"Why don't we go inside," said Maggie.

"I can't talk long. Aunt Nettie called; she's hungry. Said I didn't leave her enough for lunch." He shook his head. "She may just be bored. But I promised to get home right away. I assume you heard what the medical examiner said about Eric."

"Yes. Horrible situation."

"It is. I was at The Great Blue for lunch," Will continued.

Then he hadn't seen her there. If he had, he would have said so.

"I talked with Hay Johnson before I left. He said people in town think Annie killed Eric. They had a fight that night."

"But I thought she went home."

"Maybe she did. But Hay told me the rest of their crew was down at the wharf drinking, and she joined them an hour or so later, and started arguing with Eric again. He said he and Brian and Jill left them there; they didn't want to get involved."

That wasn't what Annie had said.

But that might explain why Jenny said Annie wasn't home early that morning.

Maggie grimaced. "The whole situation is awful. I can't believe Annie killed Eric, but her name keeps coming up. Brian told me Eric and Jill had something going. I don't know how involved they were, but what if Annie found out about it?"

"She'd have a motive."

"She's being questioned again at the station right now."

"I hope it wasn't her, Maggie. She seems like a good kid. Plus, Brian's upset enough about losing Eric. For him to lose two of his friends would be rough. Not to mention, we'd need to find someone else to finish our website, pronto."

The website had not been on the top of Maggie's mind. But Will was right.

"Anyway, I need to get home to Aunt Nettie. Are you all right? After last night, I mean," Will asked.

"I'm sorry you didn't trust me enough to tell me earlier," said Maggie. "But I'm okay. Although we may need to talk about it again if it affects my adopting Brook. I'm hoping there aren't any records of what you were accused of that an adoption agency could find."

"I know." Will reached his arms out and Maggie walked into them. His arms around her were solid. Dependable. Like coming home.

She hoped that was true.

"Give my best to Aunt Nettie. Don't tell her, but I almost made her some cookies today. But before I do that I need to do some more shopping."

"You know she loves your cookies." Will reached down and kissed Maggie's forehead. "And so do I. Whenever you're in the mood to bake, just let me know. I'll volunteer to be a taster."

She stood on the porch and watched as he got into the little sedan that had been Aunt Nettie's, and now was his.

Then she unlocked Victorian House and went home.

44. A Young Maine Fisherman

Young man wearing a tan shirt and hat, steering his boat on calm seas just offshore. The fish he's caught are in a barrel on board. One of the illustrations of Maine history that N.C. Wyeth (1882–1945) painted for Kenneth Roberts's *Trending into Maine* (1938). Wyeth and Roberts both had homes in Maine and were close friends.
5.5 x 6.25 inches. Price: $50.

*W*INSLOW HOMER'S purred thank-yous for his dinner were the only sounds in Maggie's apartment. Three stories above the street, with her windows closed against temperatures in the high forties, the rooms were silent.

She could have filled the void with the evening news, or music. But the day had been exhausting. Maggie kicked off her shoes, poured a glass of sherry, took a sip, and then put a pan of water on to boil for macaroni while she grated the bits and pieces of hard cheese left in the refrigerator. Cooked macaroni baked with the cheese, dry mustard, milk, and a few shakes of cayenne would make a simple and satisfying dinner. A few frozen peas would be good, too.

As she moved around her small kitchen, Maggie found herself comforted by the silence.

After Brook moved in she'd miss the peace she'd learned to cherish at the end of a long day.

But the joy of sharing those days with someone else, someone who needed a family as much as she did, would more than make up for her need for quiet.

She hoped.

It was already Friday night.

So far the only people who were possible suspects in Eric's

death were Brian, Hay, Jill, and Annie. It was hard to think of any of the four longtime friends as killers.

An article she'd read once said a murderer had to have MOM. Not a parent. Motive, Opportunity, and Means.

Brian had been drinking heavily the night before Eric's body was found. His memories of the evening were cloudy. Or at least he said they were. He'd certainly been with Eric and the others Wednesday night, and into early Thursday morning. So, yes, he'd had the opportunity. Means? Perhaps Owen and Nick knew more, but all she knew was that Eric had been shot.

Everyone who was a suspect knew how to shoot. But who would have had a gun with them that night at The Great Blue?

Although Annie had gone home after work. Had she picked up a gun there?

Or would a bartender have had a gun, maybe behind the bar? It was possible, if Hay was expected to be a bouncer as well as a bartender. She had no idea. The only person she'd seen thrown out of The Great Blue was Abe, and Nick had done that.

Abe. He had guns. He'd even muttered something about losing one. And he was no friend of seals. But did Abe had a reason to shoot Eric?

Maggie didn't know.

Motivation? Brian was younger than the others. He didn't have a girlfriend, as Eric and Hay did. He didn't work on the waters, the way Eric did and Hay did occasionally. Maggie thought through everything Brian had said. He'd known, or at least strongly suspected, that Eric hadn't been totally faithful to Annie. He must have known it for some time. But he hadn't told anyone about it. Of course, something could have happened that night that no one was talking about. Anything was possible. But Brian didn't seem to have a motive.

Two years ago the girl he'd loved was killed. He still mourned her death. It didn't make sense that he'd be a murderer.

What about the others?

Did Hay know Eric had a relationship with Jill? He hadn't said so, but she suspected Hay didn't totally trust Jill, even if everyone said she was his girl. Jealousy was a classic motivation for murder.

Jill herself? Maybe she was jealous of Annie. Although Annie and Eric seemed to have broken up Wednesday night, certainly Annie hadn't seen their argument as a permanent rift. Did Jill?

She'd met Jill a few times, but only once had she talked with her: that afternoon, at Annie's house. Under the circumstances she hadn't been as understanding as a best friend might be expected to be. But, then, both Hay and Annie had excused her rudeness. "Jill's Jill," Hay had said.

That didn't explain a lot. It raised more questions.

And what about Annie?

Annie was a hard worker. A bit premature about planning a wedding before an engagement, but…

Unfortunately, it wasn't surprising the police had called her back for more questioning. She'd had a loud argument with Eric only hours before he'd been killed.

On the other hand, she was the only one of the group who didn't drink. She'd been working at The Great Blue, but not sneaking drinks at the bar. She said she'd gone straight home after her shift was over.

But what if Jenny was right when she'd said Annie wasn't in her bed in the middle of the night? And Hay had told Will that Annie had joined them later at the wharf. Jenny was only six. She could have been mistaken about the time, or even about the night.

But even Annie had said she'd left her house, and gone down to the wharf early in the morning. What if she and Eric had argued again—either late at night or early in the morning?

Maggie was sure about only one thing. If she was going to make any sense of this, she needed to find out more.

She knew what Brian had been doing that night. Annie wouldn't say any more than she already had. Hay hadn't said much, and although he'd helped Eric out sometimes, Hay was pretty easygoing. What better job than tending bar and drinking? Not exactly a career. But, then, nothing she'd heard about Hay said he was planning for the future.

On the other hand, Eric and Annie, separately or together, were dreaming and planning. Brian was saving money and hoping to have his own company one day.

Jill? She needed to know more about Jill. She was Hay's girl. Annie's best friend. Eric's…whatever.

And she'd be back at The Great Blue waitressing tonight.

Maggie finished her macaroni and cheese. Part of her wanted to stay home. Watch *Jeopardy!* Read a book.

But if she could do anything to help Nick solve Eric's murder before Brook came back to Waymouth, she had only a little over twenty-four hours.

She put her shoes back on, and headed to The Great Blue.

Jill was seating people. "No table tonight," Maggie said. "I'll just sit at the bar. But when you have a few minutes, I'd like to talk to you."

"What about?" asked Jill, suspiciously.

"Annie. The police called her back again for more questioning this afternoon," said Maggie. "And Eric."

"I don't see that's any of your business," said Jill defiantly. "You don't even live in this town."

"I do now," said Maggie. "And Annie works for me at Victorian House, and Brian's my guy's cousin. Plus, I'm trying to adopt a little girl who's already upset that seals were killed here. I don't want her to think people get murdered here, too."

"I'll talk to you about seals," said Jill, seeming to relax a little. "Go sit at the bar and order something."

Jill wasn't being charming. Would Hay be? Maggie slipped onto a seat at the bar.

"Hi, Maggie. Food tonight, or just a drink?"

She'd just finished her dinner. "A dessert menu? And a glass of port. Water, too, please."

"Coming up!" Hay grinned.

A few minutes later she was sipping a glass of port and ordering a scoop of vanilla ice cream.

"Jill said you were over to the Bryants, talking to Annie this afternoon," Hay said.

"I wanted to see how she was doing. She's having a rough time, but she seems to be coping."

Hay nodded. "Annie's tough. Tougher than she thinks."

"How are you doing? Eric was one of your best friends."

"I'm trying not to think about him a lot," admitted Hay. "We had our disagreements over the years, but, you're right. I'd known him all my life. It doesn't seem possible he's gone."

"You were all together down at the wharf that night. Everything seemed all right then?"

"Eric was upset; he and Annie'd had a fight. He hated confrontations of any kind. He'd never take a job like this." Hay gestured at the bar. "I have to talk with people all the time. Eric was more comfortable talking to lobsters. His argument with Annie was why he was drinking more than usual. Brian had brought some beer, but that disappeared fast, so they went back to his truck for more. That was about when Annie got there."

Annie'd come to the wharf?

Maggie asked carefully, "So, Brian and Eric went for more beer."

"Right."

"And Annie joined you all?"

"Yup. No one was feeling any pain by then. She and Eric got into it again. We finished off the beer, and then Jill and Brian and I left."

"When was that?"

"I don't know exactly. One or two?"

"Eric and Annie didn't leave?"

"Nah. His mom isn't exactly the welcoming domestic type. Eric kept a sleeping bag on his boat. Sometimes he slept there." Hay wrinkled his nose. "Pretty rank on a lobster boat, but he wouldn't have to go far to get to work the next day. I figured he and Annie didn't need an audience for their argument."

"Did you all know Eric sometimes slept on the *Lucy II*?"

"Sure. He'd been doing it for years."

Jill slipped into the seat next to Maggie. "So, you want to know about seals?"

"Someone's been killing them."

"It wasn't Eric," she said.

Eric? She hadn't even considered that Eric would have killed them.

"Eric loved those stupid seals. Even when someone on the waterfront had a problem with the seals, they knew not to mention it in front of Eric. He'd get all righteous, and 'They have a right to live in the river.'"

"I see."

"Two of those seals were killed near the *Lucy II*."

Maggie'd known that, but hadn't considered it was important.

"Eric figured someone was pissed at him and killed the seals there, or left them there, intentionally, because they knew he'd be upset."

"Who would have done that?"

"Could have been anyone. Anyone mad at Eric." Jill stood up. "Got to get back to work."

Maggie glanced around. Hay was filling beer glasses at the other end of the bar. She reached out to stop Jill from leaving. "Jill, were you sleeping with Eric?"

"What business is that of yours?"

"It would explain why Eric broke off with Annie that night."

"Fine, then. Sure. We had a thing going. He didn't love Annie. They'd just been together so long everyone expected them to be together forever. But they wouldn't have been. I told Eric he needed to break it off. She'd made him feel guilty for needing a little free-dom. He deserved to do what he wanted to do." Jill hurried back to the entrance, where two couples were waiting to be seated.

Eric might have deserved to choose what he wanted to do with his life. But he hadn't deserved to die.

Hay put Maggie's ice cream in front of her. "So, what did Jill have to say for herself?"

"She told me Eric didn't kill the seals."

Hay grinned. "Did she? Then it must be true. Enjoy your dessert."

He went to fill more orders. The ice cream was soothing, and so was the port.

She finished, and left Hay a good tip for the second time that day.

Had she learned anything?

She walked back to Victorian House by way of Water Street. The crime scene tape was gone from the town wharf.

She walked down the ramp and stared at the *Lucy II*. Brian had told her one of the other lobstermen had been checking Eric's traps for now, but soon they'd all have to be pulled permanently.

The *Lucy II* was securely tied to the wharf. The bait barrel was there, and two metal lobster traps. Several of Eric's red-and-gold-striped buoys were still on the deck. They looked new. Lobstermen all had different, registered, colored buoys so they—and other lobstermen—could identify them. Eric had planned to set new traps this week. He'd said he wanted to increase the number he had. Annie had been encouraging him to do that.

But the seals he'd loved had died here, and then he had.

If he'd slept on the *Lucy II* that night, he hadn't slept long. Even assuming no one involved had been checking their watches, Eric had been drinking with friends until between one and two in the morning. And Abe and Annie had found him about five, his usual time to take the *Lucy II* out.

A window of three or four hours at most.

Tonight the moon was full, and the security lights over the town wharf lit the whole area. No secrets there. She'd seen the security lights from her apartment. They were on all night. Anyone nearby could see what was happening on the wharf. But who would have been out here at three or four in the morning? A lobsterman getting an early start?

The boat was wood, and so was everything on it, except for the motor and the traps, of course. If Eric had been shot on his boat, the crime scene technicians would have found a bullet. Or bullethole. Or blood or… Of course, information like that was confidential. They might have found something and weren't sharing it.

In the night's silence, Maggie heard footsteps. Irregular steps. In back of her. Eric had been killed here. What did she have to defend herself with?

She froze. Her mind went blank. Then she turned around quickly, ready to confront whoever was there. "Abe!"

"You're Maggie, Will Brewer's lady. What're you doing down on the wharf at this time of the evening?"

"Just thinking. About the seals that died here, and of Eric."

"Good kid, Eric. Hard worker. Had some ideas that weren't the same as mine, but kept most of 'em to himself."

"You knew him well."

"Sterned for his grandfather, remember? Knew Eric when he was just a cunning little fellow. Always loved the water, that one. Always said he wanted to be a lobsterman, like his granddad."

"And he did."

"Yup. He did."

"But someone shot him."

Abe shook his head. "Why would someone do that?"

"A lot of people in town have guns."

"Sure." Then he shook his head. "Wish I were one of them."

Maggie stopped. "Sorry, Abe. That's right. You told me you'd misplaced your gun. But you have rifles at home."

"At home doesn't do no good unless you're there."

"True." She didn't want a gun, even at home, but this wasn't the moment to discuss gun control legislation.

Abe seemed a nice enough old guy, crusty but sad.

"That's exactly why I had me a gun. On occasion I've been known to drink a bit more than a man should. I always thought I should have something to protect me, on my way home, sometimes late in the evening, you know?"

Maggie knew what she thought about a drunk carrying a gun. But she nodded.

"But I don't have a gun now. Somehow I lost it." Abe shook his head. "No idea where. Keep thinking it'll show up somewhere. If it doesn't pretty soon, I'll have to get me another one." He shrugged. "Not a big deal. Pawn shop up on Route One has guns. But money's tight now, you know? Most people have someone to stern for 'em, and I haven't got a boat anymore. May have to look for some job on land." He shook his head sadly.

Abe was a little under the weather, but he was making sense.

Maggie hadn't considered that Abe might have killed Eric, but now she was certain he wouldn't have. With Eric gone, Abe had no way to support himself. She decided to check what she'd heard from Hay and Brian. "Hay Johnson said Eric sometimes slept on his boat."

"Ayuh. He did. I'd come down in the morning to meet him and he'd be rolling up that old green sleeping bag of his." Abe lowered his voice. "Sometimes he'd had company for the night. If you know what I mean." He winked broadly. "Not always his Annie, either. But I wouldn't tell no one on him. He was a young man, and young men have to find their own ways."

"You're right about that, Abe. It's just sad he won't get the chance to grow up. You know—get married, have a family."

"Not all men are interested in doing that. Eric was wicked stubborn, but he did all right. Have a fine evening, Maggie. I'm off to get myself a nightcap."

Maggie stared as Abe walked toward The Great Blue. She'd assumed he'd already had his nightcap.

And Eric was "wicked stubborn."

Wasn't everyone once in a while?

It had been a long day. She had too much to think about.

Too many questions. Too few answers.

45. Quatrain XXIV

Wizard-like man standing among his books, looking out
the window of a tower room in the Middle East, pon-
dering his next move. Edmund Dulac illustration for
The Rubaiyat of Omar Khayyam, rendered into English
verse by Edward Fitzgerald, 1930.

5 x 7 inches. Price: $70.

*F*RIDAY NIGHT. Maggie stood in the cupola of Victorian House and looked out at the end of the sunset. The
sky over the river reminded her of a Turner painting: a
gray-and-pink sky streaked with white clouds. As she watched,
winds blew the clouds into darkness.

Winslow was by her side. "Keeping me company?" she asked
him.

He rubbed himself on her legs. "Or, more likely, telling me
you're hungry."

He followed her down the narrow flight of stairs to her kitchen,
where, indeed, his food bowl was empty. "Sunday," Maggie said
as she filled the bowl with Winslow's preferred brand of dry food,
"Sunday, I hope Brook will come to visit."

Winslow ignored her and focused on his dinner.

"And no one's caught whoever killed those seals. Or whoever
killed Eric." Maggie looked down at her cat. "You may not care,
Winslow, but I do. And Brook does. We don't even know whether
the same person killed Eric and the seals, or if Waymouth has two
crazies in town."

Winslow was a good listener, but tonight he had food, and
probably a nap, on his mind. The banging and loud voices that accompanied the elevator construction had been disturbing his afternoon
siestas for two weeks now. Thank goodness that was almost over.

Maggie'd heard one of the workmen saying the elevator was installed and working. All that was left was finishing details around the doors.

His bowl empty, Winslow curled up at the opposite end of the couch from Maggie.

"I don't even know how to begin to find out who shot those seals. But Eric had to have been killed during a short window early Thursday morning."

She picked up the pad of paper she'd left on the coffee table. On it was a shopping list she'd made up two days ago.

Maggie read over the list of spices and baking essentials, pasta and couscous, and bouillons and beans she'd planned to use as the basis for soups. Then, as Winslow watched intently, she tore the list into small shreds. Kitchen details seemed unimportant right now.

She started a new list.

TIMELINE: Wednesday night/Thursday morning

10:30 in evening. The Great Blue closed. Annie started home. Eric either went with her, or joined her along the way. They argued. Brian, Hay and Jill stayed at the bar.

11–11:30. Eric rejoined group at The Great Blue. They picked up beer from Brian's pickup, and went to the town wharf.

Maggie paused. What had happened next? How long had the friends stayed drinking at the wharf? Some of her details were educated guesses.

12:30 A.M. Brian and Eric went back to Brian's pickup for more beer. According to Hay, Annie joined them at the wharf and argued with Eric. According to Annie, she was at home.

1:30–2:00. Beer finished. Jill, Hay, and Brian left. Annie still at wharf (?).

??? Eric went to sleep on the *Lucy II* and/or was shot.

3:47 Jenny woke up; Annie not home. (Jenny was the only one who knew exactly when something had happened that night.)

4:45 Annie took coffee to wharf as peace-offering for Eric. Didn't see him.

5:00 Abe arrived at wharf for work. He and Annie see Eric's body in river and call police.

5:30 Sirens.

None of the times were in concrete, except Jenny's contribution. If she'd been right.

Four of the close friends were still alive. She'd talked with them all. But their stories didn't match.

Most significant, Annie'd said she'd stayed home, in bed, until she'd taken coffee down to the pier in the morning. Hay had said she'd joined the group at the wharf after they'd been there about an hour.

Why would Annie have lied? Or—why had Hay lied? Brian hadn't mentioned Annie joining the group at the wharf. But Brian had also said his memories of the whole evening were hazy.

Jill hadn't wanted to talk about the evening at all. She'd just said Eric loved seals.

Eric had said that himself.

As Jill had pointed out, two of the dead seals had been shot near Eric's boat.

Everyone in town seemed to have access to one or more guns. But the only gun Maggie'd seen in Waymouth was Abe's. Probably the handgun he'd said he'd lost. When had she seen it?

She was almost positive it had been last Sunday, down at the wharf, when the body of the third seal had been found. Maggie focused on what else she'd heard that day. Yes, Jill had said something about Eric's keeping his gun on the *Lucy II*.

Was his gun still there?

Could someone who knew about that gun have killed Eric with it?

After the others left, Annie had been alone with Eric, according to Hay.

Why hadn't the others mentioned that?

Annie already had a motive for killing Eric. And if she was the last person to see him alive…no wonder the police considered her their chief suspect.

Maggie sat and stared at the notes she'd written down. It all looked obvious. Annie had to have murdered Eric.

She hadn't killed the seals, though. At least she hadn't killed one. She and Eric were out on his boat when one of them was killed.

Eric loved the seals. Why had Jill kept repeating that?

By midnight, Maggie had an idea.

It might not work. But it was the only plan she could come up with.

46. The Lobsterman
(Hauling in a Light Fog)

Man standing in dory, checking the wooden lobster trap he's just hauled. Seas are mild, but waves evident. A flock of gulls follows his boat, their color muted by the fog surrounding the scene. No land is visible. Print from the oil painting by American artist N.C. Wyeth illustrating Kenneth Roberts's *Trending into Maine*, 1938.

5.5 x 6.25 inches. Price: $50.

*A*T EIGHT SATURDAY MORNING Maggie was at the Waymouth Sheriff's Office waiting for Owen Trask or Nick Strait to show up.

"Don't call either of them in," she repeated to the clerk who was puzzled someone would just sit in the outer office and wait. "They'll be here soon. Give them time to finish their coffee."

She'd been up for over an hour and had finished a Diet Coke, the rest of the macaroni and cheese, and a couple of chocolate kisses she'd found at the bottom of the red canvas bag she used as a pocketbook. Caffeine, sugar, protein, carbs...she was ready for whatever might happen.

For the first time in ten days she was optimistic that the mysteries of both the seal killings and Eric's murder could be, and would be, solved. And soon.

"Just listen to me for a few minutes," she said to Owen when he arrived.

"Maggie, you've had some good ideas in other cases. But we're talking about several different major crimes here. Killing seals is a federal offense. It's not even something we'd deal with at a local or state level. And murder?" He shook his head. "I get that you're trying to tie both cases up with a bow before that little girl you want to adopt comes to visit again. But we already have a serious suspect.

We're close to collecting enough evidence to make an arrest. We don't have the time or manpower to play games."

"I agree. No games. But I'm not sure Annie killed Eric. And if you were sure, then she'd be under arrest. Right?"

Owen nodded, reluctantly. "We don't have all the ends tied up yet."

"If my plan works, then you'll have your proof Annie was the killer. Or you'll know someone else was." She smiled her sweetest smile. "That would help you make your case, wouldn't it? Whatever the result?"

Owen sighed. "Okay. So what's your plan?"

"It's simple. We all agree the chances are pretty high that either Annie killed Eric, or, if not, then it was Brian, Jill, or Hay. Right?"

"Right," Owen agreed. "We haven't found evidence leading to anyone else."

"And they all know they're at least persons of interest. You've questioned each of them at least once."

"And talked to the owner of The Great Blue, and some of their parents and friends," Owen confirmed.

"So it's simple. I'll let each of them know, confidentially, that you've decided to declare the *Lucy II* a crime scene, and confiscate it. That there's evidence on board you're certain will lead to the killer."

"We've already searched the *Lucy II*," said Owen. "And the crime scene folks have gone over it. There was no blood, and no evidence of a crime. All four of our suspects had left fingerprints there, but that wasn't surprising."

"Did you find Eric's gun?" asked Maggie.

"His gun?"

"He told me he kept a gun on board."

"We didn't find a gun on board. Are you sure?"

"Have you identified the gun that killed Eric? Or killed those seals?"

"Remember, the seals aren't our problem. Marine mammals are covered by another law enforcement agency. But, no. We haven't found the gun that killed Eric."

"Maybe it was the same gun that killed the seals," Maggie continued.

"Those killings aren't in our jurisdiction, but we have been in touch with the officers investigating them. So far, nothing definite about the gun."

"Oh." Maggie'd hoped the solution would be easier than it was turning out to be. "Then we'll just focus on Eric's murderer for now. Although I still think they're connected."

"Maggie, you're getting too involved with all of this. I don't see where you're going."

"It's simple. I'll make sure Brian and Annie and Hay and Jill all know you think there's evidence on the *Lucy II*. That you're going to trailer it up and take it to the crime lab in Augusta tomorrow."

"Even though that's not true."

"It doesn't matter if it's not true. You won't be the one saying it is. I will. What matters is whoever killed Eric will think they made a mistake; they left something on Eric's boat."

"And?"

"And tonight they'll go to the *Lucy II* to try to figure out what they did wrong. What they forgot."

"We don't even know if Eric was killed on the boat. Since we didn't find any evidence there, or on the wharf, chances are he fell in the water when he was shot. He could even have been in the river when he was shot. We just don't know."

"But his killer knows. And if you and Nick are watching the *Lucy II*, you'll find the killer."

Owen threw up his hands. "Okay. You may be right. But I'm going to have to talk Nick into agreeing to this plan of yours."

Maggie stood up. "Tell him it was my idea; I'm the crazy one. But I'm going to tell Brian, Jill, Hay, and Annie about the evidence you're sure you'll find. If I'm right, by dawn tomorrow you'll know who killed Eric. If I'm not right, you'll just have wasted some time."

47. The manager appears before the curtain, in doublet and hose

Man in red, taking a bow on a stage in front of a green curtain. Lithograph by Maxfield Parrish from *The Knave of Hearts*, 1921.

8 x 10 inches. Price: $250.

*W*HAT ARE YOU DOING HERE?" whispered Nick. "I agreed to go along with this ridiculous plan of yours because we didn't have any better ideas. I never agreed you could be here."

"It was my plan. I wanted to see if it worked," said Maggie, calmly. She perched precariously on a large rock partially covered with rockweed, just below the high-tide mark. Nick was ten feet in front of her, under the wharf. "I was sure one of you would hide near where the *Lucy II* is moored. Those bright lights on the wharf make it hard to hide anywhere but in the shadows. Where's Owen?"

Nick frowned. "You shouldn't be here. Owen's behind the Bowmans' barn, just down the street. He's watching for foot traffic or cars." Nick pointed at his cell phone. "He'll let me know if anyone heads toward the wharf."

Maggie noted Nick's holster wasn't hidden tonight. "Lucky the tide is going out. Although this rock is still wet." Her rear end was increasingly damp.

"Tide was high a little after nine o'clock," said Nick. "I decided if we were going to see if your ploy worked, we should get here shortly after sunset. I've been hanging around these mud flats for about an hour. So far no one's shown up. Were you able to talk to all four of the suspects?"

"Mission accomplished. I talked to Hay and Jill over at The Great Blue. A couple of other people heard me, but no one else seemed to care. I stopped in to see Annie—she's still taking this whole situation hard—and casually mentioned it to her. She seemed relieved you guys might have some real clues. And Brian was working at Victorian House today, so I had no problem chatting with him."

Nick shook his head. "I wish you weren't here, Maggie. But in case someone shows up, I don't want you climbing up onto the shore now. Does Will know you're here?"

"I didn't tell Will," said Maggie, stretching one of her legs to avoid the sharp barnacles on the rock. "He isn't as interested in this situation as I am." She paused. "I don't mean he doesn't care that Eric was murdered. He just has other priorities right now. He believes you'll find the killer."

"Which you didn't think I could do on my own?"

Luckily, Nick was smiling. Slightly.

"Of course I trust you, Nick. I just want this case to be solved before tomorrow at noon."

"When your new daughter will be visiting."

"Exactly. I don't want her to hear anything about unsolved killings in Waymouth. Killings of people, or of seals." Maggie paused. "I can't make the whole world safe for Brook. Or even the whole state. But I'll do everything I can to make this town a place she's comfortable living in. Growing up in."

"I understand. And if this plan of yours doesn't work?"

"Then I promise to hand the whole situation back to you. I'll have my hands full keeping Brook in the dark about what's happened in Waymouth."

"And Will doesn't know you're here."

"He doesn't need to know. I told him I had a headache tonight."

Nick shook his head and grinned. "The old headache ruse, eh?"

Maggie shrugged. "Will doesn't understand when I get involved with solving crimes."

"Somehow that doesn't surprise me," Nick said, drily. "And have you thought what's going to happen after Brook comes to live with you?"

"I'm doing this for Brook."

"Those words won't mean a lot if you get hurt. It's dangerous for you to be here, Maggie. You're going to be a single parent. What would happen to Brook if you were killed? She'd be left alone again. You can't do that to her."

Maggie hesitated. "You're a single parent."

"Sure. Hadn't planned to be, but after my wife left me with the baby, yes. But I already had a career in law enforcement. And if the worst happened, my mom was there to look after Zelda. You're not a state trooper, Maggie. If you were badly injured or killed Brook would go back into foster care."

Maggie shook her head. "I've thought about that. But Brook doesn't live with me yet. And if whoever killed Eric—and those seals—isn't found, than she may decide not ever to live with me. I have to be here, Nick. If I weren't here I'd be going crazy up in my apartment, looking down at the wharf and wondering what was happening."

Just then Nick's cell phone buzzed. He looked down. "It's Owen. Someone's coming. He can't see who—it's too dark. Shh!"

Nick stayed under the pier but moved a little farther toward the float where the *Lucy II* was tied. The water was deep and cold. But the *Lucy II* was only about fifteen feet away. He and Maggie could see it. For the first time Maggie realized a ladder was part of the wharf, so someone could get down to the mud flats or the water. Or Nick could climb up. Right now the ladder led down to three or four feet of water.

The only sounds were the soft lapping of waves hitting the pilings and shore.

Somewhere in the distance an owl cried. The shrill, repetitive sound of spring peepers echoed across the river.

Maggie forced herself to be still. Her pulse was racing. She didn't get off the rock, but she stretched as far as she could so she could see the float.

Nick had moved into the water, and was standing on the ladder. The sounds of water dripping from his clothes into the river seemed loud. But that was because she was so conscious of any noise.

Every moment, waiting, seemed to last forever. To calm herself Maggie matched her breaths to the pattern of the waves. Nick hadn't moved from the ladder.

Then, above them, she heard footsteps on the wharf. Heavy footsteps, coming from the shore side of the wharf. Boards creaked as the steps kept coming. *Step. Step. Creak. Step. Step.*

Who was it? Not Jill; she usually wore high heels. These steps were steady and strong. Not hesitant. A man's steps.

The footsteps passed over Maggie's head. Whoever was there was heading toward the *Lucy II*, just as she'd anticipated. She crossed her fingers and prayed this was the ending she'd hoped for. That whoever those footsteps belonged to had killed Eric.

As the footsteps continued, Nick climbed higher. One rung. Then another. His head was still below the wharf. Unless someone on the ramp or float was looking for him, he was invisible, hidden by dark shadows under the wharf.

The footsteps quickened as the man went down the ramp to the float. The tide was still high enough so the ramp was a gentle incline.

Now Maggie could see a man's back. Whoever he was, he was now on the float. Five boats were moored there, tied to the float, their movements cushioned by plastic bumpers. Would he approach the *Lucy II* ?

He did. And stepped on board with the familiarity of someone who knew boats. Frustratingly, his back was still to Maggie. He moved forward and seemed to be opening one of the storage compartments under the bow.

Nick quickly climbed the rest of the rungs of the ladder, slippery with salt water and seaweed, until he was on the wharf. Maggie leaned forward, trying to see, as he ran down the ramp toward the *Lucy II*.

"Hold it!" Nick called, as the man on the boat turned around. "Police! Don't touch anything. Just turn around slowly and put your hands up."

Maggie shifted her weight on the rock so she could see what was happening.

The lights on the wharf were placed to illuminate the boats, and anyone on them. Nick was standing on the float, his gun out.

Slowly the man on the boat straightened up and turned around. "Ah, shit, Nick. What're you down here for?"

It was Abe Palmer.

Nick didn't move his weapon. "What're *you* doing here, Abe? Eric's dead. That's private property you're trespassing on."

"I'm not trespassing! I worked for the guy. You know that, Nick."

"So what're you here for tonight? Going lighting for lobsters?"

"Put your gun away, Nick. I just thought… See, Eric kept his gun on board the *Lucy II*. Never could figure why, except maybe he didn't want that mother of his to get hold of it when she was in one of her tempers."

"And?"

"Last week I lost my gun. Don't know what happened to it, Nick. I had it one day and it was gone the next. Looked everywhere; couldn't find it." Abe shrugged. "Must have somehow dropped out of my holster."

"Did you report it missing?"

"Nah. Didn't bother. But this afternoon I was over to The Great Blue and heard that friend of Will Brewer's, Maggie something? She told Hay and Jill you guys were going to take the *Lucy II* up to one of the crime labs; check to see if anything in here would tell you who killed Eric. I figured, he wouldn't have been killed by his own gun, and he wouldn't be needing it where he is now, so I'd come and get it. A replacement for mine that was lost, see?"

Nick lowered his weapon. "So where's this gun of Eric's?"

"He kept it in the port-side compartment, under his sleeping bag."

Nick waved Abe back to the float. "Just stay there. I'll look."

Maggie watched as Nick rummaged through the compartment, shaking Eric's sleeping bag out, and moving some other things she couldn't make out.

"Not here," he announced, turning back to Abe. "You sure it *was* here?"

"Ain't seen it fer a couple of weeks. But, yeah. That's where Eric kept it. Been there for a year or two, far's I know."

"It's not here now." Nick climbed back onto the float. "You have anything to do with killing Eric, Abe?"

"No way," Abe backed up on the float. "Eric was my meal ticket, you know? Without him, I've got no way to pay the rent."

"And the bar bills," Nick commiserated. "Okay. I believe you. What about those seals? You shoot them?"

"I ain't a fan of seals, Nick. No secret about that. When I was a kid, when there was a bounty on 'em, I killed my share. But I'm a law-abidin' citizen now. I wouldn't hurt 'em. Seals ain't worth getting caught, for sure."

"You know anything about who did shoot them?"

Abe shook his head, and most of his body. "Not a clue, Nick. If I did, I'd tell you. Don't know what idiot killed those seals." He paused. "Got Eric all uptight, for sure. He loved those animals."

Maggie watched as Nick reached into his pocket and pulled out his cell phone.

He glanced at it, and then waved Abe up the ramp. "Get going, Abe. There's nothing you want here. But don't be telling anyone I'm down here."

"Got it, Nick. No problem." Abe walked up the ramp onto the wharf twice as fast as he'd walked down it.

Nick went behind the ramp and hunkered down on the float.

Maggie took a deep breath. Owen must have called. Someone else was on their way to the town wharf

48. Fairies are all more or less in hiding until dark

Arthur Rackham lithograph for *Peter Pan in Kensington Gardens*, 1940. A small girl with a hoop and an older boy are looking for fairies near the trunk of a large tree. They can't see any, but the viewer can. The fairies are under the ground, sleeping cozily in rooms between the tree's roots.

5.5 x 8 inches. Price: $60.

*M*AGGIE GLANCED AT her phone. Past eleven. The Great Blue had closed, and most Waymouth residents were at home, many of them already asleep.

No cars had passed the wharf in a long time, although she'd been so focused on what was happening on the float and the *Lucy II* that she hadn't been paying much attention in the past few minutes.

Wherever Abe had gone, he was now off the wharf. All was silent again.

Had she been right? Had Nick's call been from Owen?

Nick was still hunkered down on the float, beneath the ramp.

He must think something was happening since he hadn't taken the time to climb down under the wharf again. Or he just didn't want to get into the water again. Maine water temperatures in May were in the low fifties at best. Not exactly bathtub temperatures.

Maggie moved up a few feet to another damp rock the tide had just left. Sharp barnacles cut through her pants. She cussed silently and tried to find a spot where there was only slippery rockweed. Not a good choice under the circumstances.

Then there were more footsteps from the wharf above her head. This time they were accompanied by words.

"I still think this is a stupid idea. I should have let you do it on your own. If we get caught, we'll be in big trouble."

"Hurry up. The can's heavy. It'll only take a minute, and then it'll be over and we can leave."

The voices were a man's and a woman's.

"I should never have let you talk me into this. This is serious. I wish you'd never told me what you did."

"You love me, don't you?"

Above her, the footsteps stopped, just ahead of where Maggie was crouching.

"I'm here, aren't I? Which doesn't say I love you. It says I'm stupid. You got yourself into this mess. If you'd stayed away from Eric none of this would have happened." Hay. It had to be Hay, with Jill.

"But I do love you. Eric was our friend. If I hadn't done something, he'd have been stuck with Mrs. Housewife Annie for the rest of his life. C'mon. Let's get this over with. Then we can go back to my place."

"Yeah. So you say. When it was just the seals, I went along with it. We all knew Eric loved those stupid seals."

"The plan was so simple. I told him the seals would keep dying if he didn't dump Annie."

"For you."

"Well, yeah, he got that."

"So how do you think I feel, my girl planning to blackmail my best friend?"

Jill giggled. "Cool. I like that. Guess that was what I was doing."

"So how'd Eric end up dead in all this? You never explained that."

"After we all left the wharf that night, and Eric was so drunk, I went home and got Abe's gun. The one he'd dropped at the restaurant. I figured I'd try to shoot one more seal, right near where Eric was sleeping. He was so out of it he wouldn't even hear. But when I got back down here, Annie was with him. They sure weren't sleeping. And they didn't look as though they'd broken up, no matter what Eric had told us earlier. I hung out up on Water Street until finally Annie left. Then I went down to the *Lucy II*. I thought Eric would've been asleep by then. But he wasn't. So I told him I'd seen him. He hadn't broken up with Annie, like he promised. I told him I'd kill every seal in the Madoc River if I needed to, until he figured out what to do to stop me."

"He believed you were there to shoot seals? At night?"

"So, we'd both had a few too many. I wasn't exactly thinking straight. And he was pretty angry to see me. He kept saying I was spying on him, and Annie—Annie!—was worth two of me. That he was through with me. That I should go home and sober up."

"Wow."

"The ramp was steep. I had to hold on to the railing. I almost dropped the gun. By the time I got down to the float, Eric was standing there, holding his gun. He started yelling about how he'd had enough. That I should stay away from him. That he'd kill me if I touched another seal, or was nasty to Annie."

"So why didn't you turn around and leave? The guy had a gun. You were both drunk."

"I didn't believe he had the guts to shoot me," said Jill. "But then…he did shoot at me. But he missed. And I shot back."

"And you didn't miss."

"I'm pretty good with a gun. Always have been. How'd you think I got all those seals?"

"So why wasn't there any blood on anything?"

"Eric was standing on the edge of the float. When I hit him he fell into the river. It was low tide. The river wasn't more than four or five feet deep there. I didn't know I'd killed him. I figured he'd get to the shore and be angrier than he had been before. So I just got the hell out of there."

"But you'd killed him."

"Yeah. Turned out that way."

"And now the police must have found something. Otherwise why would they take Eric's boat to the crime lab?"

"I don't know what they've found. But that's why we brought the gasoline."

"If Eric shot at you first, it was self-defense. Why didn't you go to the police?"

"I didn't think. And I'd killed the seals. And I had Abe's gun.

Anyway, I threw the gun in the river and went home. I just wanted to get away. But now it's too late. We have to burn the boat. That way no one'll ever know what happened that night."

"Oh, yes they will."

Nick ran up the ramp toward the two on the wharf. "Police! Stop! Put those cans of gasoline down. You're both coming with me."

49. Fashions for June

Hand-colored engraving from *The Lady's Friend*, 1880, showing four elegantly dressed women and a young girl who is holding a bouquet of wild flowers. The women's dresses are violet, gold, brown, and rose; the child is dressed in blue. Originally a double-sized illustration, so there is a fold mark.

9.5 x 11.5 inches. Price: $75.

*B*ROOK SAT ON THE COUCH in Maggie's apartment next to Winslow, who was enjoying having his head scratched. "I never had a cat before," she said. "Once I had a puppy, but my dad took him away because he peed on the floor." She bent down to look at Winslow. "You won't pee on the floor, will you?"

Aunt Nettie laughed. "Winslow's a good cat, isn't he, Maggie? This is the first time I've met him, but I can tell. And he likes you, too, Brook."

"Do you think he'll sleep on my bed?" asked Brook.

"Cats do whatever they want to do," Maggie cautioned her. "He may sleep on your bed, or he may not. He's an independent cat."

"Does he have any toys?" Brook asked.

"They're in a box on the floor of my study. You can go and get a couple for him," said Maggie. "With all these people here, I don't know if he'll want to play. Cats can be shy."

Brook hopped off the couch, and headed to the study.

Happily, Winslow followed her.

"She's doing so well," said Aunt Nettie, quietly. "And so are you."

"I hope so. Let me check on how the chicken is coming. We should be able to eat soon."

"Can I help?" asked Will.

In the kitchen he gestured that she should come closer. "I

haven't had a chance to talk with you, with the excitement last night, and Brook here this afternoon. But I told Nick about what happened in Buffalo."

"And?" Maggie suddenly was nervous. What would Nick have said?

"He understood our concerns. So he checked New York State and national records. There's no mention anywhere of what happened at that school where I worked. They must have managed to keep it quiet."

"So if anyone were to investigate you?"

"They wouldn't find anything."

Maggie gave him a hug that lasted long enough for the timer on the stove to go off.

"Are you two kissing?" Brook was standing near the kitchen, grinning, and holding a small gray cat toy stuffed with catnip.

"Just hugging. But sometimes we do kiss," said Maggie, reaching up and giving Nick a small kiss on his cheek, above his beard.

"Yuck," said Brook. "Grown-ups are weird."

"Dinner's almost ready," said Maggie. "Why don't you go and get your seal picture to show to Aunt Nettie while I get our dinner out of the oven?"

Brook ran into her room, as Will gave Maggie another hug.

"So far, so good," he said. "Your daughter didn't freak out when she saw us together."

Last night had been a success. Nick and the Marine Patrol were trying to figure out what to do about Jill. Right now they were holding her locally. Had she shot Eric in self-defense? Maybe. But the seals hadn't had guns.

And today had gone better than she'd expected. Brook had loved the seal prints, and had chosen her favorite.

A stuffed roast chicken and yams were in the oven, and Will and Aunt Nettie were joining them for dinner, since the elevator now worked. And now Will had shared his good news about what she'd been thinking of as The Buffalo Incident.

She removed the chicken from the oven, put it on a platter, and then filled bowls with yams, peas, and cranberry sauce. "Will, would you help me put these on the table?" she instructed. "And, Brook? Would you help Aunt Nettie to the place we set for her?"

Within a few minutes all four of them were seated and Maggie was carving the chicken.

After everyone was served, Brook asked, "Can Winslow have chicken? Cats like chicken, I think."

"No. This is people food," said Maggie. "Winslow has his own food."

Will had gotten up from the table. He returned with a bottle and four glasses. "I think this is a good time to share that champagne I've been saving," he said. He opened the bottle with a loud pop.

"Can I have champagne?" asked Brook.

"No. But you can have ginger ale in a champagne glass," Maggie decided. "Ginger ale looks like champagne. It even has bubbles." As she poured Brook's "champagne" she tried to ignore Winslow, sitting at Brook's feet and happily gulping a small piece of chicken.

"A toast," said Will, raising his glass. They all followed him. "To Maggie and Brook."

"And to you and Aunt Nettie," added Maggie.

"And Winslow," Brook put in. "To the whole family."

ACKNOWLEDGMENTS

Thank you to everyone, everywhere, in the adoption triangle: adoptees, birth parents, and adoptive parents, who prove every day that families are created by love. To my friends in ASPNJ and, especially, to Elizabeth Park, Joan Jacobus, Diane Veith and their families. For years we shared day-to-day joys, traumas, and sorrows, and formed an extended adoption community. I couldn't have done it without you.

Thank you, again, to Meredith Phillips and John and Susan Daniel of Perseverance Press/John Daniel & Company, who bring Maggie and her friends to readers.

To my wonderful husband, Bob Thomas, who patiently listens to plot dilemmas, cooks meals, does errands…and is my first critical reader.

To the memory of my mother, Sally Wait, who introduced me to antique prints.

To my wonderful daughters, Caroline Childs, Ali Hall, Becky Wynne, and Elizabeth Wait, who taught me that adopting older children is always challenging, but always wonderful.

To my fellow Maine Crime Writers (www.mainecrimewriters. com) especially Kate Flora, Kathy Lynn Emerson and Barbara Ross, who blog with me and share advice and counsel.

To my readers, whose support has ensured that the Shadows series has continued.

To the librarians and bookstore owners who order copies and introduce Maggie to their patrons.

To everyone at Malice Domestic, the wonderful conference that celebrates traditional mysteries, and to the real Sandy Sechrest, who won a charity auction at Malice to share her name with a Maine social worker.

And to readers everywhere, without whom there would be no (published) writers.

ABOUT THE AUTHOR

Maine author and speaker Lea Wait writes the Shadows Antique Print Mystery series and the Mainely Needlepoint series, as well as historical novels for ages eight and up set in nineteenth-century Maine, and a memoir, *Living and Writing on the Coast of Maine*. She is an antique print dealer. As a single parent, Lea adopted four older girls from Asia; now she is married to artist Bob Thomas. For more information about Lea and her books, see http://www.leawait.com, friend her on Facebook and Goodreads, and read the blog she writes with other writers from the often mysterious state of Maine, http://www.mainecrimewriters.com

More Traditional Mysteries from Perseverance Press
For the New Golden Age

K.K. Beck
Tipping the Valet
ISBN 978-1-56474-563-7

Albert A. Bell, Jr.
PLINY THE YOUNGER SERIES
Death in the Ashes
ISBN 978-1-56474-532-3

The Eyes of Aurora
ISBN 978-1-56474-549-1

Fortune's Fool (forthcoming)
ISBN 978-1-56474-587-3

Taffy Cannon
ROXANNE PRESCOTT SERIES
Guns and Roses
Agatha and Macavity awards nominee, Best Novel
ISBN 978-1-880284-34-6

Blood Matters
ISBN 978-1-880284-86-5

Open Season on Lawyers
ISBN 978-1-880284-51-3

Paradise Lost
ISBN 978-1-880284-80-3

Laura Crum
GAIL MCCARTHY SERIES
Moonblind
ISBN 978-1-880284-90-2

Chasing Cans
ISBN 978-1-880284-94-0

Going, Gone
ISBN 978-1-880284-98-8

Barnstorming
ISBN 978-1-56474-508-8

Jeanne M. Dams
HILDA JOHANSSON SERIES
Crimson Snow
ISBN 978-1-880284-79-7

Indigo Christmas
ISBN 978-1-880284-95-7

Murder in Burnt Orange
ISBN 978-1-56474-503-3

Janet Dawson
JERI HOWARD SERIES
Bit Player
Golden Nugget Award nominee
ISBN 978-1-56474-494-4

Cold Trail
ISBN 978-1-56474-555-2

Water Signs (forthcoming)
ISBN 978-1-56474-586-6

What You Wish For
ISBN 978-1-56474-518-7
TRAIN SERIES
Death Rides the Zephyr
ISBN 978-1-56474-530-9

Death Deals a Hand
ISBN 978-1-56474-569-9

Kathy Lynn Emerson
LADY APPLETON SERIES
Face Down Below the Banqueting House
ISBN 978-1-880284-71-1

Face Down Beside St. Anne's Well
ISBN 978-1-880284-82-7

Face Down O'er the Border
ISBN 978-1-880284-91-9

Sara Hoskinson Frommer
JOAN SPENCER SERIES
Her Brother's Keeper
ISBN 978-1-56474-525-5

Hal Glatzer
KATY GREEN SERIES
Too Dead To Swing
ISBN 978-1-880284-53-7

A Fugue in Hell's Kitchen
ISBN 978-1-880284-70-4

The Last Full Measure
ISBN 978-1-880284-84-1

Margaret Grace
MINIATURE SERIES
Mix-up in Miniature
ISBN 978-1-56474-510-1

Madness in Miniature
ISBN 978-1-56474-543-9

Manhattan in Miniature
ISBN 978-1-56474-562-0

Matrimony in Miniature
ISBN 978-1-56474-575-0

Tony Hays
Shakespeare No More
ISBN 978-1-56474-566-8

Wendy Hornsby
MAGGIE MACGOWEN SERIES
In the Guise of Mercy
ISBN 978-1-56474-482-1

The Paramour's Daughter
ISBN 978-1-56474-496-8

The Hanging
ISBN 978-1-56474-526-2

The Color of Light
ISBN 978-1-56474-542-2

Disturbing the Dark
ISBN 978-1-56474-576-7

Janet LaPierre
PORT SILVA SERIES
Baby Mine
ISBN 978-1-880284-32-2

Keepers
Shamus Award nominee, Best Paperback Original
ISBN 978-1-880284-44-5

Death Duties
ISBN 978-1-880284-74-2

Family Business
ISBN 978-1-880284-85-8

Run a Crooked Mile
ISBN 978-1-880284-88-9

Hailey Lind
ART LOVER'S SERIES
Arsenic and Old Paint
ISBN 978-1-56474-490-6

Lev Raphael
NICK HOFFMAN SERIES
Tropic of Murder
ISBN 978-1-880284-68-1

Hot Rocks
ISBN 978-1-880284-83-4

Lora Roberts
BRIDGET MONTROSE SERIES
Another Fine Mess
ISBN 978-1-880284-54-4

SHERLOCK HOLMES SERIES
The Affair of the Incognito Tenant
ISBN 978-1-880284-67-4

Rebecca Rothenberg
BOTANICAL SERIES
The Tumbleweed Murders
(completed by Taffy Cannon)
ISBN 978-1-880284-43-8

Sheila Simonson
LATOUCHE COUNTY SERIES
Buffalo Bill's Defunct
WILLA Award, Best Softcover Fiction
ISBN 978-1-880284-96-4

An Old Chaos
ISBN 978-1-880284-99-5

Beyond Confusion
ISBN 978-1-56474-519-4

Lea Wait
SHADOWS ANTIQUES SERIES
Shadows of a Down East Summer
ISBN 978-1-56474-497-5

Shadows on a Cape Cod Wedding
ISBN 1-978-56474-531-6

Shadows on a Maine Christmas
ISBN 978-1-56474-531-6

Shadows on a Morning in Maine
ISBN 978-1-56474-577-4

Eric Wright
JOE BARLEY SERIES
The Kidnapping of Rosie Dawn
Barry Award, Best Paperback Original. Edgar,
Ellis, and Anthony awards nominee
ISBN 978-1-880284-40-7

Nancy Means Wright
MARY WOLLSTONECRAFT SERIES
Midnight Fires
ISBN 978-1-56474-488-3

The Nightmare
ISBN 978-1-56474-509-5

REFERENCE/MYSTERY WRITING

Kathy Lynn Emerson
*How To Write Killer Historical
Mysteries: The Art and Adventure of
Sleuthing Through the Past*
Agatha Award, Best Nonfiction. Anthony and
Macavity awards nominee
ISBN 978-1-880284-92-6

Carolyn Wheat
*How To Write Killer Fiction:
The Funhouse of Mystery & the Roller
Coaster of Suspense*
ISBN 978-1-880284-62-9

**Available from your local bookstore
or from Perseverance Press/John Daniel & Company
(800) 662–8351 or www.danielpublishing.com/perseverance**